The Mirror

Written by KRISTI OLSON Edited by JAMES OLSON
Cover Illustrated by RICHARD OLSON

TRAFFORD
USA ▪ Canada ▪ UK ▪ Ireland

I thank my husband James who continually fills my mind with great and wonderful ideas which I sift through on a daily basis.

I thank Jennifer Landsberg who read the rough story before it was published, and then for saying she'd actually buy a copy anyway.

I thank Richard Olson for his Mirror illustration.

Angelina Spear has lost everything, including her memory. Can the rose pendant she's found help her recover what she's lost?

William Wade is finally coming to terms with his Pa's 'illness' when he meets the memory deprived Ann. Can he keep her safe?

Nora Anderson and son Scott have just arrived at their new home, an old Inn on the Oregon Coast. Scott, who has a mild case of muscular disease and moments of telepathy , senses something evil within the newly purchased Inn. Something his Uncle didn't mention. What Uncle Ed did mention was an old mirror, a secret surprise for Nora. But Uncle Ed hasn't been completely honest with Scott.

On the run from his Pa, William and Ann are drawn to the old Inn by the rose pendant where fate and the mirror await them.

Note for Librarians: A cataloguing record for this book is available from Library and Archives Canada at www.collectionscanada.ca/amicus/index-e.html

ISBN: 978-1-4120-8367-6 (sc)

Copyright acknowledgements:

"The Continuing Story of Bungalow Bill"
"Let it Be"
"Drive my Car"
Written by John Lennon and Paul McCartney
Published by Northern Songs (PRS)/Sony/ATV Tunes LLC (ASCAP)
Northern Songs (PRS) and Sony/ATV Tunes LLC (ASCAP) administered by
Sony/ATV Music Publishing Canada, 1670 Bayview Ave.,Suite 408, Toronto, ON. M4G 3C2
All rights reserved
Used by Permission
The Stand: 1978 Stephen King

Printed in the United States of America. Printed on paper with minimum 30% recycled fibre. Trafford's print shop runs on "green energy" from solar, wind and other environmentally-friendly power sources.

Offices in Canada, USA, Ireland and UK

Book sales for North America and international:
Trafford Publishing, 6E–2333 Government St.,
Victoria, BC V8T 4P4 CANADA
phone 250 383 6864 (toll-free 1 888 232 4444)
fax 250 383 6804; email to orders@trafford.com
Book sales in Europe:
Trafford Publishing (UK) Limited, 9 Park End Street, 2nd Floor
Oxford, UK OX1 1HH UNITED KINGDOM
phone +44 (0)1865 722 113 (local rate 0845 230 9601)
facsimile +44 (0)1865 722 868; info.uk@trafford.com
Order online at:
trafford.com/06-0122

10   9   8   7   6   5   4   3   2   1

TABLE OF CONTENTS

PROLOGUE: THE MIRROR   11

DAY ONE: SUNDAY

CHAPTER 1:   LIGHTNING STRIKES   19
CHAPTER 2:   THE VISIT   26

DAY TWO: MONDAY

CHAPTER 3:   WHAT'S YOUR NAME, WHO'S YOUR DADDY? 39
CHAPTER 4:   THERE'S NO PLACE LIKE HOME   50
CHAPTER 5:   DESTINATION SEAL CAPE   58
CHAPTER 6:   HOMEWARD BOUND?   70

DAY THREE: TUESDAY

CHAPTER 7:   ROOM AND BOARD   83
CHAPTER 8:   FAMILIAR FACES   97
CHAPTER 9:   WILLIAM FINDS TROUBLE   112

DAY FOUR: WEDNESDAY

CHAPTER 10:   THE PORTAL   125
CHAPTER 11:   REUNITED   137
CHAPTER 12:   STEPPIN IN   142
CHAPTER 13:   MEET THE DEAD   147
CHAPTER 14:   IMPOSTER   151
CHAPTER 15:   VISIONS   157

CHAPTER 16:   PARAISO   161

CHAPTER 17:   QUICKSAND   168

CHAPTER 18:   SCOTT TAKES A WALK   171

CHAPTER 19:   PLANS   175

CHAPTER 20:   VENGEANCE   178

CHAPTER 21:   A WAY OUT?   184

DAY FIVE: THURSDAY

CHAPTER 22:   INVESTIGATIONS   195

CHAPTER 23:   RACE AGAINST TIME   202

CHAPTER 24:   JONNY DELIVERS   208

CHAPTER 25:   ELIZABETH'S GHOST   209

CHAPTER 26:   THE GATHERING   215

CHAPTER 27:   KIDNAPPED   223

CHAPTER 28:   KISMET   227

CHAPTER 29:   ESCAPE   245

CHAPTER 30:   NEW LIVES   256

EPILOGUE: THE TWINS   262

THE MIRROR

·· 1 ··

Elizabeth and Jonathan Reed stand in the foyer, wide-eyed, watching their mother, normally a sane woman, insanely ripping the sheet covered mirror from the wall. "Don't look at it kids, don't ever look at it!" she exclaims, frightening them all the more.

"It'll be safe in the cellar," she mutters, dragging the huge mirror passed them, down the hallway to the new elevator, and inside with it.

Confused, the children race downstairs to the kitchen just in time to see their mother disappearing through the cellar door. A blast of hot air shoots from the opening, engulfing them in a wave of blistering heat. Cautiously approaching the cellar door they decide, without words, to wait at the top of the rickety old stairs.

Hours pass.

Then, as if released from a trance, the children run from the cellar door back to the penthouse and the safety of Elizabeth's big four poster bed.

The long stormy night passes without sleep or parents.

Early the next morning they huddle together in the big bed, the covers pulled up to their wide, blue eyes, only the tops of their little blonde heads peeking out. Daylight seeps into the room through a space under the heavy drapes that cover the door to the balcony.

"Lizzy," Jonathan whispers. "I'm scared."

"Me too, Jonny, me too," Elizabeth whispers back.

"Why'd she do that? Why'd she take that old mirror to the cellar?"

"I don't know," Elizabeth replies. The old mirror was their mother's newest addition to the redecorated interior of the Light Keeper's Inn. It was the biggest mirror Elizabeth had ever seen in her whole entire life.

"Doesn't she like it anymore?" Jonny asks.

"I guess not," Elizabeth answers.

"Is she coming back?"

"Of course," Elizabeth lies, chewing her bottom lip, knowing she shouldn't lie; knowing their parents would never be back.

"I'm hungry," Jonny whispers.

"Me too, c'mon."

They climb from the warm, safe bed. Jonny clutches his two favorite stuffed animals, home sewn by his mother, tightly in his arms. Donning her robe and slippers, Elizabeth escorts her five year old brother down the two flights of carpeted stairs, both afraid of using the new elevator, through the dining room and into the warm kitchen.

Come, a friendly voice invites.

The steep, narrow cellar stairs beckon. Slowly the children descend; no longer aware of their hunger, their fear, anything.

Inside the lighted cellar, with its dusty wine bottles stacked in dusty racks, the children stand before the uncovered mirror. The sheet lay crumpled in a pile on the dirt floor beside it. The age's old mirror frame encircled with the vines of perfect, wild roses, some in full bloom, and others just buds, is beautiful, mesmerizing, hypnotizing . . .

Heat bursts from the mirror, blowing their blonde hair away from their faces. A black claw shoots out and seizes Jonathan by the waist. He wriggles to get away, clutching his stuffed animals firmly to his chest, gasping from the explosive heat, eyes squeezed shut. Elizabeth grabs for him, but misses just as the monstrous arm and Jonathan disappear into the mirror, together. Momentarily frozen, her jaw hanging open in disbelief, Elizabeth stands there.

Then she turns and bolts up the stairs.

Across the library she sees Father's glass gun cabinet standing beside the massive rock fireplace, his 30-30 inside. She races toward the cabinet, throws open the door and snatches the rifle from its place. A box of shells sits on the bottom shelf. She grabs one bullet from the box and quickly stuffs it into the rifle, unaware of the cold sweat drenching her brow, the rapid pounding of her heart, the bonging of the old library clock.

"God help me," she whispers.

A wave of heat laps at her brow.

Lizzy, don't be afraid, Jonny's voice fills her mind. *I'll take you to play with Mommy and Daddy. Come find me.* But Elizabeth knows it's not Jonny, she's no dummy. She is, after all, nearly thirteen.

With the loaded rifle clutched in her small hands Elizabeth races down the stairs, the red and blue ribbon in her long hair flying out behind her. Insane laughter from the cellar burns her ears, her brain, like the heat of a fever, yet she is not deterred. Down the narrow stairs and into the sweltering cellar she goes. Her only thoughts are of saving Jonny.

With steadfast determination Elizabeth marches toward the mirror. "I'm coming to kill you," she says, stepping into it, disappearing forever.

· ·2· ·

Five years later a stocky, bald-headed man stands on the cobblestone walkway in his yellow rain slicker, one leg of his blue jeans stuffed inside his black rubber boot, the other one out. He gazes over the grounds surrounding the abandoned Inn; at the flower buds sprouting on the untrimmed rose bushes in the neglected garden, the once manicured lawn grown wildly out of control. Tall prairie grass covering the formerly desolate bluff sways in the gentle breeze of spring's mid-morning. Sunlight brightens the flowering stalks, and then fades as a cloud passes by. Just over the bluff the Pacific Ocean meets the land where sea lions bask in the sun.

Sam Jacobs has been caretaking Seal Bay properties for a long time. It's his first job at the Light Keeper's Inn. He starts with the garden and lawn, trimming, mowing, and weeding. Overhead a few billowy white clouds hang in a sky of blue. Darker clouds gather around the red, cone like roof tops of the looming twin towers and just above the roof garden of the main house that stands between them.

Sam halts his weeding and stares at the Inn, feeling a dark presence there, unfriendly.

Ci'del, a voice whispers deep inside his head.

Slowly Sam rises from the garden, crosses the cobblestone walk and mounts the five marble stairs. The massive, cathedral doors with their oval shaped and brightly colored mosaic insets greet him.

He hesitates momentarily.

Come in, the voice inside his head invites.

Reluctantly Sam enters; it's his job.

Sunlight flows through the mosaic glass, throwing a stream of colors into the foyer. He sits on the cushioned bench across from the smooth, mahogany counter, and removes his muddy boots and dirty coat.

The cellar, it directs.

Now in stocking feet, he hypnotically crosses the foyer to the stairs.

Your medal of honor awaits you, it whispers. *Hurry!*

Sam quickly descends the beige carpeted stairs to the dining room, enters the hot kitchen where the cellar door stands wide open, and thinks, *I need to turn down the furnace.* Even though there is no furnace, has never been a furnace.

He enters the superheated cellar and sees the ancient mirror. The glass ripples and an image appears, a black armored beast with yellow lizard eyes and carving knife teeth. It holds Sam's horrified gaze in its hypnotic stare as it speaks to him. Sam hears and understands his mission, his purpose.

· ·3· ·

For five years he's heard it calling to him, guiding him closer to its location, careful not to reveal too much, too soon. He thinks he knows where it is but he's not quite sure, not yet. So until the creature reveals more, Edwin Anderson will continue to drive the West Coast Highway in search of it.

Today the sun is out from behind the billowy clouds, heating up the cool spring air. Evergreens line the road, swaying in the freshening breeze. It's a pleasant drive.

Jailer.

The voice is out of the past, but the old man recognizes it instantly and slams on the brakes of his classic Plymouth sedan bringing the tires to a screeching halt on the dry asphalt road, throwing his wife, Sarah, forward in her seat against her lap belt. Several cars skid to a halt behind them, horns blaring, voices shouting, fists with fingers flying. She stares at him through wide gray eyes and asks, "What is it Eddie?" Knowing she really doesn't want to know.

"It's here," he says. "I can feel it, calling me. I knew we were close."

Sarah raises her weathered hand to her thin throat, feeling the knot of terror there; it was calling him. "Are you sure?"

Edwin nods. "Aye, right down there," he says, pointing a long, thin finger passed her to a one-lane road leading through a sparse, freshly burnt forest.

"We're not going there, are we?" Sarah asks.

DAY ONE
SUNDAY

LIGHTNING STRIKES

• • 1 • •

Her parents could be a royal pain in the ass; and this wet, October day was proof of that, Angelina Spear was certain of it. Rain drops thumped her hooded, lime-green poncho as she hurried down the trail, ahead of them. Finally they were going home. She should have been at the high school football game with Jen and Gayle cheering on Jess and the other Wildcats. It wasn't fair – just because Jess had gotten her home half an hour late, *half an hour!* It wasn't like they'd done anything, *yet.*

The scene unfolded in her memory. Her dad (a military man) greeting her at the door, his face stern. *Now because you weren't home at the agreed upon time, you get to spend Friday and Saturday nights with your mom and me up at the lake, no friends, and no phone, just the three of us out in the woods, enjoying nature.* Then they made her come out here in the frickin rain for a frickin hike, *to cleanse the mind, become one with nature, and contemplate her future.* Sometimes she hated them, their rules, and their punishments. Why couldn't they be like other parents?

Maybe she'd just run away.

The thought crossed her mind for about half a second.

No, she *couldn't* run away. If she did that she'd lose the car they promised her for graduation. Angie had every intention of getting that car, a primo 1965 Impala convertible with a 396 cubic inch motor and a Turbo 350 tranny her dad had put in; a hot rod, red with white interior. Granddad bought it brand new in 65. He gave it to her dad in his will, long before Angie was ever born. It was the coolest car in town and soon it would be hers. Angie imagined herself behind the large, white steering wheel, cruising down the boulevard with the top down, her short hair standing up in the breeze, the sun blazing down on her face.

She smiled and placed the IPOD earpiece back in her ear, half covering the sound of the pattering rain. Paul McCartney was singing one of her favorite tunes. Angie liked a lot of the older bands from the 60's, although she sometimes got flack about it from her friends. She and her parents had driven the red and white convertible all the way to Portland, Oregon to see Sir Paul in concert in October of 2002. It was awesome. Their seats had been so close to the stage Angie felt she could almost reach out and touch him.

Glancing back over her shoulder she sighed at the sight of her parents still strolling along hand in hand across the grassy meadow. *How can they be so damn happy walking around in a rain storm?*

Beside the trail ahead of her stood a tall Ponderosa Pine, probably the tallest one in this forest. Setting her day pack at its base she turned back toward the meadow, shoved the poncho's hood from her head, lifted her pale face into the rain and gazed at the dark, gray clouds gathering overhead, crashing together.

Thunder rumbled across the sky.

"Angie," her mother called. "Get away from there!"

She paid no attention as the rain suddenly turned to hail, pelting her upturned face.

"Angelina!" Her parents shouted.

Electricity snapped in her ears, standing her hair on end. A sudden, white flash ripped through the sky, the blinding zigzag of light pierced her eyes, thunder slammed through her body.

Then there was darkness; nothing.

After a time she struggled to open her heavy eye lids. Pounding waves of pain washed though her temples, sending a shrill ringing to her ears. Tall trees loomed overhead. Wet grass and ground lay beneath her as she looked into the gray sky above. Where was she? Another jolt of pain shot through her body as she tried to sit up. Raising one lead filled hand to her face she saw the blackened tips of her fingers then dropped the hand back to the ground. She closed her eyes, and slept.

· ·2· ·

Lightning flashed across the darkening sky. The young teenaged boy in faded blue jeans and a black tee-shirt, red baseball cap perched backwards on his head, slowly strolled along the wooded path toward his favorite fishing hole and campsite. He wasn't worried about being out in a thunder storm, in fact,

he rather enjoyed it. It was something he could always count on at the end of a
long, hot summer; although this year it was way later in the season than usual.
Most years the summers of Northern California didn't last into October; but
thunder and lightning was his favorite kind of weather, no matter what month
it was.

Who knows, he thought, *maybe one of these days I'll get killed by lightning,
or better yet, get shot by some stupid red neck hunter.* Even though he knew it
unlikely he'd ever be struck by lightning, and there was no hunting allowed in
this part of the park.

He'd been thinking about death a lot lately, looking forward to it really. He
wasn't sure how much longer he could go on hiding Pa's secret. He seemed to
be thinking about *that* more and more these last few days, too. It was getting
to be that time again, he could tell. He shook these thoughts from his head.
William Wade didn't want to think about his Pa.

On the trail ahead, a small wild rabbit stood on its haunches, looking for a
safe place to get out of the storm. William stopped, knelt to the ground while
removing the knapsack from his back and dug the stolen, high velocity sling
shot (an accurate, high impact weapon, the best on today's market, and the
most expensive) from it, loaded the small steel ball into the leather pouch, and
aimed it at the unsuspecting bunny. He was just about to let the shot fly when
an old memory flooded his vision. He lowered the weapon and squeezed his
eyes shut, unable to control the sudden flow of heart wrenching guilt. Why had
he let it go on? Why hadn't he stopped it? What the hell was the matter with
him anyway? Again he shook the thoughts away, and then opened his eyes.

Today was the second of three (well, it was really only about two and a
half) days away from Pa, and William hoped to enjoy his time away from the
murdering bastard, in every way. That meant not thinking about the past. The
past was a trap, a place where nothing could be changed. A place where dark
memories stirred up emotions William didn't like; emotions and feelings that
could get him in deep shit.

A crack of lightning split the sky.

The bunny hopped away into the underlying ferns at the base of a fir tree,
away from William and his weapon.

William stuffed the sling shot back into his pack. It had been an easy steal.
The clerks were so used to seeing him and his Pa in the store buying rifle shells
for Pa's gun and the ball bearings for his old, home made sling shot (which he

proudly showed off to them) that they never even noticed him stuffing this one into his back pocket. Someday he'd put it to good use.

• •3• •

One large, fat raindrop fell from the sky, splashing across her pale face. She opened her brown eyes and sat up, shivered. Ten feet away, a once tall and massive tree, now blackened and split in half, lay on the ground.

Lightning? She couldn't remember.

Wooziness gave way as she got to her hands and knees, slowly standing, scanning the perimeter. Tall evergreens surrounded the small grassy meadow dotted with wilting red, yellow, and orange wildflowers. A knapsack lay at the base of the fallen tree.

Near the small meadow's center a huge, black bird with a small, red head and long tail feathers snacked on a dead (human?) body. Actually there were two bodies. It was like a bad accident; she couldn't turn away – instead the girl watched in morbid fascination as the bird pecked and pulled an eye from the dead owners socket, held it in its white, pointed beak for a moment, and then swallowed it whole. The girl's large brown eyes took in the horrible, fascinating scene. The couple lay on their backs. Blackened flesh that had once been their faces hung from their skulls, like marshmallows left too long in the campfire. They were wearing yellow ponchos and blue jeans. A mangle of flesh and bone and fabric was all that was left of their shoes and feet.

Looking down at her own shoes, she saw the numb, blackened tips of her bare toes hanging out the open ends. She jumped as an unseen animal in a nearby tree rapidly sent out its warning to others. A crow squawked overhead.

Turning her back on the dead, she proceeded to investigate the pack. Sitting cross-legged on the ground she grabbed the knapsack. Inside the large, bulging exterior pocket she found a full water bottle. She popped the bottle's top and took a long, long drink. Her stomach rolled with sudden nausea, which she managed to keep down, this time. Setting the bottle aside she reached in a second time and produced a pocket knife. It was silver with three black semi-circles on each side at one end. On the other end was a small ring, to hang from a chain, she supposed. The handle contained a screw driver, nail file and cork screw on one side. The other side was a bottle opener, a knife blade, scissors and something she wasn't sure of, some kind of hook. She set the knife aside.

Reaching in a third time she felt a small, smooth, cylinder shape. She pulled it from the pocket. It was the smallest flashlight she'd ever seen.

Inside the main compartment was a hairbrush covered with short strands of light brown hair, and a black compact mirror that used to have some kind of picture and writing on it that was now faded and unreadable. Under the hairbrush and mirror was a small blanket and a pair of dark blue sweats (matching top and bottom), and white, slip on sneakers with a three inch sole. She scowled at the shoes thinking they weren't much of a walking shoe, and then placed them on the ground with the other items. The last thing she pulled from the knapsack was a candy bar. She ravenously ripped the wrapper from it and wolfed the candy down only to have it come back up seconds later along with the water she'd consumed earlier.

A while later, after her stomach settled, she took the knife and extra clothing and disappeared behind the fallen tree, out of sight from the open meadow. With great pain and caring she cut through and peeled off the soggy cardboard clothing, the melted socks to shoes. The warming air played lightly over her bare skin. Then she slipped into the dry (one size fits all) sweat pants and hooded, pullover shirt and tried on the impractical sneakers, a perfect fit.

Picking up the discarded clothing she hurried back around the tree and into the meadow as a feeling of urgency swelled inside her. A slight twinge, like an electrical pulse, beat in the middle of her forehead, and there was something else, her whole body felt . . .electrified.

Somewhere faint music was playing.

Scanning the meadow again she noticed the pathway leading through it, and passed her and wondered, *was I coming or going? Which way is out? Where in the blazes am I?*

She gazed up at thin, wispy white clouds sailing by. Then she looked around the meadow again. The dead couple (bird food) was now covered with the flapping, fighting, flopping, pecking scavenger birds. They made no bird like screeches, as one might think, but their flapping wings made up for it.

"Well," she asked herself. "Which way ya goin?"

Looking toward the feasting birds, a sick feeling fell over her. "The other way," she said.

Dropping the torn up, cut up, melted clothing and shoes to the ground the girl then picked up the pack, stuffing the blanket and knife back inside. She opened the compact mirror and looked into it, into a face she didn't know;

short, brown hair comically standing on end, a black spot right in the middle of her forehead. It hurt a little as she touched it. Snapping the mirror closed she put it and the brush into the pack as well and zipped it closed. She took a small sip of water from the bottle, swished it around in her mouth then spit it out, putting the water bottle back in the bag's exterior pocket where she'd found it. Then she stuffed the tiny flashlight into her sweatshirt pocket and slung the pack over her shoulder.

The girl turned and walked into the forest.

Beneath the tree's thinning canopy, needles and cones littered the damp, well trodden path. She breathed in the fresh scent of the sun-warmed forest and smiled, it was a beautiful day. But her smile began to fade as she strolled along, her thoughts returning to the two dead people. She'd left them there, the birds having a feast of them. Perhaps she should've covered them with the blanket from the pack. But what if she needed that blanket, what if she ended up spending the night in the wilderness? The blanket was all she had. If she didn't find shelter or the end of the forest soon she would, would what? Freeze? Was it that cold? She didn't feel cold. In fact she felt quite warm; now that she was dry.

Stepping into a grassy clearing, at the end of the path, she saw one car, barely lit by the dusky light. An old Chevy, she knew by the bow tie emblem on the grill (funny, what she knew and didn't). Cautiously she approached the car and peered into its dirty windows. The seats were quite worn out; the springs almost poking through in places, mostly the driver's side. The dash was cracked down the center. She reached for the door handle.

Zap!

Small sparks flew from her fingertips, like tiny lightning bolts, to the handle.

"Ouch," she cried, pulling back her hand, shaking it rapidly to deaden the sudden, shocking pain. Then she reached out again. This time seeing the sparks leap from her fingertips, unable to pull back in time to stop it.

Zap!

When the pain in her hand subsided, she licked her blackened fingertips, held her breath and slapped the metal handle, feeling no shock. Grabbing the handle she flung the heavy door open and tossed her pack onto the backseat. She then slid in behind the wheel, feeling the poking springs of the old seat in her butt. Did she know how to drive? She couldn't remember.

The car's musty, earthy smell seeped into her nose, but she didn't care, it was shelter for the night, as long as the owner's didn't come back. *And what if they do?*

She'd cross that bridge when and if it ever came. Sliding into the passenger seat, she pushed the button opening the glove box. Old papers exploded out of it. Fishing the flashlight from her pocket, she shinned its bright light on them; old receipts for tires and tune ups.

Pointing the flashlight's beam into the deep, dark box she noticed something way in the back corner, something that sparkled as the light crossed over it. Reaching in she retrieved the shiny object; a small, red rosebud pendant, its perfect petals closed up tightly, three green leaves cupped its bottom; it had no stem. The feeling it was something important fell over her. Was it hers?

Quickly she stuffed the papers back into the box and shut it. For a long time she sat and stared at the intricate rose pendant in the palm of her hand and before she knew it the car was completely shrouded in darkness and the sounds of the woods at night. Finally turning off her flashlight, the girl stuffed it and the rosebud into her sweatshirt pocket. Crawling into the backseat of the old car she fished the blanket out of the pack. Using the pack as a pillow she curled up under the blanket. She was exhausted, but sleep didn't come easy. The image of the birds and the two dead people kept floating into her mind as faint, familiar music played somewhere in the distance.

THE VISIT

· · 1 · ·

He looked up from his reading to see the dawn of another fall day as a puff of cool, desert air blew in through the open bedroom window, caressing his young, stubbly face. Outside the birds were singing their morning songs. Marking his place with the gold and silver plated book marker and setting the red covered book aside Scott Anderson stretched his thick, muscular arms toward the unfinished ceiling. Twisting from side to side, he could hear the popping and snapping from his spine. It felt good. He ran his fingers through his curly, reddish brown hair. Swinging his scrawny, ailing legs over the edge of the bed, he stuffed his stocking covered feet into the shoes and strapped on the steel reinforced leather leg braces. He grabbed the pale green overalls Uncle Ed had gotten him at the army surplus store from the bedpost and slipped them on. Each leg zipped up the outside making it easier to get those big shoes into. Plus, they were Gore-Tex (made in Germany), *Heil!* Not that he liked Hitler, he didn't. In his opinion, Hitler was a wacko.

In the kitchen Scott started the coffee maker for his mom. He didn't drink coffee, in his opinion it was nasty, especially the way she liked it. Instead he ate a piece of her homemade banana bread (now that was good stuff), chugged a big glass of milk and headed outside, grabbing his windbreaker jacket and the keys from their hooks on the way. It wouldn't be real coat weather for another month or two, by that time they'd be long gone from this dust bowl.

The old truck was parked across the yard in the dirt driveway. Scott hobbled down the porch steps and over to it where he keyed open the door (even out here in the boonies you had to lock stuff up) and reached in, sniffing the aroma of the still new vinyl as he pulled the release cable (custom installed by Scott himself) for the hood.

"Gotta get you ready," he said. "Uncle Ed says we're moving, finally getting a new place over at the Coast, an old Inn. You'll be right at home there." He patted the new dashboard. "Says he found the missing mirror, too. Can't tell

Mom though. It's a surprise." *Shouldn't be talking to yourself,* Rachel's voice spoke inside his head, *it's a sign your crazy.*

Ignoring his dead twin, as usual, Scott propped one side of the hood open and checked the truck's oil and water. Overhead, puffy dark clouds drifted by, the kind of clouds that would suddenly burst open without warning, drenching everything for about five minutes with rain drops the size of quarters, then close up and move on, leaving behind the smell of damp dust. A smell he hated. A smell he would not miss once they were gone from here.

Late last night, Uncle Ed had promised to stop by today with good news. And Scott knew exactly what that news was. They had discussed it many times, in their minds, late at night, while his mother slept. Whenever Scott needed him, Uncle Ed was there, telepathically. Now, it seemed, Uncle Ed needed Scott. *I need you to help me recapture the mirror*; his Uncle had said. It seemed an odd way to put it, odd indeed. As if it were some escaped prisoner rather than a missing piece of his art collection. Uncle Ed had hundreds of pieces of art stored in the basement of his Nevada Mountain home; someday they'd be Scott's, if he lived long enough. This piece though, this secret mirror was a surprise for his mom's collection, he was pretty sure about that. Why else would they keep it a secret?

Inside Scott's consciousness the soul of his dead twin kept quiet. She only spoke *her* mind when it served her purpose to butt in. Unlike Uncle Ed, Rachel was *always* there, whether Scott needed her or not. When the kids had teased him that day back in kindergarten, calling him a cripple, it was Rachel who dug inside their thoughts, it was Rachel who invaded their privacy, and it was Rachel who made his mouth say those terrible, awful, truthful things, and boy did he get into hot water for it! But that was long ago, and didn't really matter anymore. He learned his lesson that day.

What mattered today was the truck and getting it ready for their big move. He'd been working on the old 1953 Dodge since he was able to read the shop manual, and the tune up and wiring chart he'd found under the seat. The flat-head six cylinder engine was in bad need of a rebuild by the time he understood the workings of it. Now, she ran like a champ. The body was straight; had never been wrecked. However, the box was full of rust, and the wood flooring in the bed, wasted. The interior was eaten through by years of sitting in the sun. But Bob's Junkyard, which was owned and operated by a guy named Gus, a guy his mom used to go to school with and didn't like, was right across the street from the liquor store in Kingston and Scott had been buying parts there (after market new and used) as often as he could afford, which meant as often as he could get the money from his mom, which was sometimes like pulling teeth from a tiger. After rebuilding the motor and tranny, he repaired the box and replaced the wood flooring in the bed. The cushy bucket seats were from a wrecked 1963 Buick Wildcat. He also replaced the door panels, and the interior workings of the doors, the headliner, the arm rests and the dash. After all that he replaced the six volt wiring system with a much more efficient twelve volt system. Now all she needed was a paint job, and maybe those fancy hand controls and an automatic tranny, so he could drive it. But he probably wouldn't live that long anyway. According to The Doctors, he should've been in a wheelchair eight to ten years ago. The disease hadn't gone at all the way The Doctors had thought it would, his arms were not affected, his heart was not affected, nor was his brain affected, unless you considered Rachel an affliction.

The only part of Scott that didn't work correctly were his lower legs. Recently though, he'd been having some problems with the muscles in his thighs, and that concerned him a great deal. More than he liked to admit.

· ·2· ·

In the upstairs bedroom she opened her eyes at the sound of the front door closing. The sun was barely up this Sunday morning, and so was Scott. No surprise, Scott was always awake before the crack of dawn, always had some project to complete, book to read, wood to chop, weights to lift, photos to take (although he was doing that less and less these days) . . .and the pick-up truck. She wondered what the hurry was *this* morning as she pulled on her colorful silk pajamas, slipped into her bunny slippers (a present from Scott) and headed down the steep stairs to the kitchen.

She stood at the large window looking out, sipping the morning's first cup of coffee and rum, eating her toast. It was the only way to start the day and Nora Anderson had been starting her days that way for years. She watched as Scott tinkered under the hood of the old truck, her mind a complete blank on who'd left it there all those years ago, before Scott was born. Scott had it fixed up and running by the time he was ten.

A stab of guilt pierced Nora's heart. Scott had no real friends, friends his own age. She had sent him to the public school in Kingston, the same school she attended. There was no school at Sucker Lake, there wasn't even a store. At the age of five, he was quite brilliant, but the children made fun of his leg braces and Scott retaliated in a way that was so unlike him. As if he were a completely different boy, not the kind and loving, keep his opinions mostly to himself, boy she knew. He had said some terrible, hurtful things to them. And she'd been afraid to send him back. So Nora hired a private teacher, a very young teacher, named Miss Leeann. Scott completed his home schooling and had his Certificate of Education by the time he was fifteen, nearly three years ago.

She watched as he closed the hood of the old truck then made his way slowly across the driveway, the painful truth of his muscular disease more apparent each day, each step. At the shed he pulled out the ax and tossed it into the wheelbarrow then wheeled it over to the woodpile where he removed his jacket, the muscular arms bulging within his tee-shirt. He grabbed the ax and began chopping firewood and kindling for the guests.

The doctors called it a neuromuscular disorder. There were about a million different types. So far this one was different in every way. It started at birth, as far as they could tell, with his feet and had slowly moved up his legs. It hadn't affected any other parts of his body which is what stumped the doctors most of all. But, what the hell did doctors know anyway? It didn't take a genius to recognize that Scott would end up in a wheelchair soon. It was only a matter of time before he wouldn't be able to walk at all. All the testing done to determine if Nora was a carrier of the disease came back negative. Nor were there any other afflicted relatives, although they couldn't test Scott's father, no one knew who he was. As far as Nora was concerned, he never existed. He was a blank spot in her mind, erased by the passing of time and circumstance.

But, in spite of Scott's weakening legs, Nora knew he had other abilities, telepathic abilities. And just like their Uncle; Scott could know what she was thinking anytime he wanted to.

Nora turned from the window, crossed the living room and settled into the faded old recliner, kicking off the bunny slippers and curling her long, slender legs under her butt. She gazed around the room at the faded sofa, the wooden rocker, the two high back stools at the counter that divided the living room from the kitchen. Her old (and still working, thanks to Scott) hi-fi record player and radio combo and the stack of records she'd received for Christmas and birthdays as a kid in the sixties and a few of which she bought herself in later years, sat in one corner, silent at the moment as Nora wasn't quite ready for music yet this morning. Nor was she ready to hear of today's War casualties

Scott's framed photos taken around the forested part of Sucker Lake, west of the house and dunes, hung on the living room walls between Nora's mirror collection, and shelves. Shelves covered with books and glass water globes (each with a different kind of flower inside) that she and Scott had collected over the years, her favorite one being the two inch globe with the tiny red rosebud that Uncle Edwin had given her shortly after her father's disappearance.

It was the sound of tires on gravel that brought Nora out of her chair.

· ·3· ·

Across the grassy sand stood the eight little cabins, each with their own wood stove and outhouse, lining the alkali lake's southwest shore about a hundred yards behind and to the east side of the main house. Scott was glad the house had been built after the cabins and included a flush toilet and tub. But soon, he surmised, they'd be living in the lap of luxury; away from all this dilapidation and dust. He could hear the guests bustling around, chattering and laughing, unloading their ATVs and dune buggies, getting them ready to master the acres of sand dunes to the northeast of Sucker Lake, as he chopped their firewood, never getting to meet them or join in. It was his mother's rule to not get involved with them. Sometimes he wished he could though.

The kids from Kingston High had called it Suck Lake (leaving off the er) for years, long before it swallowed up Scott's dog, Rascal, and that rabbit he'd been chasing. Scott hadn't had a pet since. The vision of Rascal struggling to get out of the swallowing sand burned in Scott's memory. There was nothing he could do, nothing. Even the barbed-wire fence surrounding the lake couldn't keep Rascal out.

Scott stopped chopping for a moment; a familiar feeling settling over him. *We're here*; Uncle Ed's voice spoke in his mind. He looked up to see a brand spanking new black Bentley Continental GT pulling into the driveway. It stopped under the golden aspen tree. Scott's long legged Uncle unfolded from the driver's side. Under his long, open coat he wore a light blue dress shirt tucked into black slacks, and tan colored loafers on his big feet. On his head was the feathered fedora.

By God, Scott thought, *he actually got himself a new ride.*

Uncle Ed nodded in Scott's direction then sauntered over to the passenger's side and opened the door. Slender Aunt Sarah, who wasn't the prettiest girl at the ball anymore, stepped out. She was nearly as tall as her husband, although not nearly as old. Her long silver hair was up on top of her head in a pile as usual. She wore a blue sweater over a plain blouse and a pair of black slacks. They were like two peas in a pod.

Scott gradually made his way over to them, one stiff step at a time. "Uncle Ed, Aunt Sarah. How are you this fine morning?" he asked, extending a hand toward the old man.

Edwin grabbed the boy's strong hand eagerly and said, "Great, son." (Uncle Ed always called him son.) "Got great news," then winked a bright blue eye at the boy, his heir.

"Oh yeah?"

"Aye."

"Awesome car."

"Aye," Edwin replied.

"Where'd ya get it?"

"It's just a loner, Son."

"Really?"

"Aye."

"You mean you gotta give it back?"

"Aye."

"Awesome."

• •4• •

Nora watched from the large window as Edwin, Sarah and Scott slowly approached the house. She turned away sadly as Scott climbed the few stairs to the porch with agonizing, painful determination. *At least he hasn't lost all the strength in his upper legs, yet*, she thought, setting her empty cup on the kitchen counter.

The door swung open and Edwin stepped in.

"I've good news Nora," he said, proceeding passed her and into the living room. "I bought a new place, sold this one." And before anyone else could say a single word, he continued, "Just wait till you see it, you won't believe it." He removed his hat, exposing thinning, white hair. He guided Sarah over to the sofa then took a seat next to her, placing his hat on one bony knee and his hands on his thighs.

"What's it like?" Scott asked, settling into the wooden rocker. Nora resumed her place in the recliner.

"It's a stone Inn, built in 1870 right into the side of the cliff above the ocean," Uncle Ed paused. "Newly refurbished and fully furnished. It's got two round towers three stories tall. Each tower has three rooms, one on each floor, with their own private baths and small cooking facilities. On the third floor of the main house is what they call The Penthouse, for the two of you, maybe even a guest now and again. If you know what I mean. The library and sitting room are on the second floor. And on the first floor, which is underground except on the ocean side, you'll find the kitchen, dining room and laundry. All the windows have frilly little lace curtains. And every floor's got a balcony out over the ocean."

"So, what's the catch Edwin?" Nora asked.

"No catch. It's all yours. It's all paid for, and just like here, I'll take care of the bills, even the cable TV, you just have to make the place work. I'll even pay for a housekeeper, a cook and a waitress, if you think you'll need a crew. The yard work is currently farmed out to one of the town's caretakers, but I suppose Scott can still handle a pair of trimming shears and a riding lawn mower."

"So, when do we get to move?" Scott asked. He could hardly sit still.

"Right away, Son. You're expected tomorrow. Already got your business license, even put up a sign saying you'll open on November first."

"What did it cost Edwin?" Nora asked.

"Hardly worth a mention."

"And why's that?"

Edwin hesitated, and then said, "It's sat vacant a long time, and the city needed some revenue. It seems the old owners just up and vanished one day years ago, seems they haven't been seen or heard from since. "

"Awesome," Scott said.

Nora shot him an accusing glance; somehow he was at least partially responsible for this purchase. She only hoped it wasn't a mistake.

Scott smiled back at her, seeing her fear. Knowing, or at least hoping, that this would be the best thing for her, for them.

· ·5· ·

The old couple rolled out of the driveway headed for their home on the north flank of Ted's Mountain, a little place about thirty miles north-northwest of Reno, Scott and Nora still visible in the rear-view mirror.

"He doesn't know?" Sarah questioned.

Edwin shook his head.

"Maybe you should have told him Eddie, you know, with your thoughts."

"Everything's proceeding as destined."

"What if he finds it?"

"I trust he'll let me know the minute he does," Edwin replied. "We can't stop the wheels of time or destiny, my Love, no matter how much we may want to."

· ·6· ·

Scott and Nora stood at the end of the dirt driveway, under a mottled blue sky, waving as Uncle Edwin and Aunt Sarah drove off down the road toward one of their many homes. Nora wondered how much real estate her old uncle really owned. She knew about the high rise condos in Washington, the hotel in Hawaii, and the casino in Vegas, but there must be more. He always seemed to have cash, and plenty of it.

When the black car faded out of sight, Nora turned toward her son, a boy who was becoming a man, and a handsome one at that, but he didn't know everything.

"Why?" was all she said, crossing her thin arms over her small bosom, she didn't need to say anything else because Scott knew exactly what why she was talking about. The why of moving, relocating, pulling up roots. Not that she had any friends in this godforsaken place, it was the principle. She was the parent, not Scott. She was the adult here and yet he was running the show, calling the shots.

"Mom," he soothed, "you need a change. We need a change. This place has no future. What are you so worried about? Come on, it'll be a great adventure. Meeting new people, making friends, having a social life. You're a great cook and believe it or not, you *know* how to run a business. Just look what you've done here, to this place." He motioned toward the old house, the tiny cabins to the east.

Nora looked out over the sand passed the cabins to the dunes stretching for miles and miles as far as she could see. She hadn't really done anything but put up a sign and collect the money. "I don't know, Scott."

"Trust me," he said, smiling that infectious smile of his, the twinkle in his light blue eyes. "Let's get packing." He held out his arm and they escorted each other back to the old house.

Grabbing the big roll of tape and the scissors from the kitchen drawer, Scott began assembling the flattened boxes Uncle Edwin had brought, as Nora selected something from her record collection and placed it on the turntable. The old familiar music flowed from the old player.

DAY TWO
MONDAY

C·H·A·P·T·E·R 3

WHAT'S YOUR NAME, WHO'S YOUR DADDY?

·· 1 ··

Using his rolled up sleeping bag for support, William Wade sat propped against it at the end of the old wooden dock. His bare feet dangled in the cool, clear water, fishing pole in hand. His faded red cap was planted firmly on his head, backwards, black hair curling up and over its rim. William always enjoyed fishing and camping without his Pa, but it was getting time to head back. Back to where Pa was waiting. William hesitated. What if he just didn't go back?

He knew the answer to that; he'd tried it once before, long ago. The results were still visible on his backside. *Death's the only way to end it. Mine or his, don't really matter which*, he thought.

Laying his pole aside, William reached into the side pocket of his small knapsack and pulled out the baggie. There were five joints left, just enough to last till he could get more at school tomorrow from Dipshit Davy. William pulled one of the joints from the baggie and lit it, drawing in the sweet taste of the green bud. He gazed out over the crystal blue waters of the lake, the tree covered mountain tops. A gentle breeze rippled across the lake then touched his face. Honking geese flew by overhead. The last couple of days it had rained like the dickens, drenching everything. There had been an awesome thunder and lightning storm yesterday morning, but this morning the sky had cleared and the sun was shining. It seemed a wonderful day.

After a few minutes William finished his smoke, removed his bare feet from the lake and put on his steel toed shit kickers. Grabbing his gear he made way for the trail. The forest's small inhabitants scurried about just out of sight. He could hear them chattering away in their hunt for winter's storage. It was a short walk to the meadow.

He'd stepped out into the bright sunlight and was crossing the meadow when he suddenly stopped. On the far side a tree lay exploded and burned. *Smells like chicken*, he thought, *or is it pork?* Then he saw the small black bear. Its muzzle deeply rooted inside some dead animal's carcass lying in the tall grass a few yards off the trail among something yellow. William had come across black bears before in this area; this was the blackest one he'd ever seen. The last one had been a whole lot bigger and a cinnamon color. Probably a male. This one, he figured, was probably a young female.

Digging the slingshot from his pack, he loaded a ball bearing into it. He took aim at the bear, stretching the sling as far back as possible, then let it fly. The shot hit the bear square in the forehead with a *thunk*. The bear yelped, quickly got up and lumbered off into the woods, away from William and whatever it was chewing on.

William approached the spot. His dark eyes widened as he saw the remains of a woman, her face blackened and her eyes missing, the empty sockets staring back at him. She had no stomach. The yellow he'd seen was a part of her clothing; a pancho. He looked away only to spot another body, a man in the same condition. He glanced back and forth between the two for a few moments before tearing his eyes away for good.

A few steps up the trail, at the base of the shattered tree, William found another poncho, light green, that was melted to a torn (or was it cut?) shirt and a pair of cardboard jeans. Inside the poncho's pocket he found a melted IPOD. A tiny black wire hung from its side, the ear piece that should have been attached to it, was missing. A pair of women's gym shoes with no toes lay nearby. Inside them he saw melted socks.

Stuffing his sling shot into his pack he turned from the burned tree, the melted clothing, and the charred, half eaten bodies; there was nothing he could do for them. He returned to his original course.

The sunshine slipped in and out of the tall trees as William strolled along taking his time. He was in no hurry to get back to his murdering Pa. He couldn't stop thinking about the clothing he'd found, or the two dead bodies, or the bear chewing on them. That had been a very disturbing sight; he could still hear the buzzing flies. When he reached the next clearing with the old abandoned car, instead of just passing by without a glance as usual, William turned toward it.

Dropping his bag to the ground beside the car he cupped one hand to the dirty, driver's door window and looked inside; nothing but an old, worn out seat.

He moved to the rear window. His dark eyes widened. An angel lay in the back seat. She was the most beautiful girl (*woman*) he'd ever seen. Her short, wild hair was the color of golden wheat with blackened tips, her face as radiant as the morning sun. Her hands were folded together in prayer style under her cheek, knees pulled up to her chest, high heeled gym shoes on her small feet.

William took a deep breath, tightness seized his chest. He looked up from the car, scanning the empty field, yet feeling some kind of presence there. Quickly he opened the door, flipped the split bench seat forward and grabbed her ankle.

· ·2· ·

She was running as fast as she could in the ridiculous sneakers through the dark woods. Something evil and unseen crashed through the brush behind her. It was getting closer, grabbing at her tattered clothing as thunder boomed overhead. Lightning lit the dark trees, tall and branchless.

You let them eat our eyes, our brains, our souls. You let them, a voice spoke, so close to her ear that she nearly screamed from the burning heat of it.

No, she tried to yell out, but her lips were numb and wouldn't move. She was numb all over. She stumbled and fell, their dead, burning hands reaching for her . . .burning hands changing into deadly talons, black and sharp.

She opened her eyes. Someone (dead) was shaking her leg.

"Hey," the muffled voice said. "You okay?"

Startled, the girl sat straight up, her eyes blinking rapidly in the daylight. Someone was leaning toward her; a boy with dark eyes. Black curls poked out from underneath a red baseball cap. In one hand he held a fishing pole. his other hand was on her ankle. Then she remembered the car. "Sorry," she said, pulling her leg away as the fuzziness faded from her head. "There was no other place to stay."

"Hey," he shrugged. "Ain't my car. What's that on your forehead?"

"What?" She put her fingers to her forehead, wincing at the shooting pain, and felt the imprint and stubble at the hairline, right between her eyes. "I don't know," she said. "Where are we?"

William looked at her with dark, guarded eyes and wondered if she was serious. "Well, this here's the Land of Many Lakes, in the Lagarto Mountains. Jackass Peak is that way," he pointed out the car's back window, passed her with his fishing pole. "And that way," he said pointing out the side window "is Jackass Springs. Over there, through the woods a spell," he continued as he pointed out the windshield, "is the fishing hole and a bear chewing on something dead."

"Oh," she replied, with a shudder.

"I'm William Wade," he told her. "Most folks call me Billy."

"I'm . . ." she paused. *Who? What the hell is my name?* And inside her head a voice whispered; *Ann.*

"Ann," she repeated. "Glad to meet you Will." She held her hand out toward him, handshake style.

"Wow!" The boy said taking her hand as if she were royalty, feeling the slight electrical snap as he helped her closer to the door. "Your fingers is black! You been lightning struck!"

"Are you serious?" she asked, narrowing her thin brow.

William nodded, noticing something (like a small, coated wire) dangling from her ear.

Dismissing the thought of being lightning struck, as he called it, Ann slid out of the car. William leaned against it, watching as she stretched her arms over her head, swaying from side to side. Her sweatshirt pulling up with her arms revealing the silky white skin of her belly.

It was after the stretching that she really noticed the car; its rusted wheels buried in an inch of dried mud, weeds growing around them, the crunched fender and dented door, the missing trunk lid. All the things she hadn't seen the night before were now so clear in the morning light. She knew it was an old Chevy. Once it had been somebody's beautiful baby – not any more. Sadly, although she didn't know why, Ann wondered what the car had done to deserve this abandonment.

She leaned in to get the blanket and pack and that's when she saw the crushed toadstools growing in the crack of the backseat. She'd slept with the mushrooms. She giggled at the thought, grabbed her stuff and closed the rusted door with a gentle push.

"Well, I gotta get goin," William said, turning away. "Pa's waiting for me and if I'm late he'll skin my hide."

"Wait," she said. "How do I get out of here?"

"Depends on where you're going," he replied, turning his head to face her, very aware of the swelling inside his pants.

Which way am I going? She wondered. *West,* the little voice inside her head answered.

"West," Ann repeated.

The boy raised an eyebrow. "West?"

The girl nodded. Inside her head that voice was speaking again. *To Seal Cape*, it said.

"To Seal Cape," the girl repeated.

"Seal Cape? Ain't that in Oregon?"

"So?"

"Well," William said with a shrug. "It's a long ways. I guess ya just follow that path over there," he pointed his fishing pole toward Jackass Peak. "When ya get to the road, turn right and then just keep to the right. That'll take ya to the closest main highway. Ya better hurry, another storms a coming." Then he walked off toward Jackass Springs.

Ya just follow that path over there, he'd said. That sounded easy enough. *It's a long way.* She should have asked how far. She should have asked what time it was, what day. She really should have asked for food. Her stomach rumbled. She took a sip of water from the bottle. *Another storms a coming.* Ann looked into the sky, the clear blue sky. A light breeze caressed her face. It didn't look like a storm.

• •3• •

William hurried away from the girl. She was a run-a-way, he was pretty sure. But was she really lightning struck? Well, she'd struck him, there was no doubt about that. She was warm and sexy with a fire in her brown eyes he couldn't explain. Looking into them had left him feeling weak-kneed and a little light headed not to mention the boner that happened quite often these days around anything with two legs and a pussy. He really didn't like that word though, that was a word the older boys at school used. It was the same word his Pa used, like it was a bad thing. William wanted to give it a nice name, a delicate, wonderful name, but nothing came to mind.

She called him Will, he liked that. He liked it a lot. It made him feel special, important, and older than his current thirteen years. He would have let her tag along, if his murdering Pa hadn't been waiting back at camp. Pa liked run-a-ways. He called them *young women*. None of the young women William knew about though had been over sixteen; he was pretty sure about that. *The younger, the better,* his Pa always said.

William knew without a doubt that Ann was exactly the kind of young woman his Pa would want. This time however, he wouldn't let it happen; he would never let it happen again – no matter what. He passed the woodpecker tree with hardly a notice of the noisy bird pecking away at it.

Forty minutes later he stepped off the main trail at his usual spot and took a seat on the fallen log, as he had many times before. Digging into his pack he grabbed the little baggie of joints and got one out, returning the baggie to the pack. He pulled out his lighter and lit the joint. His thoughts went back to the girl (*woman*) with the strange mark on her forehead, the large brown eye, and the wire hanging from her ear. The missing IPOD earpiece. *What was she really doing out there? Was she really a run-a-way? What about those other people?*

A twig snapped.

William quickly cupped the joint in the palm of his hand and looked up.

· ·4· ·

Ann looked toward the path that Will said would lead to the main road. Is that where she wanted to go? She looked toward the path that he had taken back to the campground, a place he called Jackass Springs. Slinging her pack over her shoulder she took off after him. Perhaps she had family or friends at the campground. She hurried as fast as she could in the ridiculous sneakers, up and down small hills, to the left then to the right, amongst several different types of trees, with little animals scurrying about, warning others of her approach. There was another sound, a slow, rhythmic hammering, like the sound of a tree being chopped down, and it was getting louder, drowning out the music that seemed to be inside her head, trapped there, an echo of lost memories.

Whack. . . Whack. . . Whack. . .

Then she saw it, about fifteen feet up clinging to a tree trunk, a large black woodpecker with a red crest on its black, white and red head, gathering bugs. She stopped to watch it noticing that when she turned her head from side to side her left ear seemed not to hear as well as the right. Sticking her pinky finger inside it she felt the blockage, and the tiny wire hanging there. She pulled it out, stared at it, unable to comprehend what it was. Stuffing it into her pocket with the rose and her flashlight, she resumed her walk.

Her thoughts drifted back to the previous day. She had opened her eyes to see the sky above her as she lay in the wet grass of some unknown place. A charred and shattered tree lay a few yards away. She shuddered as she recalled the sight of the two dead bodies and the huge bird with the eyeball in its beak. Had she been lightning struck as the boy claimed? She looked at her blackened fingertips, then touched the spot on her forehead and remembered the shocking zap she'd received as she reached for the abandoned car's door handle. *Is it possible to be struck by lightning and live?*

Absolutely, the tiny voice spoke inside her head again.

The sun's radiant heat sizzled overhead making the pool of sweat around her neck run between her small breasts. Her feet were killing her. She was just rounding a corner when she saw him sitting on a log in a clearing with his head down. A twig snapped under her step and he instantly looked up. A quick whiff of something burning drifted passed her nose. Ann could see that something cupped in his hand.

She stepped into the small clearing and said, "You're not gonna burn yourself with that, are you?"

William looked back down at the joint burning close to his palm, un-cupped it and then looked back to Ann. "Ya wanna hit?"

Ann shook her head.

Will brought the home-rolled cigarette up to his thick lips and took another puff, holding the 'hit' for several seconds before exhaling. "Sure ya don't want some?"

Ann knew what it was, recognizing the smell from some distant past, but she had no recollection of ever having smoked it. "I don't think so," she said politely.

William took another hit and then let it go out. He was in deep trouble now. She followed him and the only way to keep her safe from Pa was to not go back there with her.

"I got to thinking I should see if I have family or friends staying at the campground. I know I said I was going to Seal Cape, but the truth is, I don't know where that is." Ann stepped over to the log and sat down beside Will. "The truth is I can't remember who I am or what I'm doing here."

William looked into her eyes and was nearly swept away with fear, fear for her, but mostly fear of her. Her eyes told him something he didn't yet understand.

· ·5· ·

William Wade stood up from the log he was sharing with a girl (*woman*) who had no memory of who she was; a girl his Pa would consider a run-a-way. *Run-a-ways was just asking to get it*; according to his Pa; and he was there to give it to 'em.

William cringed. "Are ya a run away?" he asked.

Ann looked up at him. "I don't think so," she said, a vision of the dead coming back to her.

"Well, I can show ya to the campground. There the Ranger can help," he said, planning to dump her at the Ranger's Station before going to Pa's camp. It was the only way to keep her safe. He offered his hand to her and felt the slight tingle of electricity as she took hold of it.

"So, where'd the name Ann come from?" he asked, helping her from the log then letting go her dainty hand. She was nearly the same height as him, in her high-heeled gym shoes.

"Just kinda popped into my head," she replied.

· ·6· ·

The walk from the log to the end of the trail was relatively short; perhaps ten minutes at most. Luckily the Ranger's Station was between the end of the trail and Pa's camp. William didn't know what time it was but hoped with all his heart that he wasn't too late; that Pa was just sitting around the campsite drinking his beer and not noticing the time, not noticing that his only son wasn't back yet.

Ann followed Will down the path toward what he'd called Jackass Springs and hopefully some recollection of her past, some resolution to her missing memory. Time marched on as the fresh warm air touched her checks. Small birds scurried about from tree branch to tree branch, perhaps looking for bugs. A bushy tailed squirrel ran across the path in front of her. Up ahead was what looked like the end of the path and someone coming their way. He was a big man with curly, wild black hair that just touched his broad shoulders. He wore a black shaggy beard and mustache of the same color, an army green tee-shirt filled with muscles, and a pair of camouflage pants stuffed into black boots. He was ruggedly handsome.

William looked up too late to do anything. Had he noticed sooner he might have been able to warn her, but what would he say? *Watch out, it's my Pa, don't let him get his raping, murdering hands on ya.* Instead William continued toward his Pa, knowing he was in deep shit and Ann was going to suffer for it. Then he had an idea.

"Pa, I gotta take this lost girl to the Ranger's Station so she can find her folks, then I'll be right back."

"Ya don't say?" Pa replied, knowing the boy was up to something.

William nodded, seeing that look in Pa's dark eyes; that look of lust and wanting. The fear he felt earlier, fear for Ann, swelled like a puss pocket in his throat. His heartbeat quickened. He swallowed hard. His Pa looked at the girl and said, "Ya hungry?"

Ann nodded, yet in the back of her mind she could hear the rising voice of caution.

"Good," he said. "I'm Billy's Pa. You can call me Joe. Come on back to camp and Billy can fix up some supper, then we'll go to see the Ranger. What'd ya say?"

Ann's stomach rumbled loudly.

Joe laughed and said, "The stomach has spoken."

William felt as if he might barf.

Ann smiled cautiously and said, "Okay." What could be the harm in supper? Joe seemed an okay kind a guy. But that little voice kept speaking, warning of danger.

"Billy," Joe commanded. "Lead the way."

William knew this was bad, very bad. If only she hadn't followed him. If only Pa hadn't come along. But maybe, if he was lucky, maybe someone would see them walking through the campground, recognize her and come to her rescue.

· ·7· ·

Supper was beans and franks, something Ann had eaten before on many a campout with people she couldn't remember, people who she assumed were her family and friends. What were their names? Why couldn't she remember them or their faces when she had the ability to remember such fine cuisine as beans and franks? She had three helpings and then belched very un-lady like.

"Pardon me," she exclaimed, a little embarrassed. The men busily shoveling beans into their mouths didn't even seem to notice, so far as she could tell.

Turning her attention from supper to the campsite she saw again the rust pitted 50's era WILLYS parked beside the brand new, at least it looked new, green tent, big enough to have a small party in she supposed. A campfire burned in the pit next to the wooden picnic table. A camp cooler sat at the end of it. Joe and Will were seated across from her. Joe had finish shoveling and was staring at her, sizing her up.

"So, what's your name?" he asked.

"Ann," she replied.

"Where ya from?"

She wasn't sure how to respond. Should she mention Seal Cape? She decided not. "Oregon," she replied.

"Ya don't say." Joe raised a thick, black eyebrow and smiled at her, and in that smile she saw something she didn't like. "Ya got a last name?" he asked.

She didn't reply.

"Well how we gonna find yer folks without a last name?"

Still no reply.

Joe sighed heavily then said, "Well, let's go see the Ranger while Billy breaks camp and packs that piece a shit WILLYS." Turning toward William he barked, "Can ya handle that boy?"

"Yes Sir, Pa," William responded. "But I wanna go with ya."

"Ya don't need ta go with, and don't ya dare leave this camp for I get back," Joe commanded. "Coz ya know the consequences if ya do, right?"

William nodded. He knew the consequences.

Joe stood up. He was a good foot taller than Ann or William. "Come on," he said, motioning Ann to follow.

Watching Ann disappear with his Pa brought a feeling of dread over William. She was being led to the end of her life; he was pretty sure about that. *But where will he do it? In the woods, back to the trail now that it was starting to get darker?* William looked up at the clear October sky darkening with the approach of dusk, wondering what he should do. If he left camp and was wrong Pa would get him good. If he didn't leave camp and he was right, Ann would die. Quickly William tossed all the trash in a bag, loaded the cooler with the leftover food, threw the paper plates into the fire and then looked over at the huge tent. No time for that, he'd already wasted enough time. William turned and marched out of the campsite, toward the Ranger's Station.

· ·8· ·

The walk to the Ranger's Station took no time at all, but Ann could see before they got there that the little shack was closed up tighter than a drum. Not only that but Joe was right, how would they find her family without a last name?

"I guess we're too late," she said, as they stepped up to the door.

"Well," Joe suggested, "ya can come on home with me and Billy, and we'll contact the local Sheriff. They otta be able to at least check a missin person's report."

That made sense to Ann, but that nagging little voice inside her head kept warning that this was dangerous, perhaps deadly.

"Okay," she said then thought; *I'll be careful.*

Together they stepped from behind the shack to see William.

He stopped dead in his tracks; surprise on his face.

"What the hell ya doing here, boy?" Joe barked. "I tol ya to stay and pack up, did ya?"

"Mostly," William replied. "I wanted to say bye to Ann, ya know, in case they was looking for her."

"No need to worry bout that," Joe said with a big smile. "Ann's comin home with us."

William's jaw fell open. *Why would she do that?*

"The Rangers have gone home for the night Will," Ann said.

C·H·A·P·T·E·R 4

THERE'S NO PLACE LIKE HOME

· · 1 · ·

I t was about thirty miles of back road from The Land of Many Lakes to the Wade Estate. Joe slowly maneuvered the rusty WILLYS down the rutted dirt road, bouncing all the way. Ann rode shot gun as William sat in the back amongst the discarded beer bottles, the camping gear and fishing poles, scowling.

Joe raised the half full beer to his fat lips and poured the remainder of it down his gullet, not spilling a single drop in the jostling jeep. He slid the empty bottle onto the floorboard behind the driver's seat and pressed the accelerator harder, making their heads bounce up and down like a bobble.

Scowling at the back of Pa's big, fat head, William was convinced they'd never make it home; Pa would just do his dirty deed right here in the old, rusty jeep. Right here in front of God and everybody. He'd just stop and do it; rape her and kill her, *it's what he does, who his is.*

Joe reached out his big hand and William watched in disgust as he placed it on Ann's shapely thigh, close to her crotch.

Ann quickly pushed Joe's sweaty hand aside.

William smiled, glad that she didn't like it; the other girls had liked it, every single one. Then a thought crossed his mind, a thought so strong he nearly acted on it without hesitation. His sling shot, the one he'd stolen for just such an occasion, was right there in his knapsack on the jeep's rusty floor board. He started to reach for it and then he did hesitate. If he shot Pa in the back of his thick head they would probably wreck and then they'd all die. Is that what he wanted? *Maybe,* he thought. *Then it'd finally be over. No more murder, no more lies, no more Pa.*

He grabbed his pack just as Pa drove passed the overgrown hedge lining their property, and into the dirt driveway. Jumping from the vehicle, even before it was completely stopped, William ran toward their home, knapsack in hand. He was on a mission to see how much beer Pa had on hand; beer could be the answer to all his problems.

"Hey Billy," Pa hollered. "What's the big hurry?" Then he laughed. It was a laugh William knew well, his lust laugh.

William pulled open the door and disappeared inside. The place was a wreck. He hadn't cleaned up before leaving. He ran to the kitchen. There was one six pack in the fridge and none in the pantry. His heart sank; six beers wouldn't be enough, he needed at least a case. His shoulders slumped as he wondered what he would do next.

··2··

A flood lamp attached to a pole high above the roof top cast its bright light over the leaning, decaying structure. Tall trees and overgrown brush populated the surrounding area. A crooked porch ran the entire length of the house.

My God, Ann thought, *it's the little pig's stick house.* The big yard was littered with old appliances, tires, junk cars, and a goat. She looked again. Sure enough, a spotted goat was chained to something behind the house as it stood chomping on a patch of briars in the side yard.

Ann didn't like being out here alone with Joe, not one bit. It had everything to do with the way he was treating Will. Quickly retrieving her shoes from her pack she slipped them on over her dirty feet. Hopping from the jeep she followed Will inside, licking her blackened fingertips (a shield against the hurting shock of electricity) before touching the metal door knob.

It was the smell of mold and stale beer that filled her nose when she opened the door on a very small living room. Two wooden, old fashioned rocking chairs with worn out cushion seats and backs were to her right, next to a coffee table where a small TV sat. Beside the TV, an opened bag of barbecued potato chips lay spilled on the table. A three light pole lamp stood between the chairs with a pile of beer bottles littering its base on the dirty, wooden floor. Beyond the chairs and coffee table were three closed doors. To her left, under the window, sat a square dining table covered with a plastic red and white checked table cloth, four chairs surrounded it. Straight ahead, the open kitchen with its sink full of dirty dishes.

Will emerged from behind the door closest to the kitchen just as Joe burst in through the front door.

"Sorry the place is such a mess," Will said with a shrug. "We never have company."

"Where's the bathroom?" Ann asked.

"Right in there," he said, pointing to the door he'd just come out of. "It's not pretty."

Inside the bathroom Ann gazed at the cracked mirror hanging above the sink, the old squeezed tubes of toothpaste, half a dozen worn out toothbrushes, a hairbrush, an old, mostly dead razor and a near empty bottle of Old Spice that littered the counter. Beside the sink was the freshly cleaned toilet. A shower curtain hung lopsidedly from a pole across the shower stall, no tub. A pair of dingy, yet clean smelling, towels hung from the towel bar. The old linoleum was faded and worn, yet clean. She'd seen worse, although she didn't know when or where.

• •3• •

Damn, William thought. He'd almost had enough time to warn Ann, but then Pa had come barging in and the chance had vanished. And even if he had been able to warn her, what good would it do? What would he say? *My Pa's a killer, a rapist and murderer of young women?*

"Billy, clean up the goddamn kitchen and get me a beer," his Pa ordered, sitting down in his rocker, turning on the tube.

"Yes Sir, Pa." William turned toward the kitchen sink with its pile of dishes; wishing he'd taken care of them three days ago. Then a vision slammed into his brain, a vision so horrible it almost made him sick. It was Lily, pale skinned, dark eyed Lily; the first he knew of Pa's young women. She was so young, so beautiful. So much like Ann. He remembered every one of Pa's young women since then and shuddered at the revelation that he never tried to help any of them. Not that he ever witnessed murder again; he didn't have to see it to know it had happened. Besides, wasn't seeing one in a lifetime one too many? William knew it was as a wave of guilt washed over him. *It's too late for them, the girls of the past, but it's not too late for Ann. Not yet. Tonight I'll . . .*

"Get me a beer," Pa barked, interrupting William's thoughts.

"That's your last six pack Pa," William said, turning toward him.

"What? You shittin me, Boy?"

"No Sir, Pa." William replied, leaning his backside against the kitchen counter, folding his arms over his small chest.

"Damn." Joe looked at his pocket watch. "Too late now, we'll go first thing in the mornin, you and me, when we take Ann to town."

William's jaw dropped open. "We're taking her to town?"

"Course we are, what else would we do?"

It was a lie. William could see it in Pa's bloodshot eyes.

"You mean I'm spending the night – *here?*" Ann asked, standing outside the bathroom door, a sick feeling stirring the pit of her stomach.

"Sure, Darlin," Joe cooed.

"Where?" she asked.

"Billy's room, he can sleep in the shed."

This was a change from Pa's regular routine and William wondered what his sick, murdering Pa was up to this time.

Looking at his boy, and then the girl, Joe knew Billy liked her, and that could be a problem, especially if the little bastard was thinking of trying something stupid, like helping her. Joe would have to discourage the boy. A little shock therapy was in order, seeing how Billy disobeyed him at camp, undermining his authority. But more important right now was a beer. "Where's my frigin beer, Boy?" he barked.

William quickly retrieved a beer from the fridge.

"Good boy," Joe said, snatching the beer from William's hand.

• •4 •

The voice was speaking again, telling her that things weren't right; she was in a trap, a snare. She'd seen it in Will's eyes too (or was it just her imagination?) as he passed her on the way to giving Joe his demanded beer. But Joe said they'd take her to town, to the Sheriff.

"Come on over here Darlin, and have a seat," Joe insisted. "Billy'll clean up this pig sty."

Ann looked toward Will instead and asked, "Do you want some help?"

"He don't need no help," Joe barked, "Now come sit here." He patted the chair next to him.

"Where's your mom?" Ann asked.

"Billy ain't got a Ma. She died when Billy was born," Joe blurted from his seat in front of the TV.

"I'm sorry," Ann said.

"No need to be sorry, she got what she deserved," Joe replied. "Now, get your ass over here girl, and sit down like I tol ya."

Ann slowly crossed the tiny room and sat down in the empty rocker. *Will's chair,* she thought.

Focusing on the small black and white TV, its screen showing some old, almost remembered TV show – Ann looked at it, through it, her thoughts wandering aimlessly within her nearly vacant memory. Thoughts of Will's mother dying at childbirth because *she deserved it,* ran through her head like a locomotive on an endless rail spur.

· ·5·

The thought of his Pa looking at Ann with those lustful, bloodthirsty eyes brought fresh guilt over William. He should have put an end to it long before they got there. He should have used his sling shot. They'd all be better off if he had. The statement about his mother, a woman he couldn't remember, brought tears to his eyes; tears he didn't want Ann to see. He took his time at the kitchen sink, his back to them, wishing for a way to sneak out for a smoke. He didn't want to leave her alone with Pa, though. Pa would soon make his move. William hoped to be ready. There were five more beers in the six pack. That wouldn't be enough. But if he could catch Pa off guard . . .then what? What would he do?

"Billy!" Pa thundered. "Quit daydreamin and get finished up there. You an me got bidness out in the shed to take care a."

Going to the shed meant the whip, or maybe a little shock therapy, as Pa liked to call it. It would also give William the chance he needed, if he *didn't* screw up. "Ya want another beer Pa, while I finish up?" he asked.

"You tryin to get me drunk, Boy?"

"No Sir, Pa."

"Okay then, get me another beer, and hurry the hell up."

· ·6 ·

Ann was still seated in Will's rocker when Joe leaned over her and said, "Now you stay right here little Missy," his breath stinking of stale beer and cigarettes, "while me and my boy take care a bidness."

Ann nodded and said, "Okay." And then thought, *where would I go?*

Follow, the voice inside her head urged.

"Come on, Boy."

"Yes Sir, Pa."

Joe shoved William out the door, closing it behind them.

Under her breath Ann counted to one hundred then got up from her chair and snuck over to the door. She reached for the knob, momentarily forgetting about her electric situation.

Zap!

Quickly she licked her fingertips and tried again. This time there was no zap and to Ann's surprise the door was not locked. Slowly opening it she peered out into the noisy night unable to see the shed. Cautiously, her heart pounding in her chest like a sledgehammer, she tip-toed out onto the porch and followed it around the side of the house.

The shed sat about ten yards off the back porch. A light showed through a tiny window in its oversized door. Climbing over the porch railing Ann cautiously approached the window. Cupping her hands to it and peeking inside she saw Will facing his Pa, their profiles to her. Will was no longer wearing his shirt. She could hear their voices through the thin plastic.

"Din't I tell ya 'bout run-a-ways?" Joe hissed.

"Yes, Sir."

"Did ya notice her nice little titties?"

William remained silent.

"How 'bout the smell a her ripe little pussy?"

Again William remained silent.

"I bet ya did. Yer little pecker was standin straight up inside yer jeans, wan't it?" Joe reached out with something, touching Will's bare chest with it. Ann saw tiny sparks fly from the devise at the same time William felt the quick jolt surging through his body. He jumped; a small whimper escaped his lips.

Unable to control the sudden burst of hate that exploded within her, Ann stepped back from the plastic window and flung open the big door. "Stop it!" she shouted.

Joe turned toward her; a wide smile erupted on his rugged face. "Well, lookie here," he sneered. "Come ta save my boy, have ya?"

He started toward her.

Ann started to back away, stumbling over something behind her. The goat bleated. Ann's feet went out from under her. She landed on her butt with a thud, biting her tongue, tasting the blood.

The goat hopped away.

· ·7·

Joe was almost to the girl when a sudden, unexplained pain exploded in his head, first one side and then the other. Ann watched Joe fold to his knees before she saw Will standing behind him, the shovel raised high over his head. Then Will brought the shovel down solidly on top of Joe's head one last time, and Joe crumpled to the ground.

Dropping the shovel William ran over to her. "Are ya okay?" he asked, reaching out. "You're bleeding."

"Bit my tongue. It's nothing," she said, taking his hand.

Zap!

"I got an idea," he said, helping her up.

"Wow. You really knocked your Pa on the head."

"Yeah," he said. "Don't know how long he'll be out. We better hurry."

Ann stared at Will, was he kidding? She looked toward Joe laying there like a bump on a log; would he really get back up?

"Come on." Will grabbed her by the wrist; and towed her toward the house. Once inside, he disappeared behind one of the closed doors. Within minutes he reappeared wearing a denim jacket over a flannel shirt with his faded jeans, a knapsack on his back. In one hand he held a black leather jacket and in the other, the matching gloves.

"Here," he said, handing her the gloves. "Put these on."

"What for?" she asked.

"Just do it."

"Okay. Jeez you don't have to be so bossy do you? You remind me of . . ." then she stopped. Reminded her of who? Shaking her head at the absence of her memory, she slipped her hands into the offered gloves. They didn't fit too badly; a little long in the fingers, otherwise, okay. "What's in the pack?" she asked.

"A few extra clothes and things," he said, holding out the jacket. "Put this on, we're leaving."

"Where we going?" Ann asked, slipping into the jacket then grabbing her own pack with its little blanket, and slinging it over her shoulder.

"Seal Cape," Will replied. "I'm gonna take ya home, Pa never would of."

Ann was sure she didn't want to know what Will meant by that.

C•H•A•P•T•E•R 5

DESTINATION SEAL CAPE

• • 1 • •

Under the pale blue sky of October's morning, Nora Anderson began hauling their stuff down the porch stairs so that Scott could wheelbarrow it out to the old black Dodge. They wouldn't be taking any of their old furniture, other than Nora's stereo, and memory chest, no need. And it was a good thing. There wasn't enough room in the truck, which means they would have had to rent another truck and spend more money on a driver. Nora didn't like to spend money unless it was absolutely necessary. Some might have called her a tight wad – she considered herself to be . . .thrifty.

In the nearly empty kitchen Nora, dressed in her navy blue cashmere sweater and black jeans, finished her first cup of coffee then poured the remaining rum from the bottle into her thermos. She then filled the rest with coffee from the pot. "That should do it," she said, just as Scott entered for a last look to make sure nothing had been forgotten.

Their eyes met for a brief moment.

"Don't start with me," she said, throwing the empty booze bottle in the trash can, the only thing left in the kitchen.

"Hey, I'm not saying anything, am I?"

"You know new studies have proven a daily drink to be good medicine."

"Sure Mom, whatever you say," he replied. But he did wish, with all his heart that she would stop, although he knew she probably never would. It wasn't that she was a drunk; he'd never seen her *drunk*. It was just that she drank every morning, first thing. One could argue that it didn't matter when or how much she drank, facts were facts. He turned from her and hobbled toward the bedroom.

When all the boxes, Scott's weight bench, Nora's stereo and her Queen Victoria memory chest, full of old family photos and her high school year books, were loaded into the somewhat restored Dodge, Scott tossed his titanium crutches in on top. Then they fastened a green tarp over the load.

Looking out over the grassy sand one last time and passed the alkali lake Scott watched the mid-morning sun cast shadows on the land as the breeze blew the top layers of sand into the air. He wouldn't be missing this place, no way.

Nora climbed into the driver's seat while Scott grabbed hold of the special bar he'd installed inside the truck just above the passenger's door, and kind of swung himself in. Nora pressed in the clutch, turned the key and pushed the starter button. The motor came to life. She put the four speed into second, and let out the clutch. They rolled out of the driveway.

An hour later, in Kingston, Nora pulled the truck into a diagonal parking spot right in front of Bob's Junkyard. Turning toward Scott she said, "Thought you might like to say good-bye."

"Thanks Mom," Scott smiled thinking, *she's really great. If only she'd quit the booze.* He got out of the truck and waddled up to the front door of the old junkyard office. Out back, Brutus was barking like crazy. The bell above the office door jingled as Scott opened it and stepped inside.

· ·2· ·

As soon as Scott disappeared into Bob's; Nora got out of the truck and sprinted across the empty road, under the cloudless sky, to the liquor store. He probably knew it but she didn't care, much. It was just in the way he sometimes looked at her through eyes that seemed to be pleading for her to stop. She had in fact stopped once, for a whole eight months after finding out she was knocked up. But what good had it done? Scott was still born diseased and Rachel was still dead. She could stop again, if she really wanted to. It was a matter of choice, and Nora figured she had no other vises, what was the harm in having a little rum with your day? After all she was well over twenty one; she didn't need any kid, even if it was her only kid, telling her what to do. It was her life.

Nora pushed her way into the store and right on passed the clerk, Thelma Robards. She knew exactly where she was going and headed straight toward the rum section, selecting two bottles of Bacardi 151. A long time ago, in another life it seemed, she and Thelma had been friends. That was years before Nora's father vanished, after which Nora chose to have no friends, none. Later Thelma became one of Kingston High School's favorite cheerleaders, and then she got the bone cancer. Her hair had never grown back and she had gained about two hundred pounds. Today she was wearing her floral moo-moo and her blonde wig.

"Thelma." Nora greeted, setting her purchase on the counter.

"Nora." Thelma returned the greeting, a requirement of the job. Had she seen Nora on the street, she would have ignored her. There was no law said you had to be cordial to anyone, and Thelma Robards hated Nora Anderson.

· ·3· ·

Inside the junkyard's small, smoke-filled office a fat man sat on a stool behind the counter; the same man who helped Scott pull many a part from his junkyard stock. The same man who never said anything bad about Scott's mother, but quite often thought unpleasant things about her whenever Scott came in. The fat man looked up at the bell jingle, raised his bushy gray eyebrows and smiled with smoke stained teeth. "Hey, Motor Head, how's it hangin?" he joked.

"Great, Gus, just stopped in to say good-bye."

"Good-bye?"

"Yeah, Mom and I got a new place out at the coast. You'll have to come visit sometime. It's an old Inn."

"Sounds lovely, Kid. We'll miss ya. Maybe me and the missus will pay ya a visit sometime." Gus had no intention of ever visiting with Nora Anderson. The kid was great, but her, well, she was nothing but a prick teaser.

"I'd like that, Gus. I'll send a postcard when we get there – give you the address. We're even getting cable TV."

"Isn't that something?" Gus mused. Everyone in Kingston knew Nora Anderson didn't like TV much, nor politics, nor religion, nor a lot of things, not since her dad up and disappeared. She just came in to town once a week for groceries and booze, and if the kid was lucky, she'd let him spend some money on that old truck. She hadn't changed at all since high school; she was still the most beautiful, stuck-up woman Gus had ever known, and she was still a prick tease. Thelma had *never* completely forgiven him for what happened. The vision of them kissing behind the church that one Sunday years ago popped into his head.

"It'll be great," Scott quipped, ignoring as much as possible Gus' vision. "Well, be seein ya."

"You take care now, Kid," Gus said as Scott opened the door, the little bell jingling again.

"Sure will, Gus. Sure will."

Scott stepped out into the bright light of the day, amusement on his face. He didn't know why a little kiss should be such a big problem and he supposed it didn't really matter because finally they were leaving this shitty little town for good. Scott didn't think they'd ever be back. There was absolutely no reason to, none what-so-ever.

Then he saw her crossing the street, red hair flying out in the breeze from a passing semi, a brown paper bag in her arms. A wave of sadness rolled over him as he realized the real reason for her stop in town. He should have known, and maybe, somewhere in the back of his mind, he had.

Nora saw that look on Scott's face as soon as the semi truck was passed. That look that said, *please stop. Don't you know you're killing yourself, committing suicide?* No, she didn't know and she didn't want to stop, not yet. And why should she have to? After all, it helped her to cope, to go on. It was her savior. Scott didn't understand the stress, the complications of having no parents, no guidance, no affection. She knew what those thing were and because of it she was always there for him, would always be there for him. It was just a matter of time before he'd be gone and she'd be alone, again; just a matter of time.

· ·4 · ·

The old pickup rolled down the long road ahead of them. Neither one said a word about Nora's purchase, they didn't have to. Scott gazed out the window as the world of sun bleached sand and flying dust disappeared and the trees appeared in a whirl-wind of colors; reds, yellows, oranges and browns. The words to an old song came to mind, *brown leaves and gray sky.* Only the sky wasn't gray, not today. Today the sky was a bright, crisp blue with a few puffy clouds touching the treetops along the tips of the mountains.

Scott rolled down his window. "Do you think we'll get there before sunset?" he asked.

"Should," Nora replied, looking at her tiny wristwatch.

"Awesome."

"You're really looking forward to this, aren't you?"

Scott nodded. "Aren't you?" He knew she wasn't, she could have stayed where they were, forever.

"I just don't know if I'm up to running a bed and breakfast. It isn't like the cabins, you know."

He saw the same fear in her green eyes that he'd seen the day before. "Don't worry," he said, "you'll be great," and then thought; *especially if you'd stop drinking.*

· ·5· ·

Nora normally drove about five miles over the speed limit, today was no different. Once they were back on the road, after stopping for a quick bite at a little diner along the way, and a cup of coffee from the thermos for Nora, she kicked the old truck up to about sixty. The cops never paid much attention to this old thing, however the Chevy she used to have, the one given to her as a gift from Uncle Edwin, if you were over the speed limit in it, the cops would be right on your ass, pulling you over and giving you a ticket, maybe even looking for drugs. Oh, yeah, they liked stopping those old Chevys. Hers had been stolen years ago; stolen by a madman – but she didn't want to think about that. She had suppressed those thoughts for a long time, no reason to recall them now.

Instead Nora turned her thoughts to their new home, her new responsibility. Would she be able to cope with real guests? Greeting them with open arms into her home? Scott said she'd do great. Nora had her doubts. Perhaps it had something to do with commitment. The very thought was unsettling. Was she committed enough? Here she was driving toward some unknown place, her lifestyle suddenly changed. She really had no choice in the matter. Edwin had sold the old place right out from under them. Why? Why would he sell his only link to her father?

Nora shook her head, the auburn curls danced across the collar of her cashmere sweater. She hadn't thought about her AWOL father in a long time. She wondered why she should think of him now.

· ·6· ·

A few dime sized rain drops splattered against the windshield then stopped. Nora turned from the coastal highway onto the one-lane, blacktop road that led out to the cape. Burned trees, twenty to forty feet tall, lined the way; most of their trunks blackened and branchless for the first ten to fifteen feet. Bits of sunlight peeked through their scorched, swept back bows as the clouds overhead tore away from each other, regrouped, then split again, several times.

Scott (who had fallen asleep) suddenly awoke with a serious case of the creeps; something was tracking their arrival. It wasn't Uncle Ed or Rachel. He was sure it wasn't even human, but whatever it was, it was trying to read his thoughts, trying to get inside his brain; and it was getting worse. The short hairs at the nape of his neck bristled, his heartbeat quickened.

A short time later they passed a driveway to their right with a faded 'Beware of Dog' sign posted on a barbed wire fence. The road then took a serious left around a bluff. Scott was sure he could hear barking. At a split in the road an old sign pointed out that Seal Bay was to the left 3 miles while Seal Cape was straight ahead 1. Half a mile later they passed a sign indicating a left turn into 'The Seal Cape Campground; OPEN'. Half a mile later they drove under a stone arch entrance, supporting a sign welcoming them to the Light Keeper's Inn, and through the open wrought iron gate onto a cobblestone drive passing an old gatehouse to their right.

A sturdy, baldheaded man, in a yellow rain slicker with the hood down stood with his back to them in the neatly trimmed yet flowerless rose garden straight ahead, a pair of clippers hanging at his side. Beyond the man, across the waving poverty grass and wilting buttercups, their new home stood; majestic and proud, overlooking the Pacific Ocean. Twin towers rose above the rounded main building, huge cathedral windows lined every floor, the pointed roof-tops looked like upside down waffle cones to Scott.

The stone lighthouse to their left with its red copper roof stabbed into the cloud-flecked sky like a spear. The soon to be setting sun, a big orange ball, hung low in the sky between a thin layer of clouds above it and the ocean below. Scott held his arms straight out in front of his face, as Uncle Ed had once shown him, using his hands to measure the time to sunset; six fingers, an hour and a half.

Nora pulled the truck to a stop in the circular drive and turned off the motor. The short man in the yellow slicker turned toward them, and then approached.

"Afternoon," the man said, leaning just slightly into the truck's open window, extending a big, beefy hand toward Scott. "Name's Sam Jacobs."

"Afternoon," Scott replied, shaking the man's clammy, wet hand.

"You the Andersons?" Sam asked, peering into the truck with his beady little eyes.

Scott nodded; the creeps subsiding, a little.

"Well, come on," Sam said. "I'll give you folks the grand tour."

· ·7· ·

The heels of Nora's black pumps clacked against the cobblestones as she and Scott approached the Inn. A light ocean breeze blew passed them carrying the many voice's of barking seals to their ears. The caretaker stood atop the five tier marble stairway which swept up from the manicured lawn below, waiting to show them in as Nora helped Scott climb the stairs.

In the entry a solid, mahogany counter stood to their left, a cushioned bench to their right. Pale lavender tiles crept under the arched doorway giving way to a beige carpet leading into the connecting library, sitting room and up the stairs to the penthouse. The walls were cedar. Large square beams crisscrossed overhead. The remodel, according to Sam, included installing an elevator, converting all the wood burning stoves to natural gas, and replacing all the rusted iron railings with new ones, with whale caricatures intricately woven around each baluster topped with a clam shell. In between the two top rails more whales playfully spouted.

Scott stepped passed the bench and into the library. His eyes widened at the sight of all the books there. Walls covered with shelves of books – books he would have to investigate later. Passed the tables and chairs, and to the right of a massive fireplace, an old grandfather clock counted off the passing of time, its pendulum swinging back and forth; tick tock, tick tock. To its left, an empty gun cabinet. *Strange*, he thought, a small frown crossing his face. He didn't like guns. Farther left was the awesome ocean view through the open French doors.

He hobbled over to them and stepped out onto the stone balcony. The vast, green ocean water stretched for miles before it met the hazy blue sky. He hobbled over to the railing; his attention drawn by the barking. He looked over the side and down the ragged cliff that served as the Inn's foundation, to the jagged rocks that lay far below; the ocean waves rolled in and out, in and out. It was low tide and hundreds of sea lions lay on the beach between the pointy spires, basking in the sunlight just out of tide's reach. He envied their ability to lie there without worry, without doubt.

I've been waiting for you, a voice whispered, hot and burning.

Scott turned and saw . . . no one.

And as he stood there wondering, a searing heat began to burn in his toe bones quickly engulfing his entire legs all the way to his groin. Darkness filled his eyes. Reaching out and grabbing the railing with both hands, he swayed in the dizzying heat. His heart thumped radically, and he could hear the blood pulsating through his body. It felt as if his head might explode and then the burning stopped and his vision returned. With his heart still racing Scott massaged his knees with the palms of his hands then slowly made his way back inside; the whispered words, *I've been waiting for you* seared in his brain.

• •8 • •

Sam, with his bald head exposed, had given them the grand tour, all the way from the roof garden, which he had just finished cleaning up that morning, to the kitchen. He wouldn't show them the cellar though. The door to the cellar was padlocked shut, *for safety;* he'd told them. If he owned the place, he'd wall it over for good. *Dangerous, very dangerous.*

"What about the previous owners?" Nora asked. "What happened to them?"

"Well," Sam began, "twas the darnedest thing. The Reeds shut the place down 'bout six years ago to remodel. Which, as you can see, they did a fine job, but then they never reopened. And when the tax man came collecting a year later, there was no one to collect from. Vanished, just like that." Sam snapped his fingers.

"Is it haunted?" Scott asked, feeling that presence again, a light touching on his brain, hot.

"Naw," the stout man said, with a nervous laugh. "Some say so, but I ain't never seen a ghost." Then he thought, *felt something though. Once on the stairway it brushed passed and then again in the library.*

Scott looked at Sam, the beady eyes quickly diverting, and knew, the place was indeed haunted. And there was something else Sam knew, something disturbing; something about the cellar. Scott tried to probe his mind but found a wall. Something was blocking his entry into Sam's puny little brain.

The town council down at Seal Bay hired me when they decided to put the place up for sale. "It's all yours now, here's the keys." Sam hung a small ring with two keys on a hook next to the swinging kitchen doors. He couldn't tell the new owner's of the thing in the cellar, his lips and mind were blinded to that subject.

· ·9· ·

After their tour of the Inn was completed, and the caretaker gone, Scott returned to the balcony outside the library. Holding onto the fancy iron railing he watched the orange sun disappear into a slow churning sea, the thin clouds turning pink and purple overhead. It was the most beautiful sight he'd ever seen. Too bad his camera was still packed away in some box in the back of the truck. *There's always tomorrow*, he thought.

In the fading light he watched the seagulls standing on the rocks below and flying in the sky beyond his reach, their screeching voices riding on the wind. The crashing, incoming tide was soothing to Scott's ears, driving the barking sea lions into the caves beneath the Inn.

Sudden stabbing, hot pain buckled Scott's knees, and he fell against the railing. *I've been waiting for you*, the hot voice repeated its welcome.

"Why?" Scott grimaced.

The jailer, it said. Then the pain vanished.

What jailer? Scott wondered.

"Scott," Nora said, startling him.

"Yeah?"

"You okay?"

"Yeah."

"Let's unpack the truck while it's not raining, shall we?"

"Sure."

· ·10· ·

Nora stood amongst the piles of boxes in their new living room wondering where to start. The brown paper bag with her bottles of rum sat on the fireplace mantle, beside the 'James Whittaker' clock. Reaching out with shaking hands she snatched the bag from the mantle, hugging it to her chest. Then she pulled out one of the bottles, unscrewed the cap and took a swig. Normally she didn't do that, but she was in dire need of a drink and there were no glasses here in the penthouse. She didn't want to go to the kitchen and risk Scott's finding out. Someday she might quit drinking, but not today. Replacing the cap, Nora placed the bottle back in the sack, setting it aside for later.

With a knife she slit the tape on the closest box marked 'fragile', knowing this was the box containing her many glass water globes. Most had been collected after her father's disappearance, but there were a few he'd given her. Reaching inside the box Nora pulled out and unwrapped the first ball, the yellow rose. After placing it on the fireplace mantle, she reached for another. The second ball was the tiny red rose. Nora gazed at it for a few moments before placing it on the mantle as well.

After emptying the first box, Nora methodically moved through the many boxes scattered about, the rum forgotten for the moment. Hours later, upon hearing the bonging of the grandfather clock in the library and looking at her wristwatch to see it was indeed after midnight, Nora grabbed her bottles of rum and headed for bed.

· ·11· ·

Scott emptied his boxes of books, each marked with a different author or series, one by one, onto the library fireplace mantel. The collection of mystery, sci-fi and fantasy books fit nicely there. Scott loved to read fiction. He opened the box marked Stephen King and pulled out 'The Stand'. Opening the cover he read the handwritten inscription there:

Scott;
May you always enjoy great fiction,
have a wonderful life, and find true love.

Your teacher,
Miss Leeann

Miss Leeann. What a great teacher she was, encouraging him to do all kinds of things, like seeing the world through photos and reading. She'd gotten him hooked on fiction, although she did have to teach him the non-fiction stuff – you know; the facts of math, science and history.

He was five when they first met. By the time he was ten and thinking more often about sex, he supposed Miss Leeann was about thirty. He could have found out, but it wouldn't be polite, according to his mom. Soon after his tenth birthday, he began asking Miss Leeann questions about sex. Not questions like, how are babies made, he knew about the physical act of sex, saw it in the magazines Gus had at Bob's. He was more interested in the psychological aspects. The chemistry, so to speak. How would he know when he'd found the right person to have sex with? Would there be only one? What about sexual preference? Those were the kind of questions he had asked. And she had answered by telling him her opinions, and then she said he would have to form his own views and opinions and to beware of myths. *Fairy tales fuck up a lot of marriages*, she said, stunning him with her use of the 'F' word.

Then one day when Scott was nearly fifteen, after his mom had gone to Kingston to shop for the day, he'd asked Miss Leeann a most serious question. *How does a man please a woman?*

She removed her school teacher glasses and looked at him through soft brown eyes, lovely eyes, captivating eyes, and Scott wondered how he'd missed their beauty all these years. Gently taking him by the hand and without a word, Miss Leeann led him to an empty cabin. He would never forget that day's lessons.

Days later, Scott was awarded his COE and Miss Leeann gave him the book he was holding in his hand, her book, a good-bye gift. His heart ached with missing her. But how he loved to disappear in the stories she most treasured, getting lost in adventures that he would never be able to physically participate in, no matter that they were fiction. Glancing up he wondered about the library's books. Would they be fact or fiction? He glanced over as the old grandfather clock bonged once. *Wow*, he thought, *time sure does fly when you're having fun.*

Relieved that he hadn't heard that awful voice again that evening, the one from the balcony, he set his book on the shelf above the fireplace mantle, with the rest of his collection, and exited the library, riding the elevator to the dark and quiet penthouse. Inside his new bedroom he opened the balcony doors, letting in that soothing ocean sound and the moonlit night air. He never knew how relaxing a sound could be till then. Crossing the room to the big bed, he unzipped the legs of his overalls, and took them off. Then he removed the steel reinforced leg braces with their huge, attached shoes, set them on the floor and climbed into bed. Outside, the ocean waves rolled in and out, back and forth, rocking Scott to sleep.

· · 12 · ·

As the new owners slept, Sam Jacobs crept in and made his way to the locked cellar door. A blast of hot air rolled out as the door swung open, Sam didn't notice. He hurried down the narrow stairs to his awaiting medal. The medal he deserved.

Standing before the ancient mirror, Sam waited as Ci'del appeared in the glass. Gazing into the lizard like eyes, he didn't see the needle tipped tail coming up over Ci'del's head.

You have done well, here is your reward.

The tail shot out of the mirror, plunging deeply into Sam's sternum with hot searing pain.

Then Ci'del pulled the caretaker's limp, dead body into the mirror.

C·H·A·P·T·E·R 6

HOMEWARD BOUND?

• • 1 • •

Illuminated in the glow of a droplight hanging from the rafters, the once Candy Ruby Red SL350KO Honda, now faded to pink and dinged up, sat in the back of the clean, straw smelling shed. A scratched up helmet hung on a peg on the wall above it. Garden tools hung from other pegs on the wall beside a tool bench. One peg, the shovel peg, was empty. Hanging on the wall above the tool bench, which ran the entire length of the small shed, were nicely arranged hand tools.

Will hustled passed his tool bench over to his bike, pulling it away from the wall. He unscrewed the gas cap, looked inside, then replaced the cap. He then pushed the bike over to where Ann was standing near the open doorway.

Keeping her eyes on Will's Pa, Ann held the shovel like a baseball bat. *Just in case,* Will told her, *he should wake up.* Wake up? He looked dead to her – dead, she sure as hell hoped he didn't wake up! It was freaking her out just thinking about it. The image of the two dead people with the birds pecking out their eyes reappeared in her mind.

"Come on," Will said, startling her, thrusting the helmet in her face. "Put this on."

Ann dropped the shovel next to the unconscious Joe, grabbed the helmet and put it on as Will hurried over to the jeep, pulling two sleeping bags from it; which he strapped to the back of the bike with a couple of bungee cords.

"What are those for?" Ann asked.

"Just in case we ain't got enough gas. Wouldn't wanna be stuck on the Oregon coast without some kinda warmth. These are 30 degree bags," he said, tapping them. Then he swung one leg over the bike and turned the key, giving the starter lever a good kick. "Get on," he yelled over the top of the motor's noise.

They rode out of the shed's doorway, passed his Pa, and into the darkness of night. Ann grasping on to Will for dear life, hoping he knew where he was going. The small head light bouncing along ahead of them barely lit the narrow, winding road. Eventually they came to a deserted highway.

William turned toward Seal Cape. His only concern now was getting as far away from Pa as possible, and quickly, and Seal Cape was certainly a ways. Again he wondered what she was doing out there in the Land of Many Lakes all alone. *How'd she get there? Who was that bear chewing on?* The image of the bear and the smell of cooked meat resurfaced in his brain. *Was she really running away?* Somehow he didn't think so, not now.

A short while later William took a sudden left hand turn onto a dirt road that led into the hills. The temperature dropped slightly, the sky darkened with the threat of rain and the trees seemed to close in on them. Ann leaned her head against his back. The trees whizzed passed in a blur; impossible to focus. She wondered how fast they were going, but then decided she really didn't want to know. Joe's words kept coming back to her. *Did ya notice her nice little titties, how 'bout the smell of her ripe little pussy?*

A car swooshed passed, going the other direction. Ann opened her eyes, unaware that she had dozed off, and looked out over Will's shoulder. They were no longer on the dirt road in the dense trees. They were on pavement again, riding along side a small stream. The three quarter moon slipped in and out of the thin cloud cover, shining down on them along with a few twinkling stars. It hadn't rained on them, and it looked like it might not. God, her butt hurt though. Unwrapping one arm from around Will's waist she tapped him on the shoulder. Will pulled over to the side of the empty highway, stopped the bike and turned it off. The non-noise was deafening. Ann slid off the bike, her legs as stiff as boards, yet rubbery at the same time; the vibration from the bike still running through them. Stretching, she then removed the helmet and shook out her short hair. Sudden dizziness swept over her, she reached out toward Will – her gloved hand skimming passed him, he caught her, steadied her.

"Thanks," she said. "I really had a cramp in my butt."

His smile was barely noticeable, very shy. He glanced at her through soft, dark eyes and nodded, then got off the bike and stretched too. His black hair poked out from under his red cap.

"Are we almost there?" she asked.

"About halfway," he said.

"Is that all?"

William nodded.

An uneasy feeling was beginning to grow just under the surface of her consciousness. Seal Cape didn't sound familiar, or even feel familiar. How would she know where to go once they got there? *What's the address?* And inside her head the voice spoke, *you will know.*

How?

Kismet, it replied.

Ann frowned. *Kismet? Just what was that supposed to mean?*

•• 2 ••

William Joseph Wade (known to most folks as Joe) came to just as Billy's motorcycle roared out of the shed passed him. He sat up. Damn his head hurt. He reached up and felt wetness behind his right ear. Son of a bitch! He looked at the blood on his fingers, the shovel on the ground next to him. *Goddamn little shit finally got some balls. Well, he'll just have to have another lesson, won't he? Him and that little bitch.*

Joe grabbed the stun gun from the ground beside him and stuffed it into his pants pocket then slowly got to his feet and stumbled to the house. Inside his hunting closet he found just what he was looking for. Reaching into the closet he pulled out the Rigel 3250 Compact Goggles. With these he wouldn't even need light to see – they were perfect for hunting pussy and dead meat. He put the goggles on his face. Then he pulled out his trusty, never had a miss, lever action Marlin M-1894 rifle and a box of shells. Now he was ready for hunting.

He was just getting ready to step out the door when a picture appeared on the TV, a picture of the young woman, *that bitch.* Joe hurried over to the TV and turned up the volume.

"Just in, Andrew Spear and wife Andrea along with their daughter Angelina pictured here have been reported missing by friends and neighbors after a two day hike in the Land of Many Lakes. The family was expected to return to their home in Mitchell by noon Sunday. Friends and neighbors became concerned when the family did not return as expected, and have not been heard from. Their abandoned vehicle and campsite were found at Jackass Springs Campground. Anyone with any information regarding the disappearance of the Spear family is urged to contact the California State Police. A one thousand dollar reward has been offered in this case for any information leading to the whereabouts of the family."

Joe chuckled, he wasn't about to tell anyone where the girl was, reward or not. He would take care of her, and the boy too, it was time. He lumbered out the door and hopped into the jeep.

At the end of the driveway Joe looked both ways through the goggles, the tiny tail light was nowhere in sight. Turning the lightless jeep to the left, down the back road, Joe floored it, driving as fast as the winding road would allow, always amazed at how good he could see with the night vision goggles. He would catch up soon and teach them both a lesson.

Where the back road met the long, straight highway, Joe stopped. To his left, an empty roadway, to his right, off in the far distance, the tiny tail light suddenly veered left off the highway. Joe smiled, and then sped after them.

· ·3· ·

Thin clouds sailed passed the face of the three quarter moon high overhead. The wind freshened, buffeting the motorcycle along its way. William was beginning to think they might get lucky and find Seal Cape before running out of gas. By his calculations they were close, very close. It was at that precise moment the motorcycle sputtered, lurched forward, and then died. Will pulled over to the side of the road and stopped. "Out of gas," he said, as Ann dismounted and removed her helmet.

"What now?" she asked.

Will got off the bike and stood in silence beside it for a moment. Then he said, "We otta be close, if I remember right. I know it's on this stretch of road, I remember that much. Don't you?"

"Will, I have something to tell you," Ann said. Bright moonlight reflected in her eyes, eyes that still made him feel woozy in the pit of his stomach every time she looked at him. "I don't really know if Seal Cape is my home." She stopped short of telling him of the little voice inside her head and the constant music there. It might not be such a good idea to admit one was crazy. "What if I'm a murderer? You know, I've blocked out all my memories because of some terrible thing I've done." Her voice grew smaller with each word, until he could barely hear her.

In the moonlight William could see that she was on the verge of tears, and they weren't just little ones, nope. It would be a major downpour. "Look, it'll be okay, you'll see. Trust me," he soothed. "You ain't a murderer." After all, he should know. He thought back to the bear in the woods chewing on *someone* and then to seeing her in the abandoned car, the spot on her forehead that now had color and looked like a rose, the blackened fingertips, the zapping of electricity every time she touched him. *Nope*, he thought, *she's just another victim.*

Releasing the bags from the back of the bike he set them on the ground. Then he removed his flashlight from his pack and flipped the switch. Shining it into the woods on the east side of the road he saw the trees were thick with underbrush on a small downward slope that quickly rose back into a steep hillside. He shoved the bike over the embankment, and into the underbrush. Grabbing the sleeping bags by the bungee cord, he took Ann by the hand and led her onward toward some unknown, unremembered home.

Ann shivered as the vision of the couple she'd left behind in the meadow with the birds pecking out their eyes resurfaced in her mind. *Who were they?* She had left them there for the birds. Did she murder them? She absently wiped the tears from her eyes, but more spilled out; a never ending flow, it seemed. Inside her head that familiar voice tried to sooth and console while music played in the distant background.

A short time later they came to a road sign. William shined his light on it:

Seal Cape Campground– 3 Miles
The Light Keeper's Inn – 3 Miles
Seal Bay – 5 Miles / Population 317

"This is it," Ann said.

Neither of them noticed the lightless jeep that was stopped, idling in the roadway a few hundred yards behind them.

· ·4· ·

Joe barreled over the crest of a small hill in the rusty WILLYS at break neck speed, nearly making his presence known to them, even though they were quite a ways ahead and walking with their backs to him.

Braking quickly, without slamming on the binders, he slowed to a crawl then stopped. He could have rushed up behind them, running them off the road, but knowing his boy, Billy would take off running through the brush dragging the girl along. Then Joe would have one hell of a time finding them. Oh, but he would find them. Then he'd teach them both a lesson. Just like the others.

This part of the country wasn't familiar to Joe. He didn't like the ocean much, it smelled like rotten fish or old pussy, both of which he detested. But he had other things to worry about right now. Looking straight ahead, through the night vision goggles, he kept a close eye on Billy and the girl as they stopped in front of a large sign. He watched as Billy shined a light on the sign. He watched the two of them stand there a moment longer, then he watched as they crossed the street and disappeared from his sight.

Go after them, a voice urged.

Joe pushed the accelerator of the old jeep to the floor and sped up to the sign where he pulled the jeep to the shoulder and read the huge words through the goggles. He peered down the tree lined road where his boy and the young woman were still in sight. Then he looked back to the sign.

• •5• •

Ann let William lead her by the hand down the semi-dark, one-lane blacktop road for a while after reading the road sign indicating it was still another three miles before they got to the Inn. The tears had stopped, but there was a growing anxiety. She had known immediately upon seeing the sign that their destination *was* the Light Keeper's Inn, but she couldn't remember for her life if she had actually ever been there. Did she really live there? Something deep down inside, way down where eternal memories live, said she didn't.

They walked on, passing a gravel driveway to their right with a 'Beware of Dog' sign hanging on a barbed wire fence. A short time later they came to a sharp bend in the road.

"Wait," she said, stopping abruptly. "What time is it?"

Will shrugged. "Don't know, ain't got a watch."

"Any guesses?"

He shrugged again. "Why?"

"This just doesn't feel right Will. Don't you think I'd remember something of this?" Ann asked, extending her arm in a gesture indicating their current surroundings.

"Dunno," Will replied with a shrug. "Amnesias kinda unpredictable; at least that's what Mr. Foote says."

"Who's Mr. Foote?"

"School teacher."

"Oh," she said.

There was a long pause.

"Will?" she asked. "How do you know about this place?"

"Ya really don't know?"

Ann shook her head.

"Murder," he said. "Maybe even more than one. It was all over the news. There's a lighthouse and an Inn, oldest ones on the Oregon coast. Some say it's haunted by the ghosts of the murdered family. Then there was the forest fire and then somebody bought the place. Hey, maybe it was your family."

"Why can't *I* remember?"

"Well, if ya got zapped by lightning it probably scrambled your brains like eggs I guess. Maybe seein it will help ya remember."

"I don't think we should be knocking on doors this late," Ann suggested. "We can do it in the morning – in the daylight." This solution was making her feel better already. Daylight would be safer.

Yes, her new inner voice agreed.

"Okay." William would do *whatever* she wanted, as long as it got them away from Pa. Shining his flashlight into the singed trees standing there opposite the bluff, William began looking for a place to enter the charred woods. A hint of burnt wood filled his nose as he led Ann in under the thin canopy of what was left of the forest. Somewhere behind them a dog was barking.

· ·6· ·

Joe hesitated at the sign, his vision blurred. The sign wavered in and out of focus. *Just where the hell is that lyin bitch leading Billy anyway?* "She don't live down there, that's for sure," Joe said aloud, the words slurring. He suddenly felt drained, it had been a goddamn long day and that lyin bitch had made Billy whack him over the head with a shovel, making his head bleed. He'd teach her a lesson for that. He'd teach them both a lesson, but right now he just couldn't keep his eyes open any longer.

Removing the goggles from his face Joe tossed them on the passenger seat. Turning the ignition key, killing the motor he then crawled into the back and curled up on the tiny seat there and immediately fell asleep.

· ·7· ·

Inside the woods William used his flashlight to scout out a place to camp. She was probably right; they shouldn't go knocking on doors this late at night. It was after midnight, he was pretty sure about that, and he was pretty sure Pa was looking for them, could in fact feel Pa looking for them. If they hung out here in the woods for the night maybe he'd drive right on passed. Maybe Pa wouldn't be able to find him, this time. Maybe that whacking on the head had really taken care of him. *You should have checked*, a voice spoke inside William's head. Yeah, William nodded, he should have checked. Then he spotted a nice little hollow under the overlapping branches of two shorter, unburned trees. "Is this okay?" he asked, shining his light into the little cove so that Ann could see it.

"Perfect," she replied, gazing in.

Once inside, William laid out the bags, sat down on one and removed his boots and jacket. He motioned Ann toward the other bag, his bag (he decided he wouldn't make her use Pa's smelly bag) and said, "That one's all yours. Don't worry, it don't smell too bad or have cooties."

Ann smiled. *The kids okay*, she thought, taking a seat, removing her shoes, gloves and jacket.

Each then climbed into their own bag and said good-night.

Ann fell asleep instantly.

William lay awake staring into the tree tops overhead. Through a clearing in the canopy he could see the moonlit sky beyond, thin clouds passing by the twinkling stars. He waited for what he thought to be about an hour, then sat up, withdrew another joint from the baggie, noted there were two left and as he wasn't going to see Dipshit Davy any time soon, figured them to be his last.

Shortly after his smoke, he fell into a dreamless sleep.

· ·8· ·

Ann, wake up.

She opened her eyes. An owl hooted nearby, not once, but twice. She sat up to the soothing roll of the ocean waves, breathed in the fresh ocean air and the slight smell of brunt wood. Faint, familiar music played inside her head. "Will?"

No answer.

Reaching into her sweatshirt pocket she fished out the tiny flashlight, turning the ring that brought forth its light. Will was completely inside his bag, apparently not the voice that had awakened her. The owl hooted again, twice. Ann laid the flashlight on her sleeping bag with the light still on and thrust her cold hands into her sweatshirt pocket. Her fingers brushed against something there. Pulling the smooth object from the pocket and holding it in the beam of light, she gazed at it for a long time. Then she moved the tiny red rose with its green leaves to the palm of her hand and something powerful and exciting began to happen. She watched in delighted fascination as the rose petals spread apart and swirls of red and pink color danced around her. Inside her head the familiar voice began to speak. It spoke of future events, secret powers, and unfamiliar worlds. It spoke of hope and love, of loss and gain. After awhile, the little red rose dimmed and closed up it petals.

Ann returned the rose to her pocket, shut off the flashlight and lay back down. Feeling drained, she faded off to sleep.

DAY THREE
TUESDAY

ROOM AND BOARD

· · 1 · ·

O n the small backseat of his piece a shit WILLYS, the inebriated, bearded man lay tangled up in sleep. Visions of rape and murder running through his sick mind.

Then the dream changes.

Joseph Wade is suddenly younger, much younger and driving through the country in his old, nearly dead pickup on a hot summer morning, sand dunes on one side, forest on the other. Up ahead is the dilapidated farm house. He pulls his old truck into the driveway where it dies under a golden tree. Through the old windshield he sees a beautiful woman sitting on the farmhouse porch steps, wearing cut off jeans and a halter top, in her hand a cup. He steps out of the truck and walks toward her. She stands on long, luscious legs. Her thick red hair is tied at the nape of her neck with a blue ribbon. Her brilliant green eyes send an electrifying jolt through his consciousness and Joe is suddenly overwhelmed by feelings he's never had before, feelings of need, desire, love. He pushes those feelings aside, he will never *love* any woman. They're nothing but trouble and heartache. His Pa told him so, and his Pa knew *everything* there was to know about women, you better believe it.

The squawk of a nearby crow startled the man awake. The dream instantly forgotten. He watched thin clouds pass by overhead, felt the morning dew on his skin and in his ragged beard, he shivered.

Joe got out of the jeep and stretched his stiffened legs. Grabbing the goggles from the passenger seat, he peered down the empty road where he'd seen Billy and that lyin bitch disappear the night before. A smile rose on his lips as the two run-a-ways emerged from the side of the roadway just where he'd seen them last. Today was his lucky day.

They will see you, a voice spoke inside his head.

Quickly Joe jumped into the jeep, started the motor, shifted into reverse and backed out of sight. He hopped out, grabbing his rifle and a handful of shells, which he stuffed into one pants pocket. Then he quickly limped across the highway on pins and needle legs, disappearing into the blackened forest.

· ·2· ·

Earlier, inside the woods, under the protection of the two unburned trees, Ann awoke in her cozy sleeping bag to the crisp early morning. She was feeling much better this morning, she had slept very well. She was no longer bothered by the uncertainties of who she was, as if her past life no longer mattered. The encounter with the rose was completely forgotten, for now. Looking toward the lump in the other bag she said, "Hey sleepyhead. Time to rise and shine."

William opened his dark eyes, rubbed the sleep from them and sat up, his black hair stuck out in varied directions on his head, a do she would have called a don't. "How long you been awake?" he asked.

"Not long," she said, grabbing her jacket and gloves from the inside of her sleeping bag and putting them on. "I don't suppose you put any food in that knapsack of yours."

Will nodded. "Yeah, there's a couple granola bars in there." He tossed the bag to her.

The granola bars were right on top. Underneath them she saw clothing, a fancy, metal handled slingshot and a box of ball bearings. She snagged one of the bars from the bag and tossed the bag back to Will. She turned the wrapped chocolate chip granola bar over in her hands before finally tearing it open and taking a dainty bite. "Got milk?" she asked.

Will shook his head, missing the joke. His mind was on other matters, matters concerning his pa.

When she finished eating, Ann used the hairbrush from her pack, hearing small snaps of static electricity. Then they rolled up their sleeping bags and made their way back to the little road leading to the Inn. As William helped Ann out of the charred woods and onto the roadway, he heard the sound of Pa's jeep starting in the distance, he was pretty sure about that. Looking up and down the empty road he saw no one, nothing. But the feeling that they weren't alone didn't go away. He knew his Pa was close by, watching.

"Did you hear that?" he asked.

"What?"

"A motor starting."

Ann shook her head. All she could hear was the crash of the ocean, the screeching seagulls, singing birds, a squirrel, the faint music, and, she thought, the distant barking of seals. *Seal Cape.* The name didn't seem to frighten her anymore, although she couldn't remember why it had. Was she afraid of seals? That seemed preposterous. Grabbing Will by the hand, she said, "Come on, we need to hurry." Not really knowing why, only knowing that it seemed important to get there.

"Whoa," William said, stopping her from dragging him forward. "What's the big hurry? Last night you were . . ." he wasn't quite sure how to put it, he didn't want to call her a chicken.

Ann stopped. "Chicken?" she asked.

"Hesitant."

She looked at him with her electrifying gaze and he saw that she was different this morning. He didn't know what had changed her, a good night's sleep? He couldn't remember how he'd slept. But it didn't seem to matter. Ann was ready to go on now; he saw it in her eyes.

·· 3 ··

This time it was Ann who led the way down the one-lane blacktop road, and she wasn't taking her time getting there. William had the insane feeling she was running toward something, something expected. *Maybe she remembers the place after all,* he thought. Still he couldn't shake the other feeling, the feeling that Pa was just a stone's throw away. He looked over his shoulder several times, but saw nothing.

A short time later, after passing the cutoff to town and then the entry to the campground, they stepped under the rock archway and onto the cobblestone drive. Ann gazed at the massive twin towers with no recollection at all, and yet she knew this was the place. For some reason they were supposed to be here. She turned toward Will and said, "I don't live here, but there's something we're supposed to do here."

William cocked his head to one side, raised an eyebrow then asked, "What'd ya mean something we're supposed to do here?"

"I'm not sure," she said.

William took in a deep breath, let it out in a long sigh and said, "Well, I guess we gotta find out."

Ann nodded in agreement and the two of them continued over the cobble-stone drive to the walkway and up the stone stairs to the entrance.

· ·4· ·

Joe lurked behind a large, unburned tree as William and Ann passed under the stone archway with its sign:

Welcome to the Light Keeper's Inn
Grand reopening November 1

When they were out of sight, he slithered through the shadows over to the archway and peeked around the corner of the stone pillar. His jaw dropped open at the sight of the stone Inn balanced on the edge of the cliff. Billy and that bitch were climbing the stone stairs to the impressive entrance, as if she really lived there.

Joe quickly moved through the gateway and around the backside of another large tree where he watched the big door to the Inn open and another boy, older yet shorter than his boy, appeared in the doorway.

"Rich little bastard," Joe muttered under his breath.

Then an idea came to Joe's sick mind, and he smiled.

· ·5· ·

Scott was looking through the books in the library, after finally getting all of his own books situated on the shelves above the huge, rock fireplace, when the door bell rang. "I wonder who that could be?" he said aloud.

Inside Scott's head Rachel spoke, *Rose.*

Rose? Rose Who? Scott thought back.

As usual, Rachel did not reply.

Scott hobbled as fast as his legs would carry him from the library out to the foyer where the sound of 'Bungalow Bill' floated down the penthouse stairs to greet him. He liked the Beatles, they were good. *The Best,* according to his mom. Luckily enough she had other music interests as well. She occasionally played the radio, if she could find a worthy station. She probably hadn't found a radio station here yet, or she just needed her Beatle fix, he supposed.

Opening one side of the heavy double doors Scott was surprised to see two young people standing there. They were both about the same height, both taller than him by a good three inches. His eyes were drawn to a mark in the middle of the girl's forehead resembling a rose,

Rose

like a third eye where her short, golden brown hair was singed. Her large brown eyes sparkled with light, like tiny lightning bolts. Scott was seized by her beauty and an unknown feeling rushed through him, something he'd never experienced before, and it wasn't lust. He knew about lust, Miss Leeann had taught him about lust, like the woman in the Kingston 7-11 who gave him a hard-on just looking at her.

Do you believe in love at first sight? Rachel asked.

The girl's cheeks were pale pink from the morning's cool air, the petite corners of her lips were drawn up in a dainty smile. She was wearing a slightly too large black leather jacket, matching gloves and blue sweat pants. Her skin was very pale, and her face, intoxicating.

Ann gazed back at the boy on the other side of the doorway. His curly, reddish hair fell over pale blue eyes that studied her for a long time, but Ann didn't mind, not one little bit.

Scott finally tore his gaze from the girl's face and looked closer at the boy. He was younger. He'd taken off his red baseball cap, revealing black, curly hair. His dark, soft eyes were almost as black. He was wearing a denim jacket and faded jeans and holding a pair of sleeping bags in one hand.

"Sorry to bother you, Sir," the boy began, "our motorcycle ran outta gas up the road a piece and well, we're outta money and need a place to stay. We could work for it."

Scott chuckled. He didn't know what to say. *Sir? Work in exchange for a room?* "Well, I'm not the boss, but I'm sure we can work something out," he said. "Come on in."

Familiar music floated down the interior staircase as Ann and William followed the boy with the strange hobble into the spacious Inn.

Kismet, Ann's inner voice said. Again she wondered just what that meant as they followed him passed a huge counter and into a room with sofas and chairs, a sitting room.

"Have a seat," he said. "I'll get the boss . . .lady." Scott wondered what they were hiding. It would be easy enough to find out, if he really wanted to.

· ·6· ·

Nora was standing at her old record player, half empty rum bottle in hand, when the doorbell rang for the first time since their arrival. She could hear the muffled voices downstairs in the foyer, then the elevator hummed to life. She glanced at the bottle in her hand, as if seeing it for the first time, wondering how it had gotten there. She glanced towards the doorway of the living room and wondered groggily if she had enough time to make it to her room before Scott arrived or if she should just stand her ground and not worry about it. This was, after all, her home and her life, she could do as she damn well pleased. She heard the swoosh of the elevator gate opening and knew there was no choice now, she'd waited too long. Quickly she set the bottle on the fireplace mantle, behind the 'Whitaker' clock, out of sight.

Scott entered the room and said, "We have guests."

Nora hadn't slept well that first night. Strange noises kept waking her, noises that sounded like voices. Although she couldn't actually hear the words, it was still unsettling.

"Who?" she asked.

"A couple of teenagers, asking to work for a place to stay," Scott replied.

· ·7· ·

Ann marveled over the Inn's interior beauty. Taking a seat on one of the rattan wicker sofas, she removed her gloves and ran her hand over the purple, crushed velvet cushion. She then felt the matching lampshade, the hanging tassels. A small table beside the sofa supported a pile of books, picture books of the Pacific Coast. She picked one up and was thumbing through it when the boy who greeted them at the door returned with *The Boss Lady*. A tall, slender woman with curly, brilliant auburn hair and emerald green eyes. She was wearing brightly colored silk pajamas and bunny slippers.

Ann smiled, put the book down and stood up. William was standing at the closed French doors leading to the balcony, looking out through the clean glass.

"Welcome to the Light Keeper's Inn," the tall woman said. "I'm Nora Anderson, and this is my son Scott."

"Hi," Ann said, looking at the boy with the light blue eyes as they exchanged greetings a second time. Then she looked at the woman, his mother, and saw the resemblance. She also saw something else, sadness.

William shot over to them, extended his hand and said, "My name's William Wade, and this is my sister, Ann. Pleased to meet ya." Ann saw a hint of recognition on Ms. Anderson's face, but remained silent, as Will introduced himself.

"What was the name?" Ms. Anderson asked, taking his offered hand.

"William Wade."

"Wade," she paused, her green eyes blazing. "I knew a Wade once, long time ago. A Joseph Wade, you know him?"

"No, Ma'am," William lied.

"No matter. Well, I'm sure we can put you to work, but right now I'll show you to one of the guest rooms where you can clean up before we have some brunch. Would that be okay?"

William and Ann nodded simultaneously.

Nora didn't look too long at the girl's tattoo. It seemed nice and delicate in comparison to some she'd seen. Had Nora not drank nearly half a fifth of rum the previous evening, she might have noticed that these kids should have been in school, and that the mark on the girl's forehead was no tattoo.

· ·8· ·

Ann and William followed Ms. Anderson out the south side sitting room door into the breezeway and up the stone spiral stairs with the wind whipping around them and the waves crashing far below, before finally arriving at the door of the third floor room. Once inside, Ms. Anderson showed them how to regulate the fireplace heat. In front of the fireplace was a sofa, two matching chairs and a coffee table. Next to the fireplace was a little kitchenette. On the fireplace mantel was a square clock, its hand showing the time to be nine o' five and above it, a colorful oil painting of a deserted beach at sunset. On the other side of the fireplace, next to the balcony's French doors, were two dining chairs and a table. A large bed was to the left of the doors with a matching six drawer dresser at its foot. In a little alcove beside the door to the bathroom was a vanity sink and counter. In the large bathroom, the oversized claw foot tub was so inviting Ann could hardly wait to use it. In the closet they found the spare roll-a-way bed and pulled it out for William to sleep on later.

After Ms. Anderson left the room Ann turned to William and asked, "Why'd you tell her you don't know Joe, isn't that your Pa?"

"Yes," he said. A pained look clouded his dark eyes. "Some things ain't worth tellin. Ya don't know my Pa."

"What is it Will? Do you want to talk about it?"

"No," he said.

"Sure?"

"Yeah."

"Okay. I'm gonna take a bath." She turned away wishing he would open up to her, tell her about his Pa, but maybe she didn't really want to know. The little voice inside her head remained silent.

· ·9· ·

Nora kicked off her bunny slippers, slid out of the silk pajamas and headed for her own bath. The name "Wade" kept coming back to her. *Who are they really and why does William seem so familiar?*

Really, who are you trying to kid? A voice asked inside her head, instantly transporting her thoughts back through the years to that hot day in August. It's early morning and she's sitting on the porch step. Out behind the house, her house since she was twelve, is the constant buzzing of ATV's on sand dunes. She watches with curiosity as an old, faded black pickup truck pulls in and stops under the shade of the golden aspen tree. She raises her hand to shield her eyes from the glaring sun and wonders, *who is that?*

A tall, young man gets out of the driver's side. His hair hangs just over his ears, jet black and curly. His muscles ripple inside a faded green tee-shirt and camouflage pants. On his feet, a pair of black, army style boots.

Nora stands as he approaches.

"Morning Miss," he says.

Her heartbeat quickens, even though she's nearly thirty five and has never been married, no one calls her miss anymore.

"Morning," she replies.

"Name's Joseph Wade," he says, extending a muscular arm toward her. His black eyes penetrate hers. There's a stirring below, long time coming. She shakes his masculine hand.

"I wonder if you might need some repairs done," he says. "I'm looking for a little work, just kinda passing through."

Nora thinks, *you could service me*, then says, "Well, the roof could use some repair."

He looks up to the roof. "Sure, I could do that."

Later that night they sit together on her sofa. Soft music from the radio plays in the background. He caresses her cheek, her neck. He kisses her lips and she eagerly responds. He unties the halter, lets it fall. Kisses her breasts, her nipples. He lifts her from the sofa and carries her to the bedroom.

The next morning, it was all over, not that she was in love, not even close. It still hurt. He came out of her room, freshly showered and all dressed up. The army fatigues and tee-shirt replaced by a nice suit. He looked and smelled fabulous. She had fixed breakfast, scrambled eggs and ham with toast. He looked at the eggs with its little pieces of ham and said, *what the hell kinda slop do ya call this? I'm not eating that shit*. And his black eyes blazed furiously at her as she shrank away. Then he grabbed the plate of eggs and threw it at her, the plate whizzing passed, just missing her head. Unexpected tears spilled over onto her cheeks, and that's when he came toward her, grabbed her by the throat with his large hand and said, *I'm leaving, Bitch*. And he did just that. He grabbed her car keys from their hook on the wall and walked out the door. Nora never saw him or her Chevy again.

• •10• •

Lounging in the sitting room Scott thought mostly about the girl. She was not William's sister, but she was beautiful. He couldn't seem to get her out of his head, the large brown eyes, the pale skin, and that mark

Rose

on her forehead. It reminded him of something, something he'd read recently or seen somewhere. He shook his head as whatever it was wouldn't reveal itself. It seemed to him that she was perhaps in trouble. Whatever trouble she was in he wanted to help her. She was enchanting, and she'd cast her spell on him, that was for sure. He wanted to be with her always, for the rest of his life; however long that might be. But did she feel the same? Would she feel the same if she knew about his disease? Would she treat him like those kids at school? Scott closed his eyes and mind to that long ago vision.

Rachel made no comments.

What about William? The kid had lied, pure and simple. Scott knew it even before it happened. He wasn't lying about his name, he really was William (most people call me Billy) Wade. The real lie was in the answer about a man named Joseph Wade, a man Scott's mother had once known, a man that might just be his father; he'd seen it in her thoughts. Why had Billy lied?

It's not important, Rachel whispered.

How would you know? Scott thought back.

Rachel said nothing.

· ·11· ·

The hot, steamy water felt good on her bare skin as Ann slowly sank into the tub, washing away all the dirt and grime from the last few days. The tips of her fingers and toes were beginning to itch, as was her forehead. She had looked in the mirror as the tub was filling, had touched the mark at her hairline that now looked like a rose, thinking it somehow important.

A look of unfamiliarity crossed the face staring back at her, the large, dark eyes, and short, mousey hair with its singed ends that stood up in a frizzy mess on her head, the nearly non-existent eye brows and lashes, the pointy nose, and thin lips, dimples. The very pale, white skin. *Why can't I remember?*

Lightning, the little voice whispered. *And kismet.*

Lightning and kismet, Ann mused, raising her thin brows.

Then her thoughts turned to Scott, thoughts of being held in his strong arms, thoughts of kissing his sweet lips. Had she ever kissed a boy before? Did he like her? God she hoped so.

· ·12· ·

While Ann bathed, William stood on the balcony, the wind pulling at his cap. He was thinking that sooner or later the lies he'd told would catch up with him. But he had to keep a low profile, had to make sure that no one knew about Pa. They couldn't find out.

He pondered the fact that Ms. Anderson seemed to know Pa yet didn't know what he did, or at least couldn't remember, and that was a good thing. But he wondered where she knew him from. His thoughts turned to the pictures he'd found years ago in the old trunk under Pa's bed, hundreds of pictures of Pa in uniform with hundreds of pretty young women, each one different yet all the same; young, sweet and innocent. Victims waiting for a hero. *But, where does Ms. Anderson fit in? Is she a victim? A survivor? Were there survivors? She's older than Pa. Maybe one of the young women in Pa's pictures was her daughter . . .*

William pushed the thought away.

Turning from the balcony railing, he headed back inside, the decision made that he would tell them the truth before something really bad happened.

Digging a fresh pair of clothes from his pack, he quickly washed up at the vanity sink and then changed into them. He placed another set of clothes on the table for Ann. Outside the bathroom door, he hollered, "I'll be downstairs." Then raced out the door.

• • 13 • •

Scott hobbled to the elevator, stepped inside and closed the gate. He pushed the down button. It was time he started the coffee. He still couldn't get his thoughts off Ann, and he was tempted to reach out for her with his mind, see what she was thinking. He could hear his mother saying that wouldn't be polite, and decided she was right.

He stepped through the swinging kitchen doors. Something was different, the room was very warm. The cellar door stood open, the padlock was gone. He hobbled over to the open door and peeked down the narrow stairs. A wave of hot air licked his face.

"Anybody down there?" he yelled, thinking his mom might have decided to investigate the cellar instead of going to her room for her morning bath, knowing she had no key to the lock. A sudden ill feeling washed over him as the voice from the balcony drifted up the cellar stairs and said, *Come on down, come on down and have some fun.*

Scott slammed the cellar door shut.

With heart racing he hurried over to the counter, grabbed the coffee pot, and fumbled for the coffee and filter. *What the hell was down there?* Not only what, but who and why also occurred to him. There was something in the cellar Uncle Ed hadn't told him about. Something to do with the missing mirror, he was sure of it. And it was really starting to get to him. Now this girl, Ann, had mysteriously shown up on their doorstep, and Rachel had called her Rose.

What did it mean? He really needed to get to the bottom of this.

A sudden noise touched his ears. Scott quickly whirled around, almost dropping the glass coffee pot, expecting the cellar door to be standing wide open with some monster lurking there, instead the cellar door was still shut and William was standing just inside the swinging doors. Scott put his hand over his heart and said, "Man you scared the shit out a me."

William grinned. "Sorry."

"It's okay." Scott studied the boy; the curly black hair, the dark eyes, and the face that slightly resembled his own. He had changed into a long sleeved green and gold, flannel shirt tucked into jeans, no belt, and no baseball cap. His boots were scuffed black and worn out. "So, should I call you William or Billy?"

"William," he replied.

"But most people call you Billy, right?" Scott asked. He finished filling the coffee maker with water, and then set the empty pot under the hopper. His mom would want coffee as soon as she was out of the tub.

William frowned, "How'd ya know that?"

"Lucky guess. How would you like to join me for a little walk?"

"Sure."

"Good, let's go then."

• •14• •

As William and Scott exited the Light Keeper's Inn, Scott said, "We'll have to take it slow, hope you don't mind."

"Not at all," William replied, "I like a slow stroll."

"Do you? We'll I'd walk faster if I could, but I was born with MD, do you know what that is?"

"Sure, Jerry's kids, right?"

Scott nodded. "The doctor's say it's a muscular disorder, not the normal kind of MD, but something they haven't seen before."

"Oh," William replied. "Ain't there a cure?"

"Not yet, but hey, they said I'd be in a wheelchair ten years ago, and here I am still walking."

"Great," William said. "After you then." He motioned Scott to lead the way then followed him down the pathway from the Inn to the bluff at the lighthouse where they stopped to gaze out over the ocean for a few minutes. Dark marine clouds hovered on the horizon. Billowy white ones floated by above as a thinner layer danced lightly on the breeze below.

They continued south on the path along the edge of the bluff for about 500 feet before coming to a set of stone stairs leading down to the beach. A stone bench sat at the top of the stairs.

"Let's sit here a few minutes, William. I want to tell you what I know," Scott said, pointing to the bench.

Once seated, Scott continued. "I know your name is William Wade, just like you said, but most people call you Billy. Even though it's not a name you're fond of. I know Ann is not your sister. Am I right so far?" Scott folded his muscular arms across his chest and leaned against the back of the bench.

William nodded, looking out over the ocean.

"I also know that your father is Joseph Wade even though you said you don't know him. Now, it is possible that this man, your father, is also my father. I'd like to know why you disclaim him."

The stone bench was cold under William's butt. He shifted a bit but didn't respond right away. He *wanted* to tell Scott everything. But could he tell him that his "father" was a killer? A rapist, a murderer of young women. That Ann would have been Pa's next victim if he hadn't whacked him over the head with a shovel. That even now Pa was probably tracking them.

"How?" Scott asked.

William looked curiously into the light blue eyes of his possible half-brother. "How what?" he asked.

Scott's mind was burning with the words Killer, Rapist, and Murderer. How could such a man be his father? How could his mother . . .he didn't want to think about how his mother could, it didn't matter and it was a long time ago. A lifetime. "Is your Pa going to show up here looking for you? You and Ann?" he asked.

"Maybe," William replied. *Yes,* he thought.

"How soon?"

"Today, tomorrow, maybe next week."

"How?" Scott asked. "How could he know you're here?"

William's thoughts slipped back to a time when he'd tried to run away from home, shortly after seeing something so terrible he never wanted to think about it, but always did, it was always there tormenting him, then said, "Dunno, but he finds me, somehow."

There was a pause.

"Tell me about Ann," Scott said.

"I found her sleepin in an old car in the woods. She seemed lost. Her fingertips was black and she had that spot on her head, the one that looks like a rose? I think she got zapped by lightning, but I didn't see it. I knew, soon as I saw her, she was the kind a girl Pa was looking for; a run-a-way. I didn't want him to find out about her, but she followed me. Then she said she don't remember her name or where she's from. I was takin her to the Ranger Station when Pa came along and stopped me."

Scott sat there a moment seeing the visions in William's memory, then asked, "How many others, before Ann?"

"Too many," was William's only reply.

FAMILIAR FACES

··1··

J oe hesitated for a long time after watching the two boys leave. There was something about the other boy that caught his eye, something in the curl of his hair, the manner in which he stood on the porch for a moment before leading Billy down the stairs and toward the lighthouse, disappearing behind it.

Finally stepping from his hiding spot behind the tree, Joe stood up a little taller, smoothing the wild black curls, the shaggy beard and mustache. With his rifle in hand he then marched off through the dewy, wet lawn toward the towering Inn. His thoughts focused on his one goal, never seeing his old pickup parked in the driveway.

At the bottom of the massive stone stairs Joe hesitated again. He'd seen Billy and the other boy leave, but who was left inside waiting for him? The little lyin bitch, that was who. He could teach her a lesson, he could sure do that. And maybe she wasn't alone, maybe she had a friend in there. He started up the stairs then stopped again as a weird sensation came over him.

Fear; a voice whispered inside his head.

Hell no! He wasn't scared a nothin.

What about love?

Ignoring the voice, Joe marched up the stairs.

··2··

It was the aroma of fresh brewed coffee drifting up through the open penthouse doors that Nora smelled all the way into her bath. She stepped out of the tub, quickly dried herself off and then slipped into a pair of stretch blue jeans and a flowered blouse. Quickly brushing through the wild, red hair she then tied it back with a blue ribbon. Looking into the mirror, seeing the tiny age lines around her eyes, she grabbed the moisturizer, dabbing it on. Afterwards she went out to their new living room. It was time for her first cup of coffee, (perhaps she would skip the rum this morning) and to restart the music.

Strolling over to her hi-fi, Nora removed the current record from the player, placed it lovingly into its jacket then put it into the crate on the floor. Selecting another Beatles LP, she put side four on the spindle. She watched as the record dropped onto the turntable and the arm swung over, setting the needle onto it. Nora loved side four of this particular LP. She felt it good for her soul, but she needed her coffee, it was already nearly ten o'clock and they had company coming for brunch.

Nora was just staring to descend the stairs when the bell rang for the second time that morning. Seemed the Light Keeper's Inn was suddenly a very popular place.

Put up a sign and they will come, she thought dryly.

· ·3· ·

Ann hopped out of the tub shortly after Will hollered that he was going downstairs. Wrapping a towel around her naked body she went out into the room. Folded nicely on the table was a pair of jeans, and a red and blue flannel shirt, with a note.

Ann,
These are for you.
Will

She slipped into the clothes, a little surprised by their clean smell. The jeans were a little snug and about two inches too long. She rolled the legs into a cuff. The shirt sleeves she rolled up to just below her elbows. Brushing through her short, clean hair, she heard the snapping static. Her stomach rumbled. She was suddenly hungry, the granola bar hadn't lasted. She hurried back to the bathroom.

While gathering her discarded clothes from the bathroom floor, something fell and went bouncing across the tile, landing under the tub. Getting down on her hands and knees, Ann peered around the tub's claw feet.

At first she saw nothing, not even dust bunnies. Then something sparkled into sight and right away she recognized the rosebud from the car. She'd forgotten all about it. Reaching far under the tub, Ann finally snagged the rose, pulling it from its hiding place. Holding it in the palm of her hand, she gazed at its smoothness, so perfect, so beautiful, and chilly to the touch yet glowing in the overhead light. She held it for a long time, turning it over and over before finally stuffing it into her shirt's breast pocket, fastening the button.

Dumping the dirty clothing on the bed Ann hurried barefoot out the door and down the cold stone stairs, stopping briefly to gaze out at the ocean, so blue and calm on the horizon – the waves crashing thunderously against the rocks below. The ocean breeze swept across her face, causing her freshly brushed hair to stand on end. A seagull landed on the railing beside her, cocked its head to look at her with one black eye then flew away against the wind.

· ·4· ·

Nora glided down the stairs, the constant ringing of the door bell getting on her nerves. Maybe she'd have that rum after all. *Who the hell do these people think they are anyway? Can't they read the damn sign? Opening November first, not October thirteenth.*

She swung the door open and gasped. The color ran from her face as her green eyes widened. Instant sobriety washed over her in a cold, numbing wave.

· ·5· ·

Nora instantly recognized the face looking back at her. Older, fatter, bearded; the hot burning furry in the dark, murderous eyes. He shoved the rifle under her nose and said, "My, my, as I live and breath. If it ain't the best pussy I ever ate. The one woman I couldn't kill, till now, that is."

"Joseph," she gasped, backing into the foyer. Joe followed her inside and closed the door.

"So, you're the rich bitch owns this place?" he asked.

Nora said nothing. *Where the hell was Scott?*

"What's a matter? Cat got your tongue?" He motioned her into the sitting room. "Nice place, who'd ya have to fuck to get it?"

Nora remained silent; thoughts of escape darted through her mind. He had a gun, she did not. Was it loaded? What about a distraction? Maybe she could trick him somehow, appeal to his sexual prowess – get him in a compromising position. But how? She had to do something, think of something. Then it hit her, an idea that just might work.

"Joseph," she began. "I've missed you."

All thoughts of the younger, lyin bitch fell from Joe's mind as The Little Head took over. His Woody raged at seeing the Number One Bitch again, the one that almost trapped him. She was still the most ravishing woman he'd ever seen. And, she still wanted him, he could tell.

"Take off your clothes," he demanded.

Nora hesitated; this wasn't exactly what she had in mind.

"Now!" He bellowed.

She flinched at the harshness of his voice then quickly unbuttoned and removed her blouse, and tossed it aside, very aware of the murderous glare in his black eyes. Then she slid out of the jeans, letting them fall to the floor, kicking them away.

"Those too," he said, referring to her bra and panties.

Removing them, Nora stood before Joe completely nude except for the bunny slippers on her feet.

"Turn around," he said.

With her back to him, Joe hung the unloaded rifle by its strap over his shoulder, grabbed the discarded blouse then roughly seized her wrists. Tugging them behind her back he tied them together with the blouse's sleeves. Then placing his big hands on her bare shoulders he swung her around to face him. Now he could do anything he wanted to her, anything. He glanced around the large, open room; no good.

"Where's the bedroom?" he snarled.

"Upstairs."

"Go!" Joe commanded.

Nora hesitated.

Joe reached inside his pocket, brought out the stun gun and touched it to her bare breast. A hurting jolt of electricity surged through her, almost making her pee.

"Now," he said, "or do ya want some more?"

· ·6· ·

Ann entered the empty sitting room. A familiar smell that hadn't been there earlier drifted passed her nose – coffee. She crossed the room to the foyer then peeked into the empty library. Perhaps everyone had gone to the kitchen for brunch. She hoped she wasn't too late as her stomach rumbled again. Following the aroma of freshly brewed coffee she made her way down the stairs to the empty dining room and then into the kitchen but found no one; only a pot full of coffee, not even a single cup gone from it.

She raced back to the sitting room, something wasn't right. She had a feeling that everything was, in fact, terribly wrong.

Danger, the familiar voice warned.

· ·7· ·

They were almost back to the Inn after their little pow-wow on the stone bench. Scott was trying his best not to think of the man who might be his father, a man who was really a monster, when those thoughts were shattered by hot needles pricking his thighs. It seemed his muscles were giving out sooner these days, especially today. With determined effort Scott ignored the pain and dragged each leg slowly forward. Normally there was no pain with the disease, at least none that he could recall, at least not until he arrived here, at the Inn. It made him wonder about the voice he'd heard on the balcony, the same voice he heard coming from the cellar. Was there really some monster waiting for him there?

The words, *I've been waiting for you*, reappeared in his brain, he shuddered. He didn't believe in monsters, did he? Suddenly the pain grew into searing, stabbing knives all along both legs. Tears sprang to his eyes. He tottered off balance, falling forward. His hands hit the rocky ground at the same time William, seeing Scott's forward motion, reached out and grabbed him by the straps of his coveralls, slowing the fall, but not completely stopping it. Scott stayed there on his hands and knees a moment until William said, "So, ya wanna shoulder to lean on?"

"Sure," Scott replied.

When they reached the Inn's steps, Scott took a seat on the first tier; he needed a little rest before climbing them. William sat down beside him. Each lost in his own thoughts.

· ·8· ·

Ann stood at the bottom of the stairs leading, she assumed, to an apartment where Scott lived with his mother, and maybe others. Familiar music drifted out of the double wide doors standing open at the top of the staircase. Was anybody up there?

Yes, her inner voice claimed.

Perhaps she would just take a quick peek. Quietly Ann mounted the stairs, stopping just inside the doorway. To her left was a living room, the décor much the same as the rest of the Inn. Straight ahead, the hallway to the elevator and another room, to her right another hallway with three closed doors.

Stepping into the living room her eyes were drawn to a large window spanning the entire southeast wall overlooking the rose garden. An unlit fireplace covered most of the south wall. Several glass water globes, each with a different flower inside, sat on its mantel surrounding a square clock sitting in the center. Flattened boxes lay in the room's corner next to it. The wall to her right was covered with small mirrors and several framed photographs of wildlife and scenery.

The familiar music flowed from an old record player sitting to the left of the fireplace. She went over to it. She hadn't seen one of those since, since when? On the floor next to it sat a wooden crate filled with record albums. The one lying on top was blue and titled, 'The Beatles 1967-1970' and had a picture of four young men on the cover. It looked nearly brand new. Ann picked it up and looked closer at the pictures then flipped it over to the backside. The same men, younger, with shorter hair, bigger ears and bigger smiles. Inside the double cover was a black and white photo spanning both sides. In the photo a crowd of people stood and stared, including the Beatles, behind a black iron fence behind a young blonde headed boy.

A new song began to pour from the record player, a vision flashed inside her mind, a memory? An auditorium filled with cheering, happy people – an older man at the piano. Instant recognition washes over her as the words flow out, *When I find myself in times of trouble, Mother Mary comes to me, speaking words of wisdom, Let it be,* a song she now recognized, actually hearing it, every note, inside her head, the same tune that had been there since waking up in that meadow, alone, with the dead. She shivered. The faces of the people surrounding her were blurred, all except the face of the singer. She looked again at the black and white photo, at Paul McCartney standing there behind that iron fence – she had seen him in concert. *When? Recently? And with who? My (bird food) parents?* Ann pushed the thought away and returned the album cover to the wooden crate.

She glanced back toward the landing, and the hallways with their closed doors. Making her way back there, Ann paused. To her left was one room and the elevator, straight ahead the other three doors. She looked back and forth between them, then decided to try the hall with the three doors first. At the first door she paused again, and then raised her hand and tapped softly three times, then waited. After a moment with no answer she turned the crystal knob and pushed the door open just enough to peek in. The large unmade bed was empty. The doors leading to the balcony stood open with the sound of the crashing waves and the bright morning light streaming in. Stacked boxes littered the room. A weight bench sat in front of the closet.

Pushing the door wide open, she stepped inside.

Beside the nightstand next to the bed, a pair of metal forearm crutches leaned against the wall. A framed photograph of four people smiled back at her from atop the nightstand. She recognized a much younger Scott and Ms. Anderson, the other two people, an older man with thinning white hair and bright blue eyes, and a woman, her silver hair piled atop her head, her eyes the color of charcoal gray, were probably grandparents. *Yeah*, she thought, *they look like loving grandparents, all smiles and glittery eyed.* Yet they were somehow familiar to her. Thoughts of her own grandparents, surely she must have them, sprang to mind. Were they looking for her? Did they know she was missing? Did they even care? Ann shook the questions from her head, and left the room, softly closing the door behind her. Behind door number two was a bathroom. The third door opened into another unoccupied bedroom.

Ann was just reaching out to knock on the forth door, the last door and the one closest to the elevator when her nose picked up a smell from her recent past. A dirty, disgusting stink. She wrinkled her nose. *It's the smell of sweat and cologne, Old Spice; the smell of Joe. Joe came looking for us and now he's here behind this closed door. Had he been invited in?*

Ann hesitated, not knowing what to do. She surely didn't want to see Joe and she didn't want Joe seeing her. Leaning against the door and pressing her ear against it she listened – unable to make out the noises – muffled voices, a familiar, buzzing sound, something she'd heard recently, and then a muffled cry.

Caution, keep low. Fear washed over her. Quickly kneeling in front of the door, she turned the crystal knob and slowly pushed the door open a crack.

Immediately inside to her left against the wall stood a beautiful, dark brown dresser on large flower bud feet and bamboo stalk legs, a rifle leaned against it. A lamp atop the matching night stand next to a big bed spilled its soft light upon Ms. Anderson tied to it, her arms stretched out over her head, her legs wide open and tied to the footboard, the bunny slippers still on her feet. Ann's view of Ms. Anderson's face was obstructed by a sight she never wanted to see; Joe's bare ass.

Ann glanced back to the rifle. Could she get her hands on it before Joe saw her? She looked back to Joe, her fear rising ever higher as she then noticed the knife, its curved blade large and shinny, in his upraised hand. Quickly she reached out, snatching the rifle from its place just as Joe turned his head, seeing her.

BEWARE! The voice inside her head screamed.

In an amazing show of speed Joe leapt toward her, the knife still in his hand. With no time to get to her feet Ann quickly brought the rifle up and pulled the trigger.

Nothing happened.

She pulled it again, and again. It simply didn't work.

At the other end of the useless rifle, the disgusting animal wearing nothing but a green tee-shirt, and a hard-on wagging out in front of him, stood laughing. Then Ann remembered something, a memory; a man in uniform showing her the importance of firearm safety. *The rifle must have a safety switch, somewhere; where?*

Before she could recall, Joe ripped the rifle from her hands, tossed it across the room, and grabbed her by the neck with one big hand. Sliding the hunting knife into its sheath on the dresser atop his pants, Joe then grabbed something else from the pile, a black plastic handle with two prongs, metal prongs. Ann's brown eyes widened as she recognized the stun gun, the one he'd used on Will. Joe brought it toward her, touching her on the breast with it, sending a jolting pain coursing through her body. She squirmed to get away. He jolted her again, exhilarated in the pain he was causing.

"Always tryin to save somebody, ain't ya, ya little bitch!" Joe snarled, slamming her hard against the wall, knocking the breath from her lungs.

She collapsed to the floor in a heap.

··9··

From her position on the bed Nora could do nothing more than watch in rage as Joseph first stunned the girl twice, while chocking her, and then slamming her against the wall. Nora thrashed from side to side against the bonds holding her wrists to the headboard. Oh how she wanted to kill him right now! The knot loosened slightly, her eyes widened with hope. If only he hadn't found something to tie her legs to the bed with, and a gag. She was in a real fine mess now. She couldn't help Ann, she couldn't scream or bite and she couldn't kick. But maybe she could get her hands free.

Nora resumed her thrashing, working to loosen the bonds around her wrists more. Joseph's face appeared above hers, and then the zapping jolt of the stun gun bore into her hip and she cried out under the bonds of the panty gag, remembering his words, *I'd use mine, if I wore em,* followed by the insane laughter.

"Now where were we?" he whispered slyly, as if all this was good fun for her. Then added, "Hold still or I'll slit the girl's throat."

Nora glared at him through tear filled eyes. Soon, she promised herself, soon she would loosen the bonds enough to escape, and then she would put an end to all of this. She would strangle him with her panties or maybe put a bullet in his head, or stick him with his own knife or better yet, stun him to death. No matter, he would be dead either way, she would see to it, and then she would celebrate with a big, stiff drink, rum without the coffee this time, she deserved it.

Joe moved from the bed back to the girl and said, "Stupid little bitch, don't worry, I'll do you next, I promise."

Ann didn't move.

The shaggy man smiled, replaced the stun gun with his hunting knife and went back to Nora.

··10··

The zapping of the stun gun the first time hurt like crazy. But, the second blast had done something else – given Ann something else. She wasn't sure how, but somehow she was different. She'd closed her eyes and slumped to the floor. She could hear Ms. Anderson thrashing back and forth on the bed. Then she heard Joe whisper, *Hold still or I'll slit the girl's throat,* and the thrashing stopped. Then he had come to check on her and she had tricked him. She'd seen his ruggedly handsome face up close, had seen it through her closed eyelids, somehow. She wanted to strike then, felt that she could strike, just like a lightning bolt. Then the vision disappeared.

Patience, the little voice urged.

Ann counted to one hundred before slowly opening her left eye, then her right. She could still see Joe standing at the bedside, but Joe was quite absorbed with the rape of Ms. Anderson. Ann scanned the room, keeping her body still so as not to attract any undue attention. She located the rifle right away, not too far from where she lay. Keeping her eyes on Joe, she slowly inched toward it. Even if it wasn't loaded or she couldn't find the safety, she was sure she could use it like a bat. And wouldn't Joe's head make a great baseball?

Yes, the familiar voice whispered.

The thought of smashing his head was delightful and sickening all at the same time. Perhaps she was a murderer after all.

Kismet, that little voice said again.

Again Ann wondered just what that meant.

·· 11 ··

Scott gazed passed the flowerless rose garden, and across the waving poverty grass with its yellow, wilting buttercups, to the towering lighthouse. He couldn't stop thinking about his mom and the man from the vision he'd seen in William's head. *He was a rapist and murderer of young women. No wonder she blocked his existence from her memory. But why would she, how could she have had sex with a murderer?* Then the answer came to him. *Maybe she was raped. That had to be it.*

Scott was sure his mom would never consent to having sex with a man that would commit murder; therefore the only explanation was that she had been raped and that was good enough for him. Her virtue was still intact, he wasn't so sure about her will to live.

She was beginning to show signs of cirrhosis, most noticeably the shaking hands. It would kill her someday, of that Scott was sure. She'd been drinking for as long as he could remember. It hadn't done any good to say stuff to her about it, doing that just pissed her off. In her opinion she could stop if she wanted to. Scott hoped a new location and new people would change all that. Maybe she would meet a nice man or woman, he didn't care which, who'd make her feel life was worth living. Scott knew about that kind of thing, he'd learned it from Miss Leeann, along with a billion other things like values, kindness and how to shoot great photos, and she had taught him how to love. Oh how he missed her.

William was trying his best not to think of anything as he sat on the step gazing out over the small manicured lawn to the rose garden. But try as he might he couldn't help wonder when his Pa would come rolling down the drive. Maybe, Will hoped, the whacking on the head with the shovel had actually put the old bastard out of commission, if he was lucky. Will didn't think that was the case. No, William thought his Pa was probably already close by. William was in fact thinking that maybe he should leave, when he saw the familiar boot print in the lawn, on the walk. "Oh shit!" He sprang to his feet. "Pa's here." He raced up the stairs and was inside before Scott had time to stand.

· ·12· ·

William sprinted passed the big counter, passed the bench and onto the landing at the foot of the stairs, taking a quick glance into the library, no one. He turned and sprinted for the sitting room. No sign of anyone there either. No sign of other boot prints. He ran back to the entry just as Scott was coming in. Frantically grabbing him by the shoulders he asked, "Where's your mom's room?"

"Up the stairs on the left," Scott replied, then wondered why he didn't know she was in trouble.

Ci'del, Rachel replied.

Who?

You'll see.

Why can't you be helpful for once? Scott thought.

There was no reply.

He hated that, it was one of the major reasons he never listened to her, that and the fact that she was a liar. He waddled as fast as he could to the elevator.

William bolted up the stairs, busting into the room at the left of the landing just passed the living room. Ms. Anderson was seated on the edge of the bed. Ann was just wrapping a blanket around Ms. Anderson's bare shoulders. William looked away and saw his Pa lying naked from the waist down on the cream-colored carpet near the foot of the bed. His dead face was smashed in and covered with blood. His head lay in a puddle of it. One hand was wrapped around his shriveled cock, his other hand held his hunting knife. His rifle lay on the bed beside the women, bloodied at the stock. His clothing and stun gun were piled on the dresser.

William looked back to Ann and asked, "What happened?" Then went over to where his Pa lay, knelt beside him and felt his neck for a pulse; nothing. *Thank God,* he thought.

"I hit a home run," Ann replied flatly.

Scott entered the room making his way over to the ladies. "Are you okay?" he asked.

Both nodded.

Scott folded Ann into his arms and held her. He stroked her hair as she laid her head against his chest. In her mind he witnessed what had happened. Why hadn't *he* known what was going on? Something was blocking his ability, again. Something in the cellar.

"Ms. Anderson?" William said, nervously running his fingers through his black, curly hair.

"Yes William?" She looked toward the boy, Joseph's son. *What a shame.*

"Sorry," he said.

"This is hardly your fault William."

He nodded. "Yeah, it is. I shoulda told the truth." His shoulders slumped as he sat down on the bed beside her.

"What truth is that William? That Joseph really *is* your father? I already knew."

"No," he replied.

She raised an eyebrow.

William looked into her green eyes, so soft and lovely, yet somehow clouded, dull. The older face surrounded by curly, dark red hair. He understood his Pa's attraction to her. "Can I ask ya somethin?"

"Sure."

"How do ya know my Pa?"

Nora sighed, she'd kept the secret for so long now it was almost impossible to recall, almost. "I met him years ago. On a hot summer morning. He was just passing through, stayed one night then left."

Scott couldn't believe his ears, a one night stand. He knew what that meant and wondered how many other one night stands there had been. How many other men? Although he couldn't remember ever having seen her with any man.

"He's Scott's Pa too?" William asked.

Nora nodded.

"Do ya have a daughter?"

"Yes, but she died long ago."

William cringed, he knew it. Pa killed her, just like all the others. *And you'll be just like me Billy Boy. you just wait and see,* Pa's voice taunted inside his head.

"Sorry," he said again. "You must really hate my Pa. How old was she?"

Nora looked at him, puzzled. "What do you mean? After Joseph left, I found out I was pregnant. Scott was born . . .Rachel," her voice wavered as tears formed in her green eyes. "Rachel was dead before she was ever born. Joseph never even knew. William, what is this all about?"

Lying bitch! Pa's voice accused inside William's head. "Pa didn't rape and kill her?" he asked.

Ann gasped, so this was what he hadn't told her?

"No, why would you think that?" Nora asked. The sickening image of Joseph's face, hot and sweaty, as he masturbated over her, loomed in her memory.

Scott saw it too.

"Because," William hesitated. "It's what he does. My Pa is, was a very bad man. The worst part is I never tried to stop it, till Ann." William hung his head.

"What do you mean, till Ann?" Nora looked to the girl still wrapped in her son's arms. "Aren't you his sister?" It dawned on her then that they didn't even resemble each other. She of the fair hair and skin; he of the darker shade.

Ann shook her head.

"No, we met just yesterday," William continued. "She don't know who she is, got lightning struck, I think." *And you wanted her, didn't you Boy!* Pa's voice taunted again.

Ms. Anderson's eyes widened. "Hit by lightning?"

William nodded, telling them of the thunderstorms, and lightning, the bear, the cardboard clothes. He told them how he tried to direct her out of the woods and how instead she followed him and everything after that. "I knew Pa liked her, he likes all the pretty young women." William looked toward Ann and blushed a little, "I had to get her outta the house, away from Pa before, well, before he could hurt her." He didn't need to explain what he meant by that.

"How'd you get away?" Nora asked.

"Hit him on the head with a shovel, three times."

There was a long pause.

"Where's your mother William?" Nora asked.

He shrugged. "Pa says she died when I was born." *I killed her, Boy. And you know it.*

Ann pulled away from Scott's comforting arms and made her way over to the curtained doors, stepping over Joe on the way. She opened the shades and then both doors as wide as she could. She needed daylight and fresh air. The stench coming off Joe was making her ill, or perhaps it was the knowledge that she killed him. She'd gotten a hold of the rifle by the barrel, ignoring the sudden electrical shock, and without hesitation had swung it like a bat toward a baseball. That familiar little voice driving her on, giving her courage.

The sound of his cracking skull, the vibration sliding up the rifle and through her hands replayed vividly in her mind. A sickening, triumphant feeling had rushed over her as his face contorted and his black eyes went vacant. She had killed him, killed him dead. He hadn't been raping Ms. Anderson – he'd been jerking off – one hand wrapped tightly around the huge erection, the other grasping the deadly hunting knife. And that's the way he laid right now, on the floor, on his back, except the erection was now just a shriveled up dick. His face was pushed in like a melon, red blood oozing from it, pooling on the carpeted floor beneath his head. She looked away in disgust, wiping the tears from her face with the back of her hand.

Scott grabbed a sheet from the closet shelf and tossed it over the dead man, the blood quickly seeped through it. The carpet would need a thorough cleaning. He wondered what they would do with the body.

Dump it in the ocean, Rachel suggested.

"William," Scott said. "Lend me a hand, would ya?"

"Sure." William left Ms. Anderson alone on the bed, joining Scott standing beside their dead, sheet-covered Pa.

"Help me move him to the balcony then we'll dump him over." Scott said.

It seemed a good idea to William.

Nora didn't care one way or the other. Thank God Ann had come along when she did. Nora looked toward the girl standing at the open doors, her savior. Somehow, even after Joseph had stunned and chocked her, Ann had still cold cocked the son of a bitch with his own rifle. It had been a repulsively, wonderful sight. She'd seen fire in the girl's eyes, like tiny lightning bolts. The rifle had glowed in her hands, as crazy as it sounded. The rifle had glowed in her God-blessed hands. Not only that, the pink-colored rose tattoo on Ann's forehead, with its red outline, had grown darker, more pronounced.

Shaking her head Nora decided to take another bath; she couldn't stand the stench of Joseph on her body any longer.

WILLIAM FINDS TROUBLE

• •1• •

Ann stood gazing at the photos hanging on the living room wall, photos of scenery and wildlife. "These are beautiful," she exclaimed.

Scott, who was fiddling with the old stereo, trying to find a worthy station, turned to her and said, "You think so?"

"Absolutely."

"Thanks."

"Did you take em?"

"Yeah, at Sucker Lake."

"Sucker Lake?"

"Where we moved from."

"You and your mom?"

"Yeah."

Ann nodded, she had no idea where Sucker Lake was.

William slouched on the sofa in front of the lit fireplace, staring into the fire, his mind a zillion miles away in thoughts of Lily and the others. Their faces and names flew through his mind like snap shots, enhancing the realization that Pa was finally dead.

Ms. Anderson entered the room after her second bath, dressed in black jeans and a sky blue cashmere sweater, just as Scott located a radio station. "Scott," she said. "I sure could use some coffee."

"No Problemo," he replied, knowing she meant right this minute and without delay as she hadn't had her morning drink yet. He turned to leave the room.

"Mind if I join you?" Ann asked.

Scott extended his elbow toward her. Wrapping her arm around his, they vacated the living room.

The square, 'Whittaker' clock on the fireplace mantle amongst the flower filled water globes showed the time was nearly noon. Nora had missed her morning coffee for the first time in years, and all because of Joseph. She didn't blame William or Ann, it wasn't their fault. Even if William had told them the truth, Nora doubted that would have changed much. How could it?

"Do you believe in God, Ms. Anderson?" William asked.

Nora looked over at the young boy seated on her sofa. How would she answer? She hadn't thought about God in a long time. "Why do you ask?"

"Just curious," he said.

"Afraid you'll go to hell because of the things your father did?"

William shrugged. "Do you think there is a hell?"

Nora glanced at the clock striking noon, seeing only the bottle stashed behind it and said, "Only those we make for ourselves." She looked back to William. "Don't worry William, if there is a God he or she knows that whatever your father did was not your fault."

"Yeah, but I *coulda* told someone. I *shoulda* told someone."

The pained look on his young face was nearly unbearable and Nora wondered how he managed to survive with Joseph all those years. "Do you have any other relatives William? Aunts, Uncles, Grandparents perhaps?"

William shook his head. "Dunno," he replied.

"Then stay here with us," she said. "We don't need to tell anyone anything."

· ·2· ·

Outside the elevator gate Scott hesitated, it might be a good idea to get a crutch; his legs weren't doing so well today. He turned to Ann and said, "Wait here a sec. I'll be right back."

"Ok," she replied. She watched him waddle away down the hall. It was a crippling disease, he'd told her, and progressive. He said it didn't hurt. She wasn't convinced. Someway, either physically or psychologically it was painful, at least for her.

A few moments later he returned with one of the forearm crutches. "This will help keep me balanced," he claimed with a smile.

Stepping into the small elevator Ann saw a row of four blue buttons. Scott pushed the bottom one labeled 'Dining Room', and the elevator descended. They rode in silence. All the while Scott hoping the cellar door would *not* be open this time. He wasn't sure what was down there. Didn't want to know what was down there. It's ability to communicate, not in his ears but inside his head, grating and scraping, was frightening. Yet he understood what it said, what it meant. It was searching for it's jailer. Uncle Ed's description of their upcoming reclaiming of the mirror popped into his head. He'd used the word 'recapture'. *Why?*

Ci'del, Rachel replied.

Stepping into the kitchen Scott sighed with relief, the cellar door was closed. The French doors were open to the soothing surf.

"You got anything to eat?" Ann asked.

"Sure," he said, "what'd ya have in mind?"

According to the clock on the wall it was noon. Right below the clock was a little framed saying 'The Hurrier I Go The Behinder I Get'. Ann smiled at the truth in the sentence, although she couldn't recall any events, and then suggested sandwiches.

Scott grabbed the full pot of coffee and said, "Sounds good. I gotta take this upstairs first. I'll see if the others are hungry. Be right back. Have a look in the pantry, see what you can find. Don't bother with the cellar, though, the stairs are dangerous."

"Okay," Ann replied.

Scott hobbled as fast as he could, using the one crutch for extra support, back to the elevator, he didn't want to leave Ann alone for too long. What if that voice spoke to her? What if it led her into the cellar? He stopped momentarily, thinking maybe he should go back and get her.

That's ridiculous, Rachel scolded.

Scott had to agree, this time. What would he say to her? *Watch out for the boogeyman in the cellar! Oh yeah, that'd be real great, wouldn't it?*

· ·3· ·

He didn't need to worry. Ann had no plans of opening that door, at least not yet. Somehow she knew that now was not the time, but there would be a time, soon. And when they did, they would have to deal with the creature that was down there.

Turning away from the cellar door Ann headed toward the pantry at the far end of the kitchen, passed the long counter, the large stainless steel fridge, the matching stove, and the double sink. The pantry was loaded with shelves and shelves of canned and dry goods; beans and corn and rice and soups. There were big bags of sugar and flour. There were cases and cases of goods. She gazed at the many items. She knew them all. Was her memory returning?

Then she heard that familiar voice inside her head. *Remember,* it said.

"The rose," she said aloud. A serene, calmness washed over her in rhythm with the rolling ocean waves. Unbuttoning her shirt pocket Ann removed the tiny, red rose and deposited it in the palm of her hand. As before, it began to change, to open; holding her . . .spellbound.

· ·4· ·

In the penthouse Scott was handing the coffee pot and an empty cup to his mom. He was just about to ask if anyone was ready for lunch, when a terrible, awful, feeling fell over him.

Nora saw the look on his face, in his eyes; fear. She hadn't seen that look in a long time, not since Rascal and the quicksand. Scott had hobbled as fast as he could toward the house yelling at the top of his lungs, the tears gushing from his eyes like the river from a busted damn. And when they returned to the sand lake, Rascal was nothing more then a nose sticking out of it. "What's wrong?" she asked.

Scott shook his head and said, "Nothing." Closing his mind to his mom's vision of Rascal's little black nose sticking out of that sucking sand.

Nora didn't believe him, not at all.

Scott couldn't tell his mom what was wrong, he didn't know for sure. But it felt as if his whole world was crashing down around him. As if any moment now, he would lose everything. That whatever was in the cellar was going to get out and devour them all and he would be able to do nothing to stop it. "It's nothing," he said a second time. "Does anyone want lunch?"

Nora nodded, still not convinced. William didn't reply.

"Hey William," Scott said.

No reply.

"Earth to William."

Still no reply.

"Yo, William!"

William looked up at Scott in dazed confusion and said, "What?"

"I said do ya want some lunch?"

"Sure, I guess."

· ·5· ·

In the pantry Ann stood staring deeply into the folds of the open rose. Its soothing voice was speaking to her; telling secrets of things to come. Suddenly it stopped. The rosebud closed up tight, became cold.

"Ann?" It was Scott.

"In the pantry," she hollered back, quickly returning the rosebud to its safe hiding place inside her shirt pocket. She grabbed two cans of tuna and a bag of potato chips from one of the many pantry shelves.

"Hope you like tuna," she said, stepping into the kitchen.

"Love it." Scott was standing at the cellar door; he could hardly take his eyes off it. But he managed to look her way. Man she was beautiful.

"Good, where's a mixing bowl?"

"Over there." He pointed to a cupboard above the counter as he opened the fridge and got out the mayo. Together they made several sandwiches and placed them on a tray. Scott grabbed the tray, Ann grabbed the chips. They headed for the kitchen doorway.

"What about some drinks?"

Ann's question stopped Scott dead in his tracks. The word drinks conjured images of his mom crossing the street in Kingston, her arms loaded down with bottles of rum, the booze she felt she had to drink everyday.

"What?"

"You know, sodas?"

"Oh, sure, absolutely." He was sure his face was about ten shades of red. Ann didn't seem to notice.

· ·6· ·

The oldies just kept flowing from the old radio as Ann and Scott cuddled on the living room floor just in front of the fireplace. In a chair next to the sofa Nora was drinking her coffee and rum, third one today, her feet scrunched up underneath her butt.

As the afternoon passed, William lay on the sofa staring into the fire, thoughts of going to hell running through his mind, but not because of hell itself. No, he worried about going to hell because that's where Pa was. Of that, William was absolutely certain. Certain because in that fire was a terrible image of his Pa commanding the flames; flames that consumed everything, everything that ever was or ever would be until the land lay barren and wasted, unable to survive the wrath of his own Pa.

Why did it have to be his Pa? Why couldn't it be someone else's Pa? What'd he ever do to deserve such a Pa? Then a voice spoke inside William's head, and it said one word.

Chicken.

William closed his eyes. It was true; he was the biggest chicken he knew. Suddenly he needed a glass of water. He opened his eyes and got up from the sofa. At the door he stopped momentarily to gaze at the collection of photos and mirrors covering the west wall. It was quite impressive. The mirrors, and he counted twenty of them, were all different, most of them small. The largest one being about twelve inches square, with intricate frames. Some were etched, some were beveled, some were round, and others were square or oblong. They all looked old, and yet untainted by the hands of time.

He looked back to Ann and Scott on the floor and Ms. Anderson still in her chair, the coffee cup raised to her lips. Then he turned and stepped out of the room. He took the stairs. There was no reason to use the elevator. Besides, you couldn't see jack shit in an elevator, and the Inn was something to see with its ceiling beams and arched windows. *Whoever decorated done an outstanding job,* he thought as he passed the entry with its double doors and their stained glass insets.

In the brightly lit kitchen William turned on the faucet in the big double sink, located the drinking glasses and was just getting ready to fill the glass with cold water from the tap when he heard a noise; the creak of an opening door. He whirled around to see the cellar door standing open. Was it open when he came in? He couldn't remember. Quickly he filled the glass, guzzled it down, then set the empty glass on the counter and walked over to the open door.

A hot gust sucked the moisture from his eyes, nose and mouth as he squinted down the rickety stairs seeing a lighted room below.

Go on, a voice said inside his head. *Yer not chicken are ya?*

William shook his head no. Then proceeded down the old staircase.

Racks and racks of dusty wine bottles and the smell of dry dirt filled the little room at the bottom of the stairs. *No moisture here,* William thought. And then he saw the mirror. *No doubt an antique.* His brow creased, *why is it here and not on the wall with the others?* It stood as tall as his Pa, six feet, and half that wide. The frame was a menagerie of wild roses complete with thorns. He wondered if he could tote it up the stairs by himself.

Moving around to the backside of it, which was leaning against one of the dusty racks, William was able to get underneath it. Hoisting the mirror onto his back, he was surprised when it wasn't as heavy at he thought it might be. However it took about fifteen minutes of huffin and puffin before he finally reached the top of the cellar stairs. He lowered one end to the floor then dragged it into the kitchen and propped it against the counter. It was a beautiful piece of artwork, flawless.

William suddenly wanted to tell everyone of his find. He bolted from the kitchen and up the stairs to the penthouse, taking two and sometimes three stairs at a time. "Hey," he said, bursting into the living room. "I found somethin really awesome."

They all looked toward him.

"What is it William?" Ms. Anderson asked.

"Oh, you'll love it especially," William replied. "It'll fit right in with your collection. C'mon, it's in the kitchen."

Scott's eyes widened with sudden dread.

· ·7· ·

In the kitchen the four of them stood looking at the ancient mirror with its rosebud frame and flawless glass.

"It's so beautiful!" Nora exclaimed, thinking it also strangely familiar. "I know right where it belongs." She grabbed one side, motioning William toward the other. Together they hauled it out to the elevator and up to the second floor where they hung it on the already mounted hooks in the foyer, above the cushioned bench, as if it had hung there before, just opposite the counter.

Scott stared at its rectangular frame and tiny roses for a long time after hanging it there. The unblemished glass rippled like water in a pool after having a pebble dropped into it. Very subtle, but it was there. And that feeling again; hot fingertips on his brain, probing. What was it looking for?

The jailer, the scratching voice whispered.

"Scott," Ann said from behind, making him jump a bit. He turned toward her intoxicating face. "I'd love to see the view from the lighthouse, would you take me there?"

"Sure. I just have to get the key."

Hand in hand they left the presence of the mirror. They took the elevator to the kitchen where Scott grabbed the lighthouse key from the hook on the wall. They returned to the sitting room and headed out the breezeway to the cobblestone walk. Ahead of them the towering lighthouse flashed out its beacon for all to see. The eastern sky was beginning to darken with the coming of sunset. A light breeze blew passed them, while seagulls screeched overhead and the seal lions barked on the beach below.

They stopped at the green door of the small white building attached to the foot of the tower. Scott inserted the key into the lock and opened the door. The vacant room had two windows facing west and two identical windows facing east. Through the west windows they could see the sun beginning its final descent toward the ocean. At the other end of the room was a door which opened to the spiral staircase. Scott slowly led Ann up the narrow stairs around and around the inside of the tall tower. Halfway to the top they passed another set of windows. At the top of the stairs was a small room with four windows, one for each compass direction. A three rung ladder hung from its low ceiling.

"What room is this?" Ann asked.

"The watch room," he replied. Reaching up as far as he could, Scott grabbed the farthest ladder rung, and using his muscular arms hoisted himself up onto it. The steel gate in the floor of the lantern room was locked. Scott hooked his left arm on the top rung, turned his key in the lock and pushed the heavy gate open. After pulling himself through, he turned and helped Ann up.

She gazed at the enormous lantern rotating inside the glassed-in room. Bright, 15000 candle watt or something like that. She didn't know anything about electricity, at least not that she could recall.

Scott reached out and turned the nearly un-seeable knob, opening a door in the glass wall surrounding them. "They call this the parapet," he said, stepping onto the walkway outside. Ann stepped out behind him. Arm in arm, in the light of the lantern they gazed out over the ocean as the sun sank into a dark blanket of clouds.

· •8• ·

The four of them were just sitting down to dinner at one of the round tables in the main dining room when the dark banner of clouds suddenly erupted. They all hurried over to the balcony doors as the squall drenched the entire coast line with sheets of rain. According to Scott, the storm was 'Awesome'. No one could disagree. Lighting pierced the sky as thunder shook the walls. The turbulent sea smashed against the rocks below in crashing waves.

This is nothing like the Oregon desert, Scott thought, thrilled with the weather and the company. He stroked Ann's hair, breathed in her heavenly scent. He was falling for her, big time. He didn't care who she used to be, not that he knew, it just didn't matter. Occasionally she'd have little snippets of memory, but nothing substantial, no names, no faces. Her mind was almost a complete blank where her personal memories should be, as if they had simply been erased. He'd read some stories on the internet in the Kingston Library about people being struck by lightning. One girl slept in a coma for five days before a full recovery. Another kid, a boy, claimed he could throw lightning bolts and fire balls from his fingertips after being struck. Scott wasn't quite sure he believed that, but Ann did seem to have a lot a static electricity surging through her body. The images in his mother's memory of Ann wielding the glowing rifle by its barrel resurfaced in his mind; the look of surprise and failure on the man's dying, broken face, the triumphant look in Ann's big brown eyes with their tiny bolts of lighting. Maybe it was crazy, maybe he was crazy, but he wanted to be with her, always.

Day Four
Wednesday

C·H·A·P·T·E·R 10

THE PORTAL

·· 1 ··

I
t was well past midnight. Everyone was asleep, everyone except Scott. Scott couldn't sleep, couldn't get Ann out of his head. So he slipped into his sweat pants, grabbed a titanium crutch and made a visit to the library.

On the shelf above the massive rock fireplace he retrieved the book he was currently reading. Cradling the beloved book in his free arm like a baby, he made his way over to the closed balcony doors. He opened them just a bit, and then sat down in the nearest chair and turned on the table lamp. He opened the book at the gold and silver plated book mark. Imprinted on the top of it was the raised impression of a rose, a golden rose. Scott gazed at the imprint for a few minutes, turning it in the light a couple of times. He was reminded of Ann, again. The girl had just kind of swept into his life.

A sudden chill settled over the room. He looked up from the book mark, toward the doorway out into the foyer. Did he see movement? Setting the book aside, Scott started to get up then stopped as something cold and unseen brushed passed him. The door of the empty gun cabinet swung open. On the other side of the lit (had it been lit before?) fireplace the pendulum on the grandfather clock stood frozen in time, the hands on the face at 5:10. Was it really that late? He didn't remember hearing the clock strike five, he didn't remember hearing the clock at all.

A faint presence, nearly transparent, appeared. A shape with long flowing hair tied back with faded red and blue ribbons. It turned toward Scott, an opaque rifle in its hand, a distraught look on its young, sheer face. Then the leg-less ghost girl moved passed him and out the door. Scott followed as quickly as he could. She seemed to wait for him, floating like a feather down the stairs. In the kitchen she floated right through the closed cellar door as if it wasn't there.

Scott opened the now lockless door and followed the apparition to the cellar. She hovered in the center of the wine room, looking his way.

Where is it? She hissed at him, her ghostly face distorting, losing its shape then reforming. *Where is the portal?*

"What are you talking about?" he asked.

My mother's mirror. Please tell me where it is. I must save Jonny, she pleaded.

Scott gulped, a ghost asking for her mother's mirror, pleading for Jonny's rescue? "This way," he said, turning and crutching his way back up the stairs to the foyer.

Hovering before the aged mirror the ghost girl looked at Scott through dead eyes. *Thank you*, she said. She faced the mirror, and Scott heard her whisper, *I'm coming to kill you.* And then she floated into it.

Scott blinked. Did that really happened? Did he really not only see but talk to a ghost? A ghost who disappeared into a mirror; what she called a portal? And who was she going to kill? *Hey Uncle Ed*, he thought. *I've really gone bonkers; absolutely, positively.*

· ·2· ·

Ann opened her eyes; it was no use trying to sleep. It was going to happen, soon. She could feel it in the deepest part of her senses. Then the little voice whispered inside her head, confirming her fears. *It is time*, it said. Ann sat up. The night light's soft glow spilled from the bathroom. The thick drapes were drawn over the doors leading out to the balcony, softening the sound of the surf outside.

She got out of bed and snuck into the bathroom, softly closing the door behind her. She changed into the clothes she'd been wearing earlier that day, checking the shirt pocket for her treasure. Smiling, it was there.

Returning to the semi-dark main room, Ann grabbed the jacket from the wall hook. Opening the door of the warm, dry room, she slipped out into the cool, rainy night. Her bare feet slapped on wet stone stairs as she glided down them, guided by little lights embedded in the stone wall at the floor. The jacket she held suspended over her head like an umbrella, the roar of the ocean waves crashed far below.

She entered the sitting room door at the end of the breezeway leading from the spiral staircase, a faint light cascaded into the dark room from the library. Perhaps Scott was still up. Hanging the wet coat over the back of the nearest chair, Ann crossed the sitting room then passed the entry on her right and the double staircase on her left, ignoring the large, old mirror hanging on the wall just inside the entry door opposite the smooth, wood counter.

Ann peeked into the library. The chair near the lit lamp was empty. The hour hand on the grandfather clock pointed to the five. The minute hand moved to the six, in one audible click. The pendulum swung slowly back and forth in time with the surf, as if time were slowing down somehow. Glancing back toward the penthouse stairs, Ann wondered if anyone was still up, if Scott was up. Quickly she mounted the stairs and entered the semi-dark living room. Rain drops ticked against the window glass. Feeling her way over to the fireplace she flipped a switch on the wall. Flames shot out and over the fake logs, casting a dim, flickering light throughout the room.

· •3• ·

Scott was lying in his bed with his eyes wide open, his escapades with the ghost still fresh in his mind. A noise out in the living room brought him out of the bed. Another ghost? Slipping back into his sweat pants he grabbed the crutches next to the bed and cautiously ventured out there where he found Ann sitting on the sofa in front of the lit fireplace. "Hey, what's up?" he asked, crutching his way across the room toward her.

"It's time," she said.

"Time for what?"

"Come." She held one delicate hand out to him.

Scott removed the crutches from his arms, leaned them against the sofa and took hold of her soft hand feeling the tingling surge of electricity. He sat down next to her, their knees touching.

Ann reached into her shirt pocket and drew something out of it. She set it in the palm of her hand.

Scott saw it was a rosebud and watched in fascination as it began to open. He hadn't realized how small her hands really were until just then. Tiny and delicate and beautiful, holding the awesome rose, the rose that spoke to him of hope and love, of loss and gain, of things to come.

· •4• ·

In her dream the faded black pickup truck pulls in and stops under the shadow of the dead aspen tree. A hot breeze drifts by. The sun fades. Nora looks up; there are no clouds, there is no sun. The once blue sky darkens to red, the color of rust. The driver's door creaks open, the black army boots hit the ground, one at a time.

Thump. Thump.

He towers over the truck. The older Joseph, Joseph of the now, smiles wickedly; the shaggy black mane outlining the ghastly, rotting, bashed in face. The bulging head wound pulsates in and out, in and out. In a kind of slow motion he moves toward her, only then she realizes it isn't slow at all. She barely has time to stand from her seated position on the porch step before he is standing over her.

Come with me, he says, extending a bloated, gray hand toward her.

She shakes her head, no. No, she won't go. *You're not real,* she thinks. *You're dead.*

I'll never be dead to you, Nora, he says with a smile. *I love you, I've always loved you.*

Nora knows this isn't right. This is just some weird, psychotic dream. Joseph never loved her. She was convenient and more than willing. Wasn't she? She looks into his black eyes, hypnotic eyes.

I've come to take you home, he says.

· ·5· ·

Neither Ann or Scott notices her heading down the stairs. They don't see the tiniest water globe atop the fireplace mantle with its red rose now open when before it was closed. They are barely aware of anything except the rose and each other.

Then the rose in Ann's palm closes it petals and Ann returns it to the safety of her pocket. She hands Scott his crutches, takes him by the arm and leads him to the elevator which they take to the second floor. As they step through the elevator's gate and into the sitting room, she asks, "Have you ever heard of Kismet?"

"Kismet?" Scott repeated, as the spell of the rose fell away from him, followed by a deep feeling that something awesome had just happened, although he couldn't remember what.

"I'll bet there's a dictionary in the library," she said.

Scott shook the fuzziness from his brain and said, "Yeah, I'm sure there are several." *But what just happened?*

Passing the foyer headed toward the library, Ann and Scott are unexpectedly stopped by the image of Nora Anderson standing before the ancient mirror, completely nude, except for the bunny slippers on her feet.

"Mom," Scott said with dismay. *Why is she standing there like that? Is she completely insane? One too many hits with the rum bottle perhaps?*

Ci'del, Rachel replied.

Scott took one crutch step toward her.

Hot air whooshed from the mirror, blowing the red hair away from her spellbound eyes. Long, black talons reached out, folding around Nora's waist, hauling her into the mirror.

"Mom!" Scott yelled, taking another crutch step toward the mirror.

· ·6· ·

A tall, thin man, the man Ann had seen in the photo in Scott's room, Uncle Ed, she later learned from Scott, was older than dirt and faster than light or sound. Appearing out of nowhere, in his tan fedora with its pheasant feather band, his long coat, and loafers, he pointed a long, slender finger in Scott's direction.

Scott suddenly plowed head first into a wall, an invisible wall. He turned and stared at his Uncle, complete confusion on his face, questions racing through his mind. *What the hell just happened? Uncle Ed using magic?*

Uncle Ed nodded his affirmation to Scott. *No time to explain, Son.* Then sauntered over to the mirror, the stolen mirror, and waved his hand in front of it. The reflective glass became like a movie screen showing the image of a black beast carrying Nora away across a desert of swirling red dust.

Edwin waved his hand in front of the mirror a second time, returning the glass to its reflective state then turned toward Ann, instantly noticing the mark. "Edwin Anderson," he announced, with a nod of his head, and a tip of his hat, "you can call me Uncle Ed."

Ann stared at the man through eyes of wonder, her jaw hanging open in awe. He looked just like the picture. He hadn't aged a day in 10 or 12 years.

Edwin turned to his confused nephew. "Son," he said, "take the elevator to the penthouse right now, change into a pair of overalls and a light weight, long sleeved shirt, put on your shoes. Then find some clothing for your mom. We'll need full water bottles, working flashlights and weapons. That rifle and stun gun could come in handy." He turned back to Ann and said, "Come with me, my child."

· ·7· ·

The gray sky was getting lighter with the approach of dawn as the rain died down to nothing. William sat at the table, in the third floor guest room, a blank stare on his adolescent face. He looked down at the hands tightly gripping the chair's arms. *The guilty, the damned. The hands of the son of a murderer,* he thought.

In his mind the images play like a rerun, over and over as he watches a much younger Billy, his Pa and the lovely Lily.

"Billy, get yer ass to yer room," Pa barks. "Me and Lily got bidness to take care a." Pa smiles that smile William has come to hate as he slaps the lovely Lily on the butt; her skirt so short Billy can almost see her private parts, almost.

Billy obeys the command, but curiosity is stronger than he. Sometime later he peeks out into the empty living room. He sneaks over to the closed door of Pa's room, and puts an ear against it. He hears something, a thump, thump, thumping noise. Quietly he turns the knob, opens the door a crack and peeks inside. The brilliant light from the lamp on the nightstand illuminates the lovely Lily lying on her back on the bed with nothing on, her bare legs dangle over the side. Her hands are tied to the bedpost, a scarf around her lovely mouth, her eyes wide open, yet unseeing. Pa stands between her parted legs, butt naked, thrusting back and forth, back and forth. Billy's dark eyes widen, he sees the knife in Pa's upraised hand; its blade glinting in the light. Suddenly Pa brings his arm down and the blade slices through her throat, bright red blood sprays everywhere. Her gurgling last breath reaches Billy's ears. He squeezes his eyes shut, clamps his hands over his ears and runs back to his room. He can't forget (no matter how tightly he closes his eyes) the image of the lovely Lily with her throat cut wide open and the blood forever gushing . . .gushing . . .gushing . . .

It's your fault, all your fault. You shoulda stopped it. You shoulda told.
No, I couldn't!
Yes, you could. But you didn't. You were afraid. Chicken!

William stood up, knocking the chair over without notice then proceeded out onto the balcony. Guided only by the voice inside his head. His eyes were blind to the world, seeing nothing; his ears deaf. Only the voice drove him forward – the voice of his dead, murderin Pa.

At the edge of the balcony William climbed up onto the wrought iron railing with its playful whales. An unfelt gust of rain-less wind caressed his young face; blew the curls around his head. He didn't notice, nor did he care.

· ·8· ·

Dark clouds hovered on the horizon, heavy with the next coming storm. Below the Inn the turbulent green sea crashed like thunder against the rocky shoreline.

Ann hurried up the stone stairs, her hair standing up in the wind, with Scott's Uncle behind her holding onto his hat, his coat flapping in the stiff breeze. Scott had other instructions and was currently gathering supplies. Supplies for what, was the question. But she liked Uncle Ed a lot. He gave her a sense of hope and a warm, familiar feeling, as if she already knew him. Everything was going to be okay, she was sure of it. Yet that nagging little voice kept telling her to *hurry up – trouble ahead – hurry up.*

They reached the guest room and Ann dashed in. "Will?"

No answer.

A quick glance around the room showed her the empty roll-a-way bed and the toppled wicker chair by the table. "Will?" She called again. *Odd, was he on the balcony?*

Yes, hurry! The voice urged.

The smell of salt air blew in through the open French doors. Ann hurried over and looked out. To her right was the roof-garden atop the main house, straight ahead and coming fast were the swelling storm clouds; loaded with rain. And to her left William stood atop the iron railing, his bare feet wedged between the clam shells of the top pinnacles. Her heartbeat quickened. Out on the horizon lightening pierced the sky.

"Will!" She yelled and ran toward him. But she was too late.

William took one step forward.

· ·9· ·

Scott rode the elevator up to the penthouse. He couldn't get over Uncle Ed's use of magic; a secret. *No time to explain now, Son.* How many other secrets did he have? Uncle Ed hadn't revealed much in their hurried communication only that Scott needed to gather clothing and some other supplies; flashlights, water bottles, weapons. Scott had a hunch that they were going in there, inside that ancient mirror, as soon as Uncle Ed and Ann returned with William. Inside his head he recalled the voice. *The jailer,* it had said. Scott was pretty sure the jailer was his uncle.

Removing his sweat pants, Scott slid his stocking feet into the gigantic shoes and buckled up the steel reinforced leather leg braces. Then he slipped into his overalls, zipping up the legs. He hurried from his room to his mother's where the blood stain still lay quite visible on the carpet at the foot of the un-used bed. His mother had chosen to sleep in the spare room after the incident. Who could blame her? Scott turned to the dresser where the camouflage pants still lay under the stun gun. Picking up the stun gun he stuffed it inside his pack then rummaged through the pants pockets for the rifle shells, which also went into the pack. Then he flung the pants onto the sticky puddle of blood, blotting as much of it up as he could. He carried the pants out to the balcony in his fingertips and pitched them over the side. Thunder rolled overhead.

He went back inside and began rummaging through the dresser drawers and closet, gathering clothes as he'd been instructed, stuffing them into his backpack, all the while thinking about Uncle Ed's magic. *Why hadn't he shared? What other secrets did he have? What'd he mean no time to explain? He's had years to explain.*

Scott had no answers; it seemed as if he didn't know his Uncle at all.

Inside his head Rachel was laughing.

· ·10· ·

Much to Ann's surprise, Will didn't plunge from her sight. Instead he floated in the air, suspended above the deadly drop like a balloon. She turned to see Scott's Uncle silently moving his old lips in some unheard magic incantation, his long, thin fingers reaching out toward the boy, guiding him back to safety. When Will was within her reach, she grabbed him by the arm. A small electrical surge from her grasp stunned him into the present.

"What the hell?" he said, a puzzled look on his young face, as one foot touched down then the other.

"Young William," Edwin said as he approached the confused boy. "Edwin Anderson, Scott's uncle." Edwin grabbed William's cold hand shaking it firmly; his bright blue eyes penetrating the dull brown eyes of the youngster. Edwin saw in William's mind the tormented years, the young women, the lovely Lily, and a six year old boy.

Gazing directly into the young lad's eyes, Edwin released William from the insanity, the grasp of his own subconscious, driven to the brink by the beast. The beast had almost succeeded, and would no doubt try again.

· · 11 · ·

In the grand library, Uncle Ed directed the children to the largest of the round tables which was near the center of the room. "Have a seat," he said. "I've a story to tell."

He stood at the table with his back to the giant rock fireplace. He had removed his fedora and placed it on the table in front of him. He held his bony hands at his sides. He was old and he was tired, but the journey was just beginning.

Once the children were seated, Edwin moved his hands from their stationary position, raising them high over his head, the fingers and arms stretching in a weird kind of taffy like manner, nearly touching the faraway ceiling. "Cloak," he whispered, bringing his thin arms down to the table. A cloud of fog fell over the group. No one could see passed the table; the library had disappeared.

Uncle Ed remained standing. His bright blue eyes penetrating, even in the fogginess of the spell. Then he told them a tale, an unbelievable tale of monsters and magic.

· · 12 · ·

In the dimly lit foyer, the foursome stood before the ancient mirror. Their faces were covered below their eyes with scraps of a sheet that Uncle Ed had torn up, just for this special occasion. Scott had also come across a better pair of tennis shoes for Ann to wear, instead of the ones she arrived in. The rifle, although

Scott disliked it very much, was now loaded and slung over his shoulder. The few remaining shells were now in his knapsack along with the stun gun. He had stopped just long enough to sop up the blood, at least most of it, from the bedroom carpet. It didn't seem right to leave it there.

William stuffed his sling shot into the back pocket of his jeans and a handful of the ball bearings went into the breast pocket of his thin flannel shirt. He filled the remainder of his bag with extra food from the pantry, like granola bars, and water, lots of water. Who knew how long they was gonna be in there, could be days, could be years. He hoped it wasn't years. *How long would it take to find and kill Ci'del?*

Ann had Scott's knapsack slung over her shoulder, loaded with the extra clothing for Ms. Anderson and more water. She had grabbed her tiny flashlight and the pocketknife, glad that both fit comfortably in the front pocket of her borrowed jeans. The tiny red rose lay securely locked away in her buttoned shirt pocket.

Edwin wondered where she found it. She wore the mark of the rose; was chosen by Rose. She had spunk, but would she succeed?

In the library, the clock began to bong.

••13••

At quarter-to-seven that stormy, rainy Wednesday morning the Sheriff's green patrol car rolled to a stop behind the old jeep. It was the second morning he'd seen it sitting there.

Sheriff Radcliff noted the old black on yellow California license plate and called it in to dispatch for any criminal activity, stolen, that kind of thing. When the plate came back negative, no warrants and not stolen he got out of his cruiser and approached it, his hand on the butt of his revolver, just in case.

The jeep was empty, except for the beer bottles littering the floor in the back, and a pair of night vision goggles on the front seat. Apparently the vehicle was abandoned or broken down, the Sheriff didn't know which nor did he care. His duty at this point was to use his red marking pen to write the day after tomorrow's date on the windshield notifying the owner of the intent to impound.

Damn! He'd left his pen in the cruiser. As it was getting time to snag some real breakfast 'cause he was getting hungry, Sheriff Radcliff quickly retrieved the red pen from his cruiser. He marked the date on the jeep then got back in his vehicle, closed the door and left, headed for Fat Patty's Cafe in town. In a couple weeks the Light Keeper's Inn & Bistro would reopen with new owners and the Sheriff thought he'd have to give that place a try as soon as possible. That brought to mind the Reeds. The whole fam-damily, had vanished from that place without a trace years before; a case that had not yet been solved.

· · 14 · ·

Sarah Anderson was dressed in her favorite slacks, blouse, and sweater vest, standing in the crisp coolness of the mountain's morning air in the open door-way of their home. Sandstone Peak stood to the north at an elevation of some six-thousand feet, the Westridge Mountain range loomed to the west. Overhead, the heavy gray clouds of snow were beginning to stack up against the mountains. A storm was brewing, and the house was over five miles from Red Puma Road at an elevation of close to five thousand feet. If she didn't hurry and make up her mind she might not be able to leave.

Should she try her rusty driving skills and go after him or not? She knew exactly where he vanished to, not that he tried to keep it a secret or anything. Usually Eddie just hopped into their old sedan and drove out to Scott when he was needed. However this time, according to Eddie, there wasn't enough time. Something unexpected happened and he had to go right now, right this minute and there was no use in trying to stop him. It was a matter of life and death. That worried Sarah greatly, she knew the whole business with the mir-ror and that devilish creature was a matter of life and death. She was afraid, so very afraid that Eddie would not survive. She didn't know if she could handle life without him. It had been hard enough losing a daughter, but now she was losing a husband too, a partner; her soul-mate.

She glanced at the clock on the entry wall. It was nearly eight a.m., little less than two hours had passed since Eddie's vanishing act. He'd told her to stay put, but did he really mean it? Did he really expect her to not go after him, to just sit there and wait?

Not at all, she heard him say. *Come now.*

Grabbing her sport jacket from the coat closet and the keys from the bu-reau Sarah hurried out into the brisk air. She looked from the old Plymouth to the new Bentley. *Which one? Bentley, automatic. Plymouth, manual on the column.* And imagined the jerking motion of trying to manipulate a clutch.

Bentley it is.

Pressing the button on the key fob, the lights flashed, and the horn honked, unlocking the door. She raced over the dirt drive in her newly washed white tennis shoes to the carport; pulled open the door of the sleek vehicle, and slid onto the plush seat, which seemed a million miles away from the pedals. Feeling the left side of the seat she found the handle for adjusting it to fit her, however it was power run and apparently the car had to be on for this feature to work.

Sarah inserted the key into the ignition to the left of the steering wheel and turned it. The car started right away. She reached back to the seat control, making it just right.

Slamming the car's shifter handle into the drive position, Sarah punched the gas pedal. There was a slight hesitation before she was suddenly thrown back against the seat, the car flying out of the carport and down the narrow, rocky driveway. Instantly ramming both feet on the brake petal she was thrown forward against the seatbelt, the car skidding to a stop, dust billowing behind.

Her heart hammered wildly. "Holy Moly!" She cried out loud. "You better take it easy girl." After several deep breaths, Sarah let off the brake and lightly pushed the gas pedal, slowly accelerating toward Red Puma Road. Glancing from the road way to the car's dash with its many buttons and knobs, Sarah wondered where the light switch might be and the wipers. What about the heater? On the steering wheel she saw other buttons. There were buttons everywhere; buttons with little pictures. *This might not be so hard after all*, she thought.

REUNITED

• • 1 • •

The black bristly beast, the one she'd seen somewhere, sometime before, with daggers for teeth and talons for hands reached out, grabbed her around the waist with its deadly hot claws and hauled her into the mirror, a mirror she'd also seen somewhere before. *But, this is all a dream isn't it? Some weird dream. It can't be real. Joseph led me here, but he's dead. Ann killed him. She swung his rifle like she was Babe Ruth. And she hit a home run, yes indeed, right out of the ball park.*

Nora could still hear the cracking of Joseph's scull, could still see the look of surprise on his sweaty face, the eruption of blood from his smashed head as he swayed backwards away from the bed.

Vertigo swept over her as the beast heaved her onto its shoulder like a sack of potatoes and took off running through the hot darkness, the gateway disappearing, along with reality, behind them. The beast's armor painfully poked into her bare torso like tiny needles.

Minutes later the darkness gave way to a reddish haze as the beast stepped from the cave out into a vast sea of desert. Dry, hot air slammed into Nora's nose and lungs, sucking the moisture from every cell in her body. Behind them, within the walls of a ragged mountain range was the entrance to the dark cave, the way back, if only she could wake up. She raised her hands to her eyes, blocking out the red, airborne powder.

The beast took a quick right and kept on running, holding Nora's bare legs with one prickly, armored arm. It packed her across the sandy desert floor through a grove of tall, black and limbless trees, and then up a steep hillside to the rim of a gigantic crater. It continued along the wide rim of the lava littered crater for a few minutes then stopped, sensing the jailer. Lifting the woman high above its head the beast roared with insane, alien laughter and then threw her to the hard packed sand. Nora landed on her ass and elbows, gulping for air. The black beast stood over her, its yellow lizard-like eyes bulging in their lidless sockets. Then its tail, its long, armored tail with its needle thin point came up over its head and shot out toward her.

Ignoring the pain racing through her body Nora quickly rolled onto her hands and feet, scrambling through the chocking dust and away from the wicked tail. Beneath her the ground shook then gave way sending her off kilter and sailing down the steep hillside, like a crazed surfer on an out of control wave. She landed in the rocky crater below, slamming her left arm hard into a large boulder, shattering her tiny gold watch. A loud snapping sound accompanied by excruciating pain burst through her elbow. Dizziness swept over her as she wavered then leaned against the boulder, cupping the broken left elbow in her right hand, squeezing her eyes shut, willing away the sudden urge to cry out. Damn it, that hurt! She leaned there several seconds before opening her eyes.

Wooziness washed over her.

She closed her eyes.

A moment later she reopened them, finding the wooziness gone. Straight ahead, at the bottom of the crater about fifty yards away, was an entrance to a cave, less than a walk down to the cabins at Sucker Lake. At least she could get out of the swirling sand.

· ·2· ·

From his seated position, at the base of the giant viper's head, the young, bare-foot, half-clothed boy, watched the scene unfolding before him. The naked, red-haired woman had come sliding down the hillside, arms flying out in all directions before hitting a huge rock just yards from where he watched. Amazingly she was still standing, looking for a place to hide from the monster. Jonny paused momentarily, remembering that day long ago when . . .

. . . Out of the old mirror comes a pair of claws, black claws, bird claws. He clutches his stuffed animals, Han and Tort, closely to his chest as he's whisked into the mirror so fast he hardly has time to realize what's happening. He doesn't scream or cry, even after dropping one of his stuffed buddies, even though the hot blackness surrounds him, as the monster carries him away; Lizzy disappearing from his view long before they reach the other end of the cave.

The monster promises to take him to play with his mother, but it lies. His mother is dead and Jonny knows it. Still he does not cry, not even when he sees her dried up body lying just inside the monster's smelly cave. He's a big boy now, and big boys don't cry. His mom said so.

The monster had sucked the life from her bones; it told Jonny so. Jonny didn't know what marrow was but only a blind person wouldn't see that she was totally dead. Jonny knew about death; he helped Lizzy burry Fluffy in the rose garden that past summer. Lizzy said it would help the roses grow better. But Lizzy was dead too.

Jonny looked out over the vast crater, the dry, barren world that was now his home. M had sent him out here on a rescue mission after seeing the monster in his magic ball carrying the woman across the desert floor. Finally Jonny had someone to rescue. "Giddy up," he said, kicking his heels into the body of the stuffed, green and blue, Honduran Palm Viper.

• •3• •

She stumbled toward the cave's entrance just a few short steps away; she was almost there, finally. It was much further and much rockier than Nora originally perceived. Golf-ball size lava rock covering the crater floor rolled under her slippered feet with each and every step. A couple of times Nora was sure she would slip and fall again, perhaps breaking her head against one of the larger boulders which also littered the crater. During those times she had accidentally let go the broken elbow, sending jolts of pain up her arm and into her head. *God, I wish I had a drink,* she thought. *A nice cold coffee with a big shot of rum would certainly ease the pain in the elbow, not to mention the head. Hell, forget the coffee; a straight shot of rum would do just fine, maybe even two or three.*

Suddenly she stopped, dead in her tracks. Directly ahead, blocking the entrance to the cave was something that certainly had to be a dream. Nora blinked her eyes several times, but the image did not go away. *Maybe it's the DTs.*

She shook her head; that was something she didn't want to believe. She could quit drinking anytime, if she wanted to. She certainly wasn't addicted to the rum.

Nora gazed at the thing blocking the cave's entrance. Its head hovered about three feet above her, the forked tongue hanging there, looking strangely unreal. Its black eyes were like the buttons on a coat she once owned. The body was kind of fuzzy with blue diamond shapes on a green background. A slender boy somewhere between the ages of eight and twelve, she guessed, straddled the creature just at the base of its head. His long, ratty blonde hair was braided with a faded red and blue ribbon.

"Down," the young voice commanded.

Nora's green eyes widened as the giant snake lowered its head and body so that it lay flat on the ground in front of her, chest high.

"Ya don't really wanna go in there," the boy said.

"I don't?" Nora asked.

The rider leaned toward her and said, "Not if ya wanna live."

Nora stared into the bright blue eyes of the young, masked boy. It was hard to tell his actual age, but his eyes spoke of long years here.

"I know a place, out of the heat and away from the monster," he boasted. "Come on, we'll take ya there. You can meet the others."

Nora gasped, "There are others?"

"A few, come on, time's running out." The boy extended a hand toward her.

Grimacing, Nora let go the broken elbow, keeping it as close to her chest as possible, grabbed the offered hand with her freed hand and was hauled up onto the snake's soft back.

"Giddy up," the snake rider commanded.

The snake lifted its head slightly off the sand and sped off smoothly down the center of the crater at an amazing, side-winding speed.

· ·4· ·

The snake glided to a stop at the entrance to a cave miles, it seemed, from where they had picked her up. It lowered its head as the boy slid off. The boy then turned and helped the woman down. Then he commanded the snake to go.

The snake slithered off into the desert.

Nora felt cooler air coming from the cave then heard the barking of a dog from deep within.

"That's Spot," the boy said. "And I'm Jonny. What's your name?"

Nora raised her eyebrow. "Spot?"

The boy removed the scarf from his face and nodded, "Yeah."

"My name's Nora," she said.

"Pleased to meet ya," Jonny replied, with a little bow.

Nora smiled and said, "I'm very pleased to meet you Jonny. What where you doing out there?"

"It's my job," he replied.

Nora looked at him with curiosity. "What do you mean?"

Jonny paused a moment. "Come, let's find M, he'll explain everything."

She followed the boy into the fresh smelling cave, its smooth walls glittering in the iridescent light from some unseen source. Something about the entire place seemed familiar to Nora; maybe some reoccurring dream. She was dreaming a lot more lately, dreaming of death. This was a dream too, had to be. Maybe she was on her way to hell right now. God knew she deserved it. She thought about what she might say to God at the pearly gates. Maybe she'd ask for a cup of coffee and rum.

It was a short walk to a spacious cavern where the ceiling shot up about a hundred feet, giving the illusion of blue sky overhead. Tall palm trees stood around a vast pool of sparkling clear water. Nestled in the midst of the trees were several little grass huts. The smell of something cooking wafted passed Nora's nose. Her stomach rolled with nausea.

"Come on," the boy said, showing her into the nearest hut.

Inside, seated on the floor, his spindly legs crisscrossed yoga style was a man with long gray hair and a matching beard. He was looking into a small glass ball he held in his old hands. Lying beside him was a dog. The dog raised its head as they entered then stood and wagged its stubby tail.

Nora stared in disbelief at the dog, a dog she recognized. But it couldn't be. Now she knew for sure she was dreaming because Rascal disappeared in Sucker Lake several years ago. Another memory tried to surface; Nora quickly pushed it away. "Rascal?" She asked.

The dog barked once then trotted toward her.

Nora reached down with her good arm and patted the dream dog's head.

The old man stood up. "Nora," he said, holding his arms out toward her.

Nora looked closer at the bearded man, into the pale eyes and suddenly her brain was flooded with a very vivid memory. Needle sharp tears stabbed her eyes. "Papa?" she gasped then collapsed to the floor.

C•H•A•P•T•E•R 12

STEPPIN IN

• • 1 • •

The ages old glass, black and void of any reflection, surrounded by its rosebud frame, stood before them. To Scott it looked like the gaping maw of some giant flesh-eater ready to devour them. A wave of heat flowed from it, drying his eyes. An old fairy tale he hadn't read in years popped into his head. *Mirror, Mirror on the wall, please don't eat me,* he thought. Then it was Uncle Ed's voice, silently telling him to stop thinking nonsense.

"Join hands," Uncle Ed said aloud, taking Scott's right hand into his left. Scott in turn took Ann's right hand into his left, feeling the slight tingle of electricity. Ann took Will's right hand into her left, passing the current on to him. He didn't mind.

"Ready?" Uncle Ed asked.

All nodded.

Uncle Ed stepped into the mirror followed one at a time by the children. Hot air and the stench of dry decay filtered into their homemade face masks. Dim light spilled in through the mirror from the foyer, fanning out a few feet then diminishing into the blackness there.

Ann let go of the boys' hands to find her flashlight. The others followed suit, their tiny lights shinning about ten feet out into total darkness. Adventuring forward, swinging their lights from side to side they checked out what appeared to be a tunnel. The walls were smooth and sparkly. The ceiling, domed and rocky. But they were not alone in here; Ann felt the presence of another. Looking back toward the mirror she wasn't surprised to see the young, long haired, ghost-girl hovering there, a ghost-rifle in her hands. A pile of dry bones lay on the dusty stone floor beneath the hovering image, a real rifle lay beside them. A battered, stuffed turtle lay nearby. Another, more recent body, that of a man still clothed, lay to the ghost-girl's right.

"Who are you?" Ann asked.

The others turned. Scott recognized the ghost at once, and then he saw the body of the caretaker, the moisture sucked from it like a grape.

Go back! The entity warned, pointing her long phantom finger toward the shriveled up body of the caretaker. *Too dangerous! Not safe! Beware Ci'del!*

Ann stepped over to the fallen toy and picked it up. Holding the dirty, stuffed turtle out toward the ghost she asked, "Who does this belong to?"

The watery image wavered, disappeared, and then reappeared. *Jonny,* she said. Then she began to wail.

Ann looked back to the others, bewildered.

Then Uncle Ed said, "Bring that," pointing toward the stuffed animal still in Ann's grasp. "And follow me." He turned and hurried off into the tunnel toward whatever lay ahead of them. "Hurry," he commanded.

Ann glanced back at the wailing ghost then turned and hurried off after the others, the turtle clutched to her chest.

In the foyer, the mirror's glass returned to its reflective state.

••2••

In the beam of her tiny flashlight she could see the backside of Scott directly ahead. She slid up beside him, extinguished her light and curled one hand around his muscular arm, the other hand tightly holding the precious turtle. "Why do you think he wants *this?*" she whispered.

Scott shook his head. "Don't know," he whispered back, loving her touch, her inner strength and courageous beauty. She was risking her life, as they all were, to dispose the creature. But for Ann, this would be the second time. And although the story his uncle had told them in the library was beginning to fade, Scott was sure he would never forget that part of the tale.

Uncle Ed could have tried to explain the possible need for the stuffed animal, but he wasn't exactly sure yet. He just had a suspicion that they might need such a creature. He did know exactly the purpose of the weapons they brought, and that their escape from the mirror would depend mostly on Sarah.

Shortly after leaving the ghost and the portal, the four adventurers emerged from the tunnel. Putting away their lights they raised a hand to shield their eyes from the red, swirling dust as they stepped into a whole new world. To their right about ten yards away through the dusty swirl stood a grove of gigantic, blackened trees; trees without limbs. A steep incline to the top of a jagged hillside stood just beyond that.

Looking passed the unusual trees and beyond the sand lake and dry river bed that lie straight ahead, Scott took in the landscape, the broken peaks of a never ending mountain range touching the red sky. There was something weird going on here. The distant mountain range looked closer now. Scott blinked his eyes and the mountains seemed further away.

"Magic," Uncle Ed said.

"Martin's?" Scott asked.

"Aye, come on." Uncle Ed motioned the children to follow as he stepped from the tunnel's doorway out into the powdery red sand.

• •3• •

William stepped out behind the others, his brown eyes gleaming with anticipation of killing the monster; his tormentor. It was just like his Pa, a murderin bastard. Only this time he would not stand by and let it continue. This time he would do the right thing. He would kill the monster before it could kill anyone else. That was the promise he'd made to himself as Scott's Uncle briefly prepared them for this trip into the mirror – a land that couldn't possibly be real, yet here they were walking through the red dust toward an unknown mountain range that lay far off in the distance, sometimes.

William dug his Pa's pocket watch (which he'd snatched from the pocket of Pa's abandoned clothes) from his own pocket and looked curiously at it. The hands stood at just a few minutes past eight. *How could that be?* Lifting the watch to his ear he listened for the tick tock of passing time and heard nothing. He returned the watch to his pocket; it was no good here. It seemed Scott's Uncle was right about that.

William eyed his new half-brother, Scott, and Scott's new girlfriend walking a few steps ahead, arm in arm; the perfect couple. Scott was one lucky guy.

You can still have her, a voice spoke inside his head.

William shook the thought away. Ann was a nice girl, and older. He didn't stand a chance against Scott.

Suddenly a stocky built man appeared beside William. He wasn't at all familiar, except for the coat he was wearing. A bright yellow rain slicker. William wondered where he'd seen it before.

I can show you where it lives, the man said through unmoving lips. *We can destroy the monster together. You'll be the hero.* The man extended a hand toward William.

Swept away by the idea of finally being the hero, doing what was right; William reached for the extended hand.

A burning heat raced through him as he touched it.

Then darkness fell.

• •4• •

The squeezing darkness took his breath away as fire raced over his entire body. In that instant William knew Ci'del had tricked him, again. Uncle Ed had warned him, had warned them all. Damn, why was he so stupid? Was he born that way?

You ARE a dumb little bastard, ain't ya? Pa's voice spoke in the darkness.

No, he thought. *This ain't real. You're dead!*

Only cuz that little bitch killed me Billy! Killed me dead, but you can pay her back for me. You'd like that, wouldn't ya?

"No!" William shouted, the heat baking him alive.

Then the darkness lifted and across the dimly lit lair he saw the ghostly image of the man. The ghost vanished and in its place Ci'del appeared in its real form; bristle black armor covering a slick, bipedal body with yellow lizard eyes, carving knife teeth pulsating in and out with each stinking breath, black bird-like talons at the end of long arms, clacking together. Then William saw the tail wagging behind Ci'del like an angry cat; a tail that was at least twenty feet long. And at the end of that tail was a spike, a needle thin, foot long spike.

You will cooperate, Ci'del's voice, grating and alien, spoke inside William's head.

William cringed at the sound, a sound resembling that of fingernails on a blackboard, a sound he heard occasionally at school, and realized Ci'del was scanning his memories. Uncle Ed had warned them.

Uncle Ed doesn't know everything, the grating fingernails on blackboard voice told him.

Magically Ci'del appeared directly in front of William, its tail wagging over its head. Then the tail shot out toward him. William tried to move but couldn't. His feet were glued to the sandy ground, his body wrapped in some kind of unseen bind. His mind seemed detached and floating in space as he watched from some distant location. He felt the sharp prick of the needle tipped tail penetrating his skin just below his navel. He felt it sliding into his pelvic bone and the pain spread out in a burning sensation from the point of entry all the way to the tips of his fingers and toes. His head felt as if it were about to explode.

Then the pain was gone and William found himself standing there, alone. He frowned. *What just happened?* Putting his hands on his chest, he felt up and down his body just to be sure he was all there. *Something strange just happened. What was it?* William shook his head as whatever it was eluded him.

He looked around the monster's lair at the dry, dusty piles of bodies littering the floor. The place had a smell to it, a nasty, dead smell. *And it's hotter than a pistol in here*, he thought. He tried to move his feet again and couldn't. Something was restraining his movement even though he couldn't see anything. He could, however, twist and turn and even bend his knees. Then a thought occurred to him, *magic*. He was being held in place by a magic spell. He still had his sling shot and ammo. He still had the use of his arms. He wasn't dead, yet.

• •5• •

In the suffocating heat William could barely stay awake, hunkered down on his haunches, the sling shot in his hand, loaded and ready. Every now and again his eyelids would droop, his head would nod and he would slip into unconsciousness. Then the thought that he couldn't be asleep when the monster came back would wave in his mind like a big red flag waving in the breeze and his head would jerk up, eyes open, because he knew he couldn't afford to sleep, he couldn't. Because if he was asleep when Ci'del returned, terrible things would happen to him, he was positive. His feet were restrained, and William knew the reason why.

That thing was going to come back any second now and eat him alive, he just knew it. And it would be easy. It would be easy if he was asleep because if he was asleep he couldn't run away. But if he remained awake, alert, he could shoot it with his sling shot.

Maybe even kill it, he thought.

MEET THE DEAD

·•1•·

I n the light of the full moon the young, red-haired girl runs across the grassy sand toward the little shack on the edge of the alkali lake. It's nearly midnight and all the other cabins, with their one little window each, are dark. Only this cabin, the fifth in a row of eight, shows any signs of life inside.

From her upstairs bedroom window, she had watched her father pull into the driveway in his old jalopy. Had watched him drag something out of it, something that glittered in the moonlight, then he hauled whatever it was across the sand and into the little shack. Moments later she had seen the light in the window. Now she was almost there.

A gust of wind howls passed, blowing her long hair away from her young face, the tail of her shirt flaps out behind her in the breeze. A chill runs up and down her spine as a feeling of dread washes over her, and she thinks, *something bad's going to happen.* But like most dreams, she can't turn back. Something drives her forward. Destiny? Stupidity?

On tip-toes at the small window she cups her hands to her face and peers inside the one room shanty. Her father is seated on a wooden stool in the center of the room, his back to her, facing a huge rectangular mirror leaning against the opposite wall. Hundreds of rosebuds surround the glass. Beautiful rosebuds of all shapes and sizes, some open, some closed.

Nora has never seen anything so beautiful, so ugly at the same time. She knows there is something wrong with the glass; she can see it wavering in and out, in and out, just before . . .

Nora sat straight up with a start, her heart jack hammering. The image of the black talons reaching from the mirror, snatching her father from the stool and dragging him into it without a sound burned in her brain. *But, that was just a dream, a horrible dream, a psychotic dream. None of it was real, not the black beast, not the mirror, none of it. It can't be real, it just can't! These things*

are just a figment of my imagination. No doubt caused by too much alcohol.
There, I've said it. Are you happy now?

Nora glared around the small room, with its straw floor and cloth door. Suddenly the door lifted and a man with a dog stepped in.

"Nora," a familiar voice said.

As he approached she realized he hadn't changed that much. His hair and beard were longer, grayer. But the voice and the pale blue eyes were exactly the same.

"Papa, is it really you or am I dreaming?"

"It's really me, Nora."

How could it be? She wondered.

Martin knelt down beside her, pulling her gently into his old, tired arms. That's when she noticed her broken elbow was mended. It didn't hurt a bit. Someone, her father most likely, had clothed her in a kind of cave woman attire; one cloth around her boobs and one around her butt. She wanted to laugh, it all seemed so ridiculous. Instead she said, "I don't suppose you have some rum."

· ·2· ·

Ignoring her statement, Martin held his daughter's shoulders at arm's length from him and said, "My how you've grown up; the spittin image of your mother. Come, there are some folks here who've been waiting for you."

Martin escorted Nora from the hut out into the open cave, with its wonderful palm trees and fresh air. A creation he was rather proud of, everything considered. It was, after all, just an illusion.

"What is this place?" Nora asked, gazing out over the sparkling pond, smelling the cooking food. Her stomach rolled again with nausea. She wiped a shaking hand across her sweat beaded brow.

"We call it Paraiso."

"Are you kidding?"

"Not at all."

"Do you know what's outside?"

"Certainly."

"Papa," she whispered. "There's a monster out there, and a giant snake."

"Yes," he agreed.

Nora stared at him through narrowing green eyes, just like her mother would have.

"Look," he said. "The monster can't harm us. The snake isn't real. It's a stuffed toy that Jonny brought with him. He wanted something unusual to ride, an imaginary friend, with a little magical help from yours truly." He bowed. "Now come, meet my friends." Placing his old hand against the small of her back, he directed her toward a small gathering of people on the far side of the sparkling pond.

· ·3· ·

Nora counted nine people standing on the other side of the pond. *Like sheep and their shepherd*, she thought. Jonny, who was among the group, seemed different, more alive. He was actually doing something while the others stood there motionless. She watched him haul a bucket of water from the pond toward the awaiting crowd, their cup holding hands extended toward him. *God, I need a drink*, she thought.

Jonny stopped at the crowd, set down the bucket and began ladling water from the pail into each raised cup. When each cup was filled the group of nine stood in a circle holding their cups to their chests, their heads bowed.

Martin guided Nora to the far side of the pond and handed her a cup, filling it with water, the same as Jonny had done. After filling a cup for himself, Martin then guided Nora to the center of the circle.

"Friends," he said. "This is a glorious day. You have all heard me speak of Nora, and here she is."

Nine pair of eyes looked up from their cups; eight pair of vacant, hopeless, dead eyes. Only one pair was alive; Jonny. Nora wanted to scream.

Jonny knew what the red-haired woman saw, he'd seen it too, the first time he met them. These people were dead, they just didn't know it. Maybe now the old man would let them die, now that *she* was here.

Nora looked at each dead person as her father introduced them to her. She looked into their dead eyes, their hopeless faces, and knew beyond a shadow of a doubt – this *was* hell. Somewhere between Sucker Lake and Seal Cape she had taken a detour into hell. They might call it Paraiso, but they were dead. They were dead and she was not.

Or was she?

"Everyone," her father's voice boomed. "Raise your cups and drink of the sweetness of life that we may all be saved."

Nora raised the cup to her trembling lips. The clear, cool water splashed down her throat, soothing the parched passageway.

C·H·A·P·T·E·R 14

IMPOSTER

·•1•·

Ann and Scott could barely keep up with Uncle Ed as they walked arm in arm across the hard, dusty land. The desert landscape wavered in and out around them; the mountain ranges close then far away, close then far away. *In time with the ocean waves in the real world*, Ann thought. But what did that mean for her? She had few memories of the *real* world in relation to *her* life. Her life had started upon awakening in that meadow. Why couldn't she remember beyond that? Was it important that she *not* remember? Maybe it was not important *to* remember. So far her memories included some bizarre knowledge about cars, franks and beans, a Paul McCartney concert, and the murder of Joe. Joe, who turned out to be a rapist, a murderer.

Then the voice of the rose spoke in her mind, *William is not himself.*

Ann stopped, stopping Scott with her.

"What's wrong?" he asked, his lips brushing passed her ear, sending tingles through her body.

"Just need a little breather," she said, stealing a glance over her shoulder. "Where's Will?"

Scott looked back and saw nothing but swirling red sand.

Ann stood on tip-toes, one hand resting on Scott's firm shoulder, the other hand still holding tightly onto the old, stuffed tortoise. *Where is he?* she wondered, and then sighed with relief at finally seeing his black hair bouncing crazily on his head as he appeared in the blowing dust behind them. *But had he been there earlier?* She shook the thought from her head remembering Uncle Ed's warning about thoughts and sights inside this place. She looked back to Scott's Uncle. He had stopped a short distance ahead of them and was looking back toward William. *He feels it too,* she thought.

Scott, who over the years had learned not to listen to his twin, barely heard her voice inside his head. He didn't know what she was saying, and he didn't care.

The truth was Rachel didn't really want him to hear, not this time. Had she wanted him to hear, he would have heard. Instead, he ignored her, which is just what Rachel wanted.

· ·2· ·

The dust swirled around them as they waited for William to catch up. When he did, Scott asked, "What happened?"

"What'd ya mean?"

Scott and Ann exchanged glances.

"What kept you?" Ann asked.

William glared at her through dark eyes, different eyes and said, "Heat stroke, took a break, drank a ton a water. I'm just about out." He held up the nearly empty container. She couldn't see his mouth under the homemade scarf, but suspected he was smiling. She suspected she wouldn't like to see that smile.

Just then Uncle Ed rejoined them. "What happened?"

William shrugged and said, "Heat stroke."

Edwin narrowed his thin eyebrows under the tan, felt hat with its colorful band of pheasant feathers. There was something different about the boy. Noticing William's knapsack missing from the boy's back, knowing this was not William, knowing he couldn't let on, he said, "Quickly, we must hurry."

· ·3· ·

Continuing across the hard sand, seeming to go nowhere, they trudged on. It was like walking on a tread mill. The wavering landscape was beginning to drive Ann crazy, and she had a terrible, awful feeling about Will. He looked like Will, talked like Will, even acted like Will. But there was something about him that wasn't right. Every now and again she'd caught him looking at her; felt him looking at her through eyes that weren't right, not quite human.

Don't trust him, the familiar, soft voice spoke. No, she wouldn't trust him, but she had to get her mind on something else, anything else; a nice cool drink of water, a cool breeze, a cooler temperature, the rose. No, she mustn't think of that.

She looked up, the mountain range had not gotten any closer. At times it seemed to fade away into the red sky, almost disappearing. Then it would return either farther away or closer but never in quite the same place, or so it seemed. It was a good thing Uncle Ed made them bring lots of water – her second bottle was almost empty, almost. She wiped her sweat-less brow. The air was terribly hot and still. The powdery dust swirled around them but was not carried on a breeze, nor did it cause a breeze. The dusty air was absolutely still.

She gazed up at the sky, it too was red, the color of rust. There were no clouds, no sun, nothing. And why would there be? They were, after all, inside a mirror. A make-believe world. At least that's what Uncle Ed had told them. An imitation of Ci'del's world. Ann didn't like it one little bit.

Of course that wasn't all he'd told them.

But Ann couldn't afford to think about those things; none of them could.

· ·4· ·

Scott and Ann graduated from walking arm in arm to Scott leaning on Ann with one arm draped over her shoulder. Ann had one arm wrapped tightly around Scott's waist to help support him, the other arm clutching the stuffed toy to her chest. Scott's legs would walk no more, but Ann didn't mind. She would carry him if she had to, if she could.

Shortly after passing between a second grove of black, stone trees to their left and a huge rock formation to their right, something Scott supposed you'd see in a place like Arizona's canyon country, Uncle Ed stopped. In the middle of the vast illusion, a small bridge spanned another dry riverbed. "We're almost there," he said, pointing toward a large hole in the side of a huge mountain. A mountain that seemed, at least to Scott, miles away just a few seconds before.

Scott stopped to look back over his shoulder passed William toward the direction they had come from. It was a long way across the valley floor to the tunnel where the portal was, if it still was. The scene was like looking through the wrong end of a telescope, and then it changed. Suddenly the tunnel's entrance was only a few feet away, within a stones throw, and then it changed back again. As his eyes passed by William a second time, Scott paused; Rachel spoke inside his head, he ignored her as usual.

· ·5· ·

They stepped inside the large mountain cavern. Its walls glittered with light. An old magic trick Edwin knew Martin had learned long ago. *Things are going well,* he thought. *If this is the place, and why wouldn't it be?* He knew the exact layout of the cell, had detected the magic to be generating from straight ahead, down this corridor. He was concerned about William. Concerned that Ci'del had perhaps become too bold. Edwin removed the home made mask from his weathered face, motioning the others to do the same; which they did. Knowing this would bring out the beast. Fate was about to show one of its hands.

Scott removed his arm from Ann's shoulder as she unclasped his waist and stepped away. The braces would hold him up as long as he wasn't trying to walk. *Why'd they have to give out now?* he wondered. *Is this part of the destiny too?* He didn't want to believe it, but what choice did he have? *I should have brought my crutches along. They would have been better than nothing, and I wouldn't have to count on others for help.* Then another thought filled his head, an outside thought. *Don't matter, you'll be dead soon anyway.*

Scott turned toward the creature charging up beside him, a creature that had William's face. Suddenly the face fluctuates; changes, brown eyes fade to yellow, teeth elongate into carving knives. A stabbing pain slices through Scott's pelvis, racing to the ends of every nerve. He screams as the world spins out of control around him. The rifle falls from his arm landing with a thud and a poof of dust on the cave's floor. Then just as suddenly, the pain stops. *Am I dead? Is it like being born? Surrounded by darkness, peace, security, tranquility?* A noise in the distance. Thu-thump, thu-thump, thu-thump. No, not outside; within. Pressure, pushing. Movement; through liquid space. Another soul joins with him, a female; his twin. More pressure on the top of his head, around his head. Sudden bright light, blurry images and colors. He blinks. Muffled voices, a stinging slap on his bottom. He opens his mouth; lungs fill with air; outside air. He exhales in a wail; just one. He is wrapped up in warmth and placed in the arms of his mother. He looks up at her unclear face, reaches out his small hand, and wraps his fingers around her thumb and smiles. Abruptly he is removed from the loving arms to a hard surface inside a glass box, a heated place. Outside, his mother weeps.

· ·6· ·

Ci'del has never tasted (drank) of anything so filthy; poison, foul and dank running through the human's bones. Pain courses through Ci'del's tail and upward toward its spinal column. Ci'del tries to jerk away from the tainted marrow and roars as the bones will not let go. Ci'del roars again as the tainted bones continue to hold. It must withdraw from the foul creature and return to the lair to repair.

Ci'del finally rips its tail from the child then slides one long, sharp talon through the thin barrier of magic space and disappears into it.

· ·7· ·

Unable to sit on his haunches any longer William stood up and stuffed the still loaded sling shot into his back pocket. Clasping his hands together he stretched his arms toward the far away ceiling. It was time to get the blood circulating. Time to figure a way out of here. He still couldn't move his feet, so he did a couple of side stretches and some twisting and turning. Then placing his hands on the ground in front of him and walking them out as far as he could reach he stretched out his legs and back. It felt good, but the feeling was cut short as Ci'del appeared out of no where.

It was hurt. William could tell by the way its black bristled armor had faded to gray. He could tell by the way it was hobbling, hobbling like Scott.

A quick retreat of hands and a bend of the knees, and William was back to standing. Grabbing the sling shot, the ball bearing still loaded inside the pouch, he aimed at Ci'del's head, thought better of it (too hard) and began looking for a more vulnerable spot, an un-armored spot as the monster came waddling toward him, its tail raised high over its head. William saw a possible target and let the shot fly, hurtling through the air toward Ci'del's left nostril. Ci'del brought up a sharp talon to block but missed. The ball bearing soared into the nostril, ripping its way through Ci'del's fleshy membranes, but the monster kept coming. It was coming to give him Scott's disease, William knew it, he didn't know how, but he knew, he knew –

He stepped aside, sudden awareness swept over him as Ci'del's tail flew passed, missing him; his feet were free. William turned and ran toward the only passage he saw.

· ·8· ·

William ran and ran and ran, and he kept on running even though he was sure he was going to pass out or die. Then he saw an opening straight ahead. With his slingshot and more ammo in hand, just in case the murderin bastard was still after him, William emerged from the long, long (or was it just a perception of time?) corridor. Red sky, red sand and the swirling dust surrounded him. A lava littered crater the size of his favorite fishing lake spread out ahead of him. But there was no lake here, no peace of mind. He took off running down an odd path through the rocky debris as fast as his legs would carry him.

C·H·A·P·T·E·R 15

VISIONS

·· 1 ··

H e spread the old tattered blanket out on the ground then motioned her to sit down beside him. In his hands he held the magic, all seeing ball.

Nora didn't know anything about magic, but she was thinking she felt somewhat better after drinking the water, which must surely be magic too. She never liked water before. It was awful; especially the stuff from the well out at Sucker Lake.

Funny thing was that now she didn't even feel like she needed a drink. Well, that wasn't quite true. Maybe just one little drink, she'd even settle for just a tablespoon full. *Oh hell, who are you trying to kid? You still want a drink, in fact you want to get bombed, totally wasted. This place, this unreal dreamland with its fake palm trees and people, who could live like this?* "Can't we go back?" she pleaded.

Her father continued to gaze into his crystal ball. "Yes," he said. "But we need a little help from our friends."

"What friends?"

"Come look."

Nora shifted closer to him, looking into the glass ball resting in the palms of his old, bony hands. At first she saw nothing but red, rust red. Then the image cleared and four people came into sight walking across a long desert. "Oh my god!" she exclaimed, raising her hand to her mouth. Where they coming for her? Then the scene changed and she saw Scott and Ann enter a glittery cave behind Edwin, with William in the rear. Suddenly William was not William. Suddenly William was the ugly monster and its needle tipped tail was sliding into Scott's pelvic bone. Scott screamed and the ball went black, then lavender; the image gone.

Nora stared at her father through huge green eyes. "What happened?" she yelled in his face. Then she was up on her knees beating him around the head and shoulders with her balled up fists yelling at him, "It's your fault, all your fault! If you hadn't brought that stupid mirror home that night, if you hadn't disappeared into it, none of this ever would have happened!" Then she was crying, racking sobs, the tears flowing down her cheeks as she remembered the panic that had overtaken her that early morning so long ago as she watched her father dragged into the mirror. Knowing she couldn't tell anyone. Who would believe such a story? She had rushed into the cabin, covering the mirror with an old blanket, and then she had left it there, locking the cabin forever. After that she poured herself a big glass of rum from her father's secret stash and she hadn't really stopped since.

Through tear filled eyes she glared at the old man for a moment and then got up and stomped off into the hut. She would have slammed the door behind her, if there had been one.

· ·2· ·

She lay down on the makeshift bedding and stared up at the straw ceiling, thinking about the vision in the glass ball. Was it real? Hadn't he told her it couldn't be trusted? That he hadn't known it was her for sure until he'd seen Jonny help her down from the make-believe snake, and he still had his doubts up until he actually saw her in the flesh? What if she was shown some future event, something she could prevent? What if it was some passed event? Wasn't this all just a dream? Was Scott really dead, no longer her responsibility? *God, I wish I had a drink*, she thought again. It would be so much easier if she at least had her morning shot. She could probably, maybe, live without the rest, but she really needed that first cup of coffee and rum; especially the rum. Wondering how long it'd been since her last drink, she glanced at the place on her wrist where her watch should have been, and recalled it shattering against the rock.

The blanket hanging over the doorway swayed inward as the dog entered.

"Rascal, what am I gonna do?"

Rascal padded over to her, nosing his way into her face. She patted his head and rubbed his ears. She couldn't believe this was the same dog, it certainly seemed to be. But dreams were like that, weren't they? "I'm just gonna go right back to sleep," she said, holding the dog's face up to hers.

"And when I wake up all this will be gone, and every frigin thing will be back to normal."

Rascal lay down beside the woman. Resting his head on his crossed forepaws he closed his multi-colored eyes.

Nora closed her eyes as well.

· ·3· ·

Jonny looked up, the woman was yelling. He wouldn't go see what was going on though, as M had warned him that this was bound to happen, *as she was a red head, and just like her mother.* Within seconds the woman stomped off into the healing hut. Soon afterwards Spot and M got up from their places on the old blanket. Spot barked once, as usual, then followed the woman into the hut as M wrapped the magic ball in the blanket, as usual, stowing it away under the fake palm tree that stood there. M then left, and Jonny knew where M was headed. It happened all the time.

He thought back to that first time, the sight of the monster sucking M's bones, its needle tail deep in the man's chest. Lizzy would have called it disgusting, gross. Lizzy would never get the chance to call anything gross ever again.

Jonny turned his thoughts to other, more pleasant things like spending most of his time altered days either riding his snake, which he named Hon (as it was a Honduran Palm Viper, according to his mom) out in Ci'del's world or exploring the massive cave in which M had created their little world. Jonny hadn't yet located the end of the cave, even though it should be close by. But everything about this place was wrong. You could walk for ever and get nowhere or you could take ten steps and be clear across the land. It wasn't so bad inside their encampment, but if you ventured out there in the desert too far you could get lost in time. And that was the real problem here, time. He didn't know how much time he'd spent in this world. It seemed like forever, but it didn't matter because they were never getting out of there alive anyway. This was something he knew, and accepted without question.

He'd been back to the mirror several times, had seen Lizzy's dried up bones and her ghost, and his stuffed tortoise, Tort. Had even tried to give Tort to Lizzy, but Lizzy was a ghost. He even tried to step back into the real world. Yet every effort to go back through the mirror was useless, it couldn't be done. M said it required a key, a key they would get from someone he called the jailer.

"How long have you been here Jonny?" The woman's voice startled him.

He turned toward her. She was tall. Her curly, red hair was nearly shoulder length. Her green eyes were rimmed with the redness of crying.

"Dunno," he replied.

"Is there a way out?"

"Maybe."

"Other than the mirror?"

"Maybe."

Nora knew there *must* be another way. Rascal could not have come through the mirror, and yet here he was – how? The only answer in her rum wanting brain was another doorway, and she wanted to find it as quickly as possible, before she couldn't. She'd been unable to go to sleep, unable to keep her eyes closed as the vision of Scott being pierced by that monster returned to her again and again. She needed a drink! "Jonny?"

"Yeah?"

"I need to find a way out of here, right now. Will you help me?" She held her hand out to the young boy. *How long have you been here?* she wondered.

Taking the offered hand Jonny was instantly reminded of his own mother. Together, and with Spot in the lead, they left the safety of the encampment.

PARAISO

• • 1 • •

Edwin Anderson scooped the fallen rifle from the ground and slung it over his own shoulder.

"Do you think he's dead?" Scott asked through lips that felt like balloons, as he lay propped against the cave's glittering wall, Ann by his side. "William, I mean."

Edwin looked toward the boy, his heir in this madness, and pondered the question then said, "Hard to say."

Scott nodded his aching head.

Edwin continued, "Right now Ci'del has returned to its lair, where William is most likely being stored. There it will regenerate. It'll be back, only next time it might be using William's body instead of his image."

Ann shivered in the heat. The thought of that hideous creature returning in William's body sent a chill up her spine. She had known it wasn't him, why hadn't she stopped him?

Kismet, the rose spoke inside her head.

She smiled a haunting, little smile. Rose was talking about fate again. Ann finally understood the word Kismet; fate, destiny. She didn't believe in fate, did she?

It matters not, that voice replied.

"Can he get away?" Ann asked.

"That's a question I can't answer," Edwin replied.

• • 2 • •

"We don't have much time, Son," Uncle Ed said, extending his long slender hand toward the boy. Scott looked up into the bright blue eyes, nodded and grabbed the old hand, getting to his feet, his legs like rubber.

Ann also stood, handed the dirty stuffed tortoise to Scott then wrapped an arm around his waist as he draped an arm over her shoulder as before. They followed Uncle Ed deeper inside.

You should have listened to me, Rachel spoke inside Scott's aching head. He hadn't listened to her seriously for a long time, not since that kindergarten episode when she raised such hell, and he'd taken the fall for it. After all, who would believe a five year old kid talking nonsense about his dead twin sister taking over his mouth?

Will you listen to me now? she asked

Do I have to? he thought back.

Do you want to get out of here alive?

Well, that's really a tough question, isn't it? Duh.

Then you do as I say, when I say. You got that?

Scott absently nodded his head, the pain had settled down to a dull roar, soon he would be able to think clearly again.

• •3• •

The three of them stood at a crossroads where six corridors met. They looked back and forth between them. Edwin knew which was the correct one but waited for Ann to decide. Ann knew the way, even if she didn't know she knew.

Inside Ann's head the voice was speaking again, *Straight ahead to Paraiso.* "I think we should go straight," she said, although there was something about the name *Paraiso* she didn't like, she knew it meant paradise and doubted that was the truth. "It's just a feeling, we don't have to."

"Aye," Uncle Ed said. "I believe we do. Would you like to lead the way whilst I take over with Scott?"

Ann handed Scott over to Ed, grabbed Scott's stubbly face in both hands, kissed him on the mouth, briefly, and then started out in the direction of *Paraiso*, ahead of the men. The leader of the pack. Had she ever been the leader of a pack? *It matters not,* she thought and smiled. She liked the cooler air on her skin, its soft caress, unlike the dusty, desert air out there; harsh and unforgiving. She stepped from the corridor into a large cavern; a cavern with palm trees, grass huts and gurgling water. Did her ears and eyes deceive her? She breathed in the scent of fresh, light air, the way it smells after a cleansing spring shower. A smell she remembered, a smell she loved. Beyond the first grass hut she saw a fountain, the water cascading over the rocks and into a little pond. Several other huts stood near by. *Is there anyone here?* "Look!" She pointed toward the fountain as Scott and Uncle Ed emerged.

Uncle Ed continued passed her toward the pond with Scott hanging from his shoulder. At the pond he then deposited the boy on the bench surrounding it, the same spot where Jonny had sat a short time before.

This is the place, Ed thought. *But where is Martin?*

· ·4· ·

While Scott and Ann sat on the bench at the pond's edge, looking deeply into each others eyes, lost in their own little world, at least for a now, Edwin began snooping around. He knew what he was looking for, could feel its low, magnetic force. It was close by, very close.

Strolling over to the largest of the huts he removed the rifle from his shoulder, propped it against the hut then squatted beside the potted palm tree at the cloth-covered doorway. He lifted the three foot tall palm out of its planter basket. Inside the basket was an old, tattered blanket wrapped around the item he was searching for, the glass ball. He lifted the ball from its hiding spot, the old blanket falling to the ground. He scooped up the blanket and returned it and the palm to the basket and then carried the ball over to the pond where he sat next to the children, next to the tattered old turtle.

A hazy lavender color swirled within the ball.

"Are you ready?" Edwin whispered.

The children turned to look.

The ball blazed a bright purple, as if in response.

"Good," Edwin replied, holding the ball out in front of him in one hand as a multitude of colors began to swirl within it.

The children looked on in breathless wonder.

"Where is Martin?" Edwin asked. Inside the lavender ball the swirl of colors began colliding together, pulling apart, and then regrouping. Images began to appear. Edwin's younger brother, Martin, wavered in and out of focus; older, grayer, bearded, standing in the iridescent light somewhere, looking for something. Suddenly Ci'del appeared beside him, faded black, ten feet tall, tail wagging, talons clacking. It spoke in broken, scarping noises, irritating noises. A flash of anger jolted Edwin, they were making a deal, Ci'del was trying to change the original deal and two could play that game. Edwin fixed upon their location, snapped his fingers and disappeared.

Ann and Scott exchanged glances.

"Your Uncle sure has a funny way of coming and going, doesn't he?"

Scott nodded.

"Has he always done that?"

"It's the first I've known of it."

"Really?"

"Yeah, I thought I knew a lot about him because of our ability to communicate through telepathy. Guess I don't know so much." *In fact*, he thought, *I don't understand any of this.*

· ·5· ·

Scott leaned his head on Ann's shoulder as they sat, hand in hand, on the bench surrounding the clear, gurgling water. The place seemed deserted, but not abandoned. The air was fresh and cool compared to the outside, if you could call it outside. *After all*, Ann mused, *we're inside a mirror.*

Hide, the familiar voice spoke. *They are coming.*

Who?

The dead.

Ann didn't like the sound of that, in fact, she didn't like it one little bit. "Scott," she said. "Someone's coming. We must leave." She slid her slender arm around his waist and helped him to stand. She scanned the area wondering which way to go when the rose spoke again, *further into the maze.*

Ann quickly dragged Scott's weightless body that way. He wasn't much help as he'd lost the use of his legs for good, it seemed. A few feet inside the lightly lit corridor, which was really just an extension of the cave, she found a little out of the way cove where she gently let Scott to the floor. "I'll be right back," she whispered.

Creeping back to the entrance, Ann peered out around the wall into the large cavern. She watched as several people entered *Paraiso*.

The dead, she thought with a shiver.

She watched as they all gathered at the far side of the pond, each one standing with a tin cup in their hand; waiting beside the pool.

Waiting for what? she wondered.

Martin.

Scott's grandfather?
Yes.
Why?
The healing water.
What does it do?
It keeps the dead alive.
Ann shuddered. *Are they dangerous?*
Perhaps.

Ann started to turn away when the rose spoke again, *Wait, the water can help Scott, at least for a while.*

Ann stopped. *What do you mean?*
The power to heal.
His legs?
Yes.
For how long?
Until the magic is gone.

Ann looked back at the pond and the gathering of the dead, could see the orphaned turtle on the bench where she'd accidentally left it. Could she get there without being seen? What about a cup or something to carry the water in? She slapped the palm of her hand to her forehead, she was still carrying two nearly empty water bottles. Removing the pack from her back, she set it on the ground, opened it up and fished out one of the bottles, removing its screw on cap. The small group of people (*the dead*) stood motionless at the far side of the pond from her. There was no one else in sight. She snuck to the vacant side of the pool, knelt down using the bench for cover and plunged the bottle deep into the clean, clear water. She wouldn't be able to retrieve the turtle, not this time.

A shriek filled the air. Ann looked up from her task; the small crowd of people stood and stared, pointing in her direction. The vision of the Beatles album cover sprang to mind. Ann snatched the bottle from the pond and raced back to the corridor. She turned once; saw that the dead were not advancing on her, yet, nor had that awful noise stopped, and then turned and disappeared inside.

· ·6 · ·

Martin knew this place like the back of his hand, and he should, he created it long ago, but now, it seemed he was lost. No, he couldn't be lost, that was ridiculous, impossible, and highly unlikely. The portal to Ci'del's lair, the one that had been right here all these long, hellish years, was simply gone, moved to some other wide spot along the way. *But where?*

He looked around again and was sure this was the place, should be the place, had to be the place. Then a thought occurred to Martin. A wonderful, delightful thought, *Ci'del is dead!*

A thunderous laugh filled his ears, his brain, and Martin knew he was wrong.

A thin line appeared to Martin's left, a doorway opened. Ci'del stepped out looking a little ill, Martin thought, even for an alien.

"What happened?" Martin asked.

The child was tainted.

"The child wasn't part of the deal." Martin replied. "Did you get it?"

NO! I have changed my mind. I want the older female and the jailer; then you will get the key.

"No, the woman was not part of the deal either, just the jailer." Martin didn't like where this was going. "What about the other boy?"

Useless!

"What do you mean?" Martin asked.

Ran away.

Martin burst into laughter, couldn't help it. The boy had gotten away from the big bad monster, what a hoot. It didn't help the current situation though. "I can get then all back for you," he said. "The jailer, his heir and the other two. Then you will give me the key and let my daughter go."

Ci'del seemed to ponder the proposition, and then nodded its big, ugly head. *Yes.*

"Good. Now might I suggest that you, my friend, get a little rest and recuperation before the big trade?"

Ci'del turned and disappeared through the doorway.

· ·7· ·

"Martin," Edwin said from behind, startling him.

Martin turned. "Edwin, long time no see."

Edwin was not impressed. "You've been making deals," he said with a scowl.

Martin nodded. "For good reason," he said.

"You can not change fate, Martin."

"I don't believe in fate."

"Explain to me how you got here then."

"Ci'del tricked me."

Edwin nodded and said, "Didn't I tell you that would happen?"

"Yes," Martin agreed. "But you also told me that you and Rose were fated to destroy Ci'del, yet that did not happen."

"Not yet," Edwin replied.

Martin raised his old eyebrows. "Where is she?

"Safely hidden," Ed said. "We must not speak of it here." He grabbed Martin by the wrist. "Viajamos," he said, and they disappeared.

· •8 · ·

"Did you see that?" Nora whispered to the boy standing at her side, behind the small outcropping of rocks. She was terribly afraid that she was starting to see things. First that hideous beast appearing and disappearing and then Edwin appearing and disappearing with Papa. And Papa had been communicating with it, had called it friend. Had offered to trade what he referred to as *the jailer, his heir and the other two* for the key and her safety. She didn't actually hear the other creature talk, but Papa had spoken to it and it seemed to understand.

Jonny nodded. He wasn't surprised. He knew there would be deals, there were always deals. "Come on," he said. "We gotta go."

Spot was already padding back the way they had come.

"No Spot," Jonny called. "This way."

Spot turned toward the boy and whimpered.

"It'll be alright this way, come."

C·H·A·P·T·E·R 17

QUICKSAND

· ·1· ·

The sand at the end of the gigantic crater was soft, dusty. William stepped out into it and turned his head, scanning the crater behind him. It seemed to stretch out for miles, the *devil* was nowhere in sight. He sighed and stuffed his sling shot into the back pocket of his jeans and the ammo into his shirt pocket.

Looking ahead he eyes followed the strange path out into the vast desert passed a stand of black, limbless trees and huge rock formations. A familiar ragged mountain range loomed in the distance. Red dust swirled passed his eyes. He wiped his brow then turned to look one last time toward where he'd just come from; still no sign of it. It was hurt though, maybe it was even dead. William really didn't believe that though. What he did believe was this; the devil was coming to gobble him up.

Then, as if the ground were reacting to his thoughts, he found himself up to his knees in the sand.

"Shit!" he yelled, struggling to lift a leg, any leg, from the sucking sand. It was no use, no use at all. Frantically looking from left to right and back again he saw there was nothing to grab onto, no tree branches, no big rocks, nothing. The sand was going to suck him in and fate (as Scott's Uncle Ed had claimed) would be the victor. He raised his hands above his head in hopes that maybe just maybe, he'd find something to grab onto before he completely disappeared.

William didn't know which was worse, being killed by that creature or drowning in sand. Either way, he'd be dead soon. *I shoulda nailed him in the jeep,* he thought. *When I had the chance then none of this would be happening.*

Not true, his inner voice spoke, remembering Uncle Ed's claims of fate, claims that they were all chosen by some higher power. Was it true? Was this all some twisted fate thing? Did he believe in fate? Did it really matter what he believed?

·•2•·

Before long William was up to his chest in the sucking sand. His arms were still raised above his head although he saw no rescue in sight. The swirling, red dust bit into his eyes. He blinked several times trying to clear them. The creature (the devil; Pa) had not yet come out of the long crater. Maybe it was dead after all. Not that it mattered much now. Nothing really mattered now. He was going to die right here in this make-believe world and he would never see Ann again. The only good thing about this whole thing was Ann.

William's heart suddenly thumped wildly in his sand covered chest at a noise from behind; a noise that could mean only one thing. Death had finally found him, and there was no escape. William closed his eyes, rested his weary arms on top of his head and waited, waited for the creature (and he was sure it would look just like his Pa) to end his short, meaningless life. He was glad actually, glad that it was finally at an end. He only wished he could see Ann one last time.

·•3•·

It was like the crunching of tires rolling over gravel that he heard, and it was slowly getting closer. Soon the nightmare would be over. But what the hell was taking so long? Seconds turned into minutes and he was still alive.

The noise stopped.

William could feel the creature close by, breathing down his neck, waiting. *For what?* He didn't want to open his eyes yet he was unable to keep them closed any longer.

His eyes widened. A brightly colored beetle the size of a dog was standing about four yards away. A big ball of stuff gathered from the desert floor lay in between its stout front legs. It seemed to be looking at him through multifaceted eyes.

"What'd ya want?" William croaked; his throat parched. He'd lost his pack somewhere along the way.

The beetle twitched its long antenna and started toward him, leaving its ball of stuff behind. William knew now that it was coming for him. This was just another disguise of Ci'del's, he was sure of it. He wondered if it would change into its real form before killing him, not that it mattered. He could see the beetle's maw, opening and closing, opening and closing. He was gonna close his eyes, call it good. But before he could, a huge green and blue snake head appeared, smashing the beetle with a loud crunch.

William's jaw dropped open. The snake bobbed its head up and down as its bright red forked tongue hung weirdly from its mouth. Black snake eyes that looked like buttons, studied William. Then the snake slithered forward and William knew this was the end.

· ·4· ·

The gigantic snake stopped just short of where William was buried almost up to his neck in the sand. It sat there, and sat there. To William it appeared to be thinking, maybe contemplating if he was worth eating.

Then it lowered its head and William saw a boy sitting on its back. Behind the boy was a woman with red hair. He shook his head, surely this couldn't be real. Looking a second time, William confirmed that his imagination was certainly playing some good tricks on him today, maybe he was already dead. He watched as the boy and woman, each dressed in something out of the old Tarzan movies, wearing coverings over their faces, slid from the snake's back.

They started toward him.

And that's when William saw the dog running up behind them.

C·H·A·P·T·E·R 18

SCOTT TAKES A WALK

· ·1· ·

Scott could no longer feel his legs, as if they no longer existed. He could no longer communicate telepathically with his Uncle, as if he also no longer existed. He needed sleep. He had never needed anything so badly; not even his need for Ann was as great. He was nearly asleep with his tired, aching head resting on her shoulder when she told him someone was coming and they had to leave the nice pond with its cascading water. He wanted to drink the water as soon as he saw its clear, clean body laying there in the rock pond, but Rachel had warned against it.

It will only make things worse in the end, she'd said. Scott didn't know what she meant by that and Uncle Ed had disappeared so fast he hadn't had the time to ask. Apparently he'd gone off to wherever Martin was. It was difficult to imagine that his grandfather had created this world inside what was nothing more than a magic spell itself. Created with magic, the whole damned place. He didn't want to think about it though. Thinking about it made his head hurt.

Scott leaned his throbbing head against the cool wall of the little alcove and closed his eyes. He was exhausted. In the recesses of his mind he could hear Rachel coaxing him to sleep.

· ·2· ·

In the depths of Scott's unconsciousness Rachel waited, as she had waited for years, for her chance to take over. She'd done it once before, long ago. He hadn't been asleep then, but this time was different. This time, his total suppression was a must, if things were to work out in *her* best interest. She had things to do and business to take care of, and she had waited a long time for pay back; a fucking long time.

She smiled as Scott finally slipped into the realm of sleep, a sleep bordering on the edge of a coma.

· ·3· ·

Ann grabbed her pack and hurried back to the spot where Scott was waiting for her, the spot where she'd left him, a feeling of urgency swelling with each step.

Something isn't right, that little voice whispered.

She stopped just short of the cove and slowly peered around the corner into it. Scott lay propped against the back of the alcove, his eyes closed. His head was rolled forward, his chin almost touching his chest. A tiny line of drool hung from his open lips. He was asleep. How could anything be wrong? The vision of the dead standing at the pool slammed into her head as the thought that Scott was dead seeped into her mind. "No," she whispered, dropping the pack and running to his side, the bottle of healing water tightly in her grip. *Please God,* she prayed, *please don't let him be dead.* She knelt down beside the boy and placed her palm against his warm, moving chest and sighed with relief. "Thank God," she said aloud.

Kismet, the rose spoke.

"I don't believe you."

It matters not.

Ann was getting tired of this place, tired of the whole damn thing. *What really happened to William? Where did Uncle Ed disappear to, and when are we getting the hell out of here?* All she really wanted was to go back to the way it was before they found the mirror, before Uncle Ed dragged them all in there.

Scott stirred and Ann sat down next to him, taking his hand into hers. His head came up and he opened his eyes. He looked toward her, with eyes the color of green, not blue; someone else's eyes. Ann pulled her hand away.

Scott opened his mouth and said, "Name's Rachel." It was Scott's voice and yet it was eerily different, harder.

"Where's Scott?" Ann asked.

"Safe."

Ann pondered the reply. Inside her head the rose was telling her to beware. *Is it really Scott's dead twin or is it some trick of Ci'del's?* Ann wondered then said, "I have water from the pond, have a drink." She held out the bottle.

Scott/Rachel grabbed the bottle from Ann's hand and drank thirstily from it, then wiped his mouth with the back of his hand. Rachel hadn't wanted Scott to drink of the water in *his* conscious state as that would benefit him and not her. This way she had *all* the benefits, and her pussy brother had none. It was better this way. She was on a mission of her own. She handed the half emptied bottle back to Ann.

"What do you mean by safe?" Ann asked.

"His consciousness needs rest. I'll take over as this occurs so that we can save mother. Then you can have him back. Help me up."

Ann raised a thin eyebrow, and then stood, extending her slender arm out toward the boy, who was now it seemed, a girl. He grabbed her hand with the same strength as always. There was a gleam in her green eyes, a gleam Ann hadn't seen before; an evil gleam. Rachel was up to no good, of that Ann was certain.

Rose agreed.

· ·4· ·

Rachel hated the girl. There was one simple reason why; Nora. The girl, Scott's 'love at first sight', had saved Nora, and for that reason, Rachel hated her, could have killed her. But Rachel would have hated the girl more if she had let that man, Joe, kill Nora. So, Rachel simply hated her. But, Rachel would be true to her word, when she was finished with Scott's body she would give it back. It wouldn't be much good for anything anyway, even if he did survive.

Rachel glared at the girl, Scott's new found love, it would be so easy to just reach out with his strong fist and smash her cute little face into it; so easy. But, Rachel needed to get her hands on the magic rose pendent first; it was the only way out of the mirror. She took hold of Ann's offered hand, and slowly stood on Scott's legs. But, could she make them walk yet? Cautiously she moved one foot forward then the other. She was still standing. She did it again. She clapped his hands twice, and smiled. Everything was working out. Somewhere down this corridor was their mother and Rachel was determined to find her and destroy her. A soul left floating without a body; it was more than their mother deserved.

· ·5· ·

Having discarded the leg braces and shoes Rachel moved swiftly through the corridor, leading the way with Scott's new, revitalized legs. Ann could hardly believe it, it was as if he'd never had any muscular disease. But she knew in the end (Rose had told her) that Scott's legs would be much worse after Rachel was done with them. The thought of it made her a little sad and a lot mad. Scott should be the one to reap the benefits of his new legs.

Just what is Rachel up to? she wondered.

Murder, Rose spoke in her head.

Ann didn't want to believe it, but so far the little voice inside her head, that unrelenting little voice, had been right more often than not. She let out a long sigh then thought; *will you be there to help me?*

Yes was the reply.

PLANS

· ·1· ·

A shriek filled the air as Edwin and Martin Anderson materialized inside Martin's vacant hut. Martin knew the sound was a warning that someone or something unknown was messing around with the healing water, and suddenly wondered where Nora and Spot had gone off too. He pulled away from Edwin's grip and hurried out the blanket covered doorway.

Edwin followed, seeing the group of people, about ten or so, standing near the pond, pointing in the direction of a tunnel leading further into the illusionary mountain. Scott and Ann were nowhere in sight. Edwin scooped up the rifle from beside the doorway and slung it over his shoulder while Martin approached the shrieking old man, silencing him. Edwin knew these people weren't alive. They were food for Ci'del, slaves. Controlled by magic. He looked down at the ball in his hand. Bright colors swirled crazily within it. Bringing it to his lips he whispered, "Where are Scott and Ann?"

The ball flashed bright purple, then red, orange, yellow, blue and finally green before their images came into focus. Scott was drinking from a water bottle. He lowered the bottle and wiped his mouth with the back of his hand and that's when Edwin saw the green eyes of Rachel. Rachel had taken over. Fate, it seemed, was right on track. Rachel had a vendetta to carry out, she thought of it often. Edwin wasn't going to stop her; it was part of his secret plan not to. He knew exactly where Rachel would end up. "Where is William?" he asked of the glass ball.

The scene within the ball faded to nothing. Moments later the swirling colors began to appear, changing to the rusty red of the outside world. In the midst of it he saw the boy's head and shoulders just poking out of the sand. Approaching the boy was a dung beetle, enlarged by the powers of magic. Something else was coming from the other direction; a giant snake carrying two riders. Next to the snake, running as if he were chasing after a rabbit, Edwin saw Rascal and considered the possibilities.

The snake made no sound as it approached at lightning speed. In one swift move it crushed the beetle, then it sat back eyeing the boy. Edwin knew right away the snake wasn't real, it was a magic creation. He wasn't surprised when two riders slid from the snake's back and approached William. He was certain that one of them was Nora. The other resembled a youngster he thought to be one of the missing Reed children. He didn't need to see anymore, they appeared to be in control of the situation.

· ·2· ·

Wrapping the lavender ball inside the tattered blanket, Edwin stowed it away under the palm tree where he'd found it and then made his way over to the pond, over to the stuffed turtle. "Well," he said, picking up the turtle, looking it over then setting it back down. "What was all the commotion about?"

"Seems someone, a girl, stole some of the healing water, and then disappeared that way," Martin replied, pointing. "I had to tell them she was a friend."

Edwin nodded then said, "We need to talk, alone."

"Back to the hut then," Martin replied, strutting passed Edwin and back toward his humble abode. He knew what this talk was all about; it didn't take a genius to figure it out. Edwin was finally here and everything that was wrong was about to be righted. It was as simple as that.

· ·3· ·

They stood face to face inside the hut, brother to brother. They hadn't seen each other in years, and in all that time nothing between them had changed. Edwin invoked the cloaking spell so that Ci'del could not hear. "Your magic is almost spent," he said.

Martin nodded.

"Then we must hurry."

"Where is Rose?" Martin asked.

"She'll be here."

"Then she's chosen the one?"

"Aye."

"The girl?"

"Perhaps. What deal have you made with Ci'del?" Edwin asked.

Martin hesitated then said, "You and the children, for the key, which Ci'del will get from you."

"You realize of course that Ci'del will never knowingly give up the key," Edwin said, clasping his slender fingers together in front of him.

"I suppose."

"Then I suppose YOU have a plan?"

"My only plan, brother dear, was to get you here," Martin replied.

"Good," Edwin said. "Do as I say and we'll all get out of here."

Martin eyed his brother with skepticism before nodding in agreement.

C·H·A·P·T·E·R 20

VENGEANCE

· · 1 · ·

R achel knew they were almost there. In her private thoughts with Ci'del and Edwin they had promised that her mother would be kept under wraps, on ice, contained, whatever, until such time that Rachel could take over Scott's body, and then she would get her revenge. It was hers and hers alone. She was entitled. It was her right. Had been her right for years now and finally she would have it, even if it was the last thing she ever did; and it probably would be, at least in this body.

They came to a three way split. Rachel veered to the left without a second thought. This was the way, she could feel it. They were very close now. She'd still have to dispose of the girl, after collecting the magic rosebud from her. She'd seen the girl toying with it a couple of times. Rachel knew something about the rose that no one else knew, not even Uncle Ed, and she wasn't about to tell anyone.

The tunnel ended. A rock wall stood in their pathway. Rachel reached out with Scott's muscular hand and felt the unreal, smooth rock. This was the place. "Yo abro," she said.

A crystal doorknob appeared there. Rachel turned the knob and a door opened into a room, gold light spilled from the doorway onto Ann's bewildered face. *What is this place?* she wondered.

The room of wishful thinking, Rose replied.

Ann shuddered.

Rachel entered the room. Rage swelled, and then bubbled over. Her mother was not here. Ci'del lied. They all lied. She turned toward the girl, Scott's face contorting, Scott's lips peeling back revealing shark-like teeth. "Give me that rose!" she bellowed.

Ann's delicate hand flew toward the pocket holding her treasure. "No!" she screamed. She would never let it go. Never. She turned to run but Rachel was quick, grabbing Ann by the straps of her pack. *Throw it aside,* the voice

inside her head urged. Ann quickly unbuttoned the pocket where the rose lay
stashed, reached in, latched onto it with two fingers and a thumb, and pulled
it out. It glowed in her hand.

Rachel spun Ann around with Scott's strong arms, saw the rose in the girl's
fingers and grabbed for it. Ann moved her hand just in time, throwing the rose
as far as she could into the golden light, hearing it hit on something with a clink
and a clatter. Bright colors swirled all around the room, washing the yellow with
reds and pinks. Then an unseen force slammed into Ann, filling her with hope
and peace, then reality. She had a job to do, and there wasn't much time.

· ·2· ·

Rachel let go of the girl, and turned in the direction of the clinking, clattering
sound of the magic rose tumbling in the litter of debris. No, it wasn't fair. How
would she ever find it in this mess? She knelt to the dirty floor on Scott's knees
and pawed through the pile of bones, throwing them helter-skelter about the
tiny room, no longer aware of anything other than finding the rose.

Ann, nodding her head in understanding, backed out of the yellow colored room, closing the door behind her. She stood there a moment longer as a
thought passed through her head. The words Rachel had spoken were familiar,
el espanol for 'I open'.

"Disappear," she said, being only mildly surprised when the doorknob did
just that.

· ·3· ·

Edwin arrived at the magic room, a creation of his own, shortly after Ann and
Rose fled as one. He knew Rachel was still searching for the magic vessel that
had housed Rose's soul for so long. Rachel didn't know its real purpose and
that's just the way Edwin planned it.

He waved his thin, weathered hand before the wall, turning it to one way
glass; he could see in, Rachel could not see out. He watched as the boy, who
was now completely possessed by his twin sister's soul, dug furiously through
the litter of discarded bones, searching.

Would she search so if she knew the outcome of finding it? Edwin doubted it. If Rachel knew what really awaited her, she would not be so eager to find it. In fact, she might be content to share Scott's body forever, if she knew. But, that was not a part of the plan or a part of fate. Rachel would cease to exist, at least as she knew existence.

· ·4· ·

"Where is it?" Rachel moaned with her brother's lips, her brother's voice, down on his hands and knees. How could it disappear without a trace? She had to find it. It was the only way out, and it had special powers, very special powers. Ed had tried to keep it from her, but she knew. Oh yes, she knew the rose pendant would get her a new body, a body of her very own. She'd seen it in Ed's thoughts, very clearly. She would get a new body, one that wasn't diseased and then she would find her mother, and this time she would finish her. *Mother doesn't deserve to live. No sir-ree. Not after wishing Rachel dead. Oh yes, she had wished to have only one child and that was a boy child, she didn't want any girl children, girl children were harder to care for, harder to raise. A boy could practically raise himself.*

These thoughts ran through Rachel's mind as she continued her frantic search through the bones, tossing them hither-thither, from one pile to another and back again. She didn't notice the puddle of slime until she put Scott's hand into it.

"Agggg," she grunted in disgust, wiping Scott's hand on the pants they were wearing. Her head, their head, was beginning to pound again from lack of water and the tension of not yet finding the rose. But she wouldn't give up, she would never give up. She couldn't give up. But what if she never found it? What if this was all a trick?

Then she saw it, plain as day; a sparkle there on the floor directly in front of Scott's face. She grabbed for it with Scott's large hand, wrapped the fingers tightly around it and brought it closer to his face where she could get a good, close look at it. It was beautiful.

She held it in the palm of Scott's large hand, the divine rosebud opening, letting all the glorious colors of the spectrum wash over her. She felt lifted to new heights she had never felt before. Excitement raced through her soul as it was whisked away on a delightful journey, a tranquil journey, a peaceful journey.

Wait, she thought. *Nooooo! I'm not ready to leave this body yet.*

But, it was too late. The rosebud closed its petals and Rachel's soul was captured within, just as Edwin knew it would be.

· ·5· ·

Edwin waited at the glass, watching. As soon as Scott's body slumped to the ground, the rose rolling from his hand to the dusty floor, he knew the task was complete. Rachel's tortured, twisted soul had left Scott's body and was now imprisoned in the rose pendant.

Edwin spoke the words to open the door, and stepped inside. He gathered the rose up and put it in his pocket, then scooped Scott into his arms. With a snap of his fingers, they disappeared into thin air.

· ·6· ·

They reappeared inside Martin's vacant hut. Edwin needed to get some of the healing water, just a simple magic solution, inside Scott's ailing body and quickly, before the magic vanished.

After laying the boy on the tattered rags that served as Martin's bed, he ventured out into the desolate camp and over to the pond. Looking up at the tall palms overhead he saw the diminishing magic, like missing pieces to a puzzle and knew it wouldn't be long now.

Feeling the approach of Ann and Rose, he wondered where Martin had taken off to. He could find out, but first things first, water for his young heir. Taking a cup from a hook on a line hanging between two of the trees, Edwin scooped some water from the pond and returned to the hut with it. Much to his surprise Scott was sitting up gazing deeply into the lavender ball nestled in his muscular hands. Where he'd gotten it, Edwin didn't know. Scott didn't look up; he only continued to gaze into the ball. A feeling swept over Edwin, something he'd not felt in a long time; fear. Suddenly it seemed as if everything might not turn out the way he planned. He hurried across the room. "Son," he said. "I have some water for you."

Scott tore his gaze from the ball and looked up at his uncle through non-comprehending eyes. "Why?" he pleaded.

Edwin snatched the ball from the boy's shaking hands, placed it under his arm inside his coat and then handed Scott the water filled cup. "Drink," he said. "Drink and forget."

Scott put the cup to his parched lips and sucked the water, every last drop, from it.

"How do you feel now?" Edwin asked, taking back the cup.

"Uncle Ed? What happened? Where's Ann?"

"Ann's fine, Son. How about you?"

Other than the fog surrounding his brain Scott felt fine. What had happened? The last thing he remembered was being so damn tired he couldn't keep his eyes open, and he had dreamed. He was pretty sure. In the dream he'd been walking, he walked with such exuberance he could hardly believe it. He and Ann had come to a small room, a room with a yellow tint that had reminded him of his mother, somehow. Then the dream disappeared and now he was here. Wherever here was. He looked around the small room with its grass walls and dirt floor. He was seated on a pile of cloth, different lengths and colors. Used clothing, torn and battered. He wondered where it came from.

"Son?" his Uncle asked.

"I feel fine," he replied, and it wasn't a lie. He felt as if he could just jump up and run. Could he? He looked at the empty cup in his hand. "Holy shit, what is this stuff?"

"Magic."

"Really?"

Uncle Ed nodded his balding head, but he had a look on his face that Scott didn't like much. It was a look that said exactly the same thing Rachel had told him; *it would make things worse in the end.*

Scott sighed and asked, "How long?"

"Hard to say. When we destroy the portal and this world, I imagine. You could get lucky." They both looked up as the cloth door swung inward and a shorter, grayer man stepped in.

· ·7· ·

He stopped abruptly upon seeing his brother and the tainted boy, his grandson. "Edwin," Martin said. "I didn't expect you back so soon."

"Where have you been?" Edwin asked.

"Looking for something," Martin replied.

Edwin narrowed his old blue eyes. "What?"

"Never mind. Who's this?"

"I'd like you to meet Scott," Edwin said. "Nora's son."

Martin nodded at Scott, but didn't approach. He couldn't get too close to the boy. Getting too close could be detrimental to the outcome of the deal, and Martin couldn't let anything screw that up. He'd been in this hell long enough.

A thought occurred to Scott, a terrible thought. This man, his mother's father, didn't give a shit about anybody else; he only cared about one thing, his own escape. Scott didn't like his grandfather, not one bit. Edwin didn't blame him.

A WAY OUT?

·· 1 ··

William blinked his sandblasted eyes several times as the kid, the dog, and the woman came toward him. He shook his head. He couldn't possibly be seeing what he thought he was seeing. "I know you guys ain't real," he croaked, as they stopped just beyond the quicksand. "So just leave me alone to die, will ya?"

Nora glanced at Jonny then back to William. "Of course we're real. Jonny says that's a way out, through the quicksand." She pointed a trembling finger toward William, quickly drawing it back to her chest, cupping her other hand around it as if that might help stop the trembles.

William shook his head again. "You're crazy," he croaked.

Nora contemplated the reply. "Perhaps," she said. "But I really need to find a way out of here. Can you understand that, William?"

William supposed he could, but that didn't change anything. It didn't change the fact that this was all just a figment of his imagination.

The blonde boy turned, placed two fingers between his lips and gave a shrill whistle.

The large green and blue snake slithered closer.

William was even more certain that this was all just his imagination when the snake wrapped its long tail around his upraised arms and pulled him from the sand, setting him on solid ground.

"Go," Jonny commanded.

The snake slithered off to a spot several yards away.

Nora stepped closer to the quicksand, wondering if it was indeed a way out. "Did you see Rascal, I mean Spot, come out of there?" she asked.

Jonny shook his head. "M told me," he said.

"Do you believe him?"

Jonny didn't answer. He *knew* they would never get out of this place alive, why were they even trying? He'd known it for a long time, perhaps always. It was one of the *first* things the monster had told him all those long years ago. And he believed it. The monster knew everything. After all, who was really the boss here? The monster, of course. M's power was pure fantasy, a fairy tale. It was almost funny in a crazy kind of way.

An image popped into Jonny's head, that of his mother dragging the mirror around the house, their nice big house on the cliff above the ocean, crazily muttering something about not looking into it. If only he hadn't looked into it, but he couldn't help it. M called it hip-something. M, who just happened to showed up one day in Ci'del's lair. Jonny was sitting on the dusty floor, playing with his one and only friend, Hon, when the hairy old man suddenly appeared. He was wearing a diaper, at least that's what it looked like to Jonny. At the man's side was a long-haired, black and white dog, its ears comically standing at attention. The dog barked once, looked up at the old man through a pair of mismatched eyes and then wagged its stubby tail. "Go Spot," the man said pointing toward Jonny. Spot padded over to Jonny, sniffing him. Jonny reached out and patted the dog's head. In that moment Jonny found the best friend he would ever have. Jonny couldn't remember what happened next, but somehow they'd gotten away.

"You don't, do you?" Nora asked.

Jonny shook his head.

A roar of wicked, alien laughter filled their ears. Looking toward that terrible sound they saw Ci'del rapidly approaching from the crater, tail wagging high above its head.

"C'mon," Jonny yelled, grabbing Nora's wrist, dragging her toward the giant snake.

Spot ran after them.

William jumped up and followed.

· ·2· ·

When they reached the snake, Nora twisted out of the boy's grip, determined to go back to the way out. "Let me go," she yelled.

The rusty red haze swirled around her as she sprinted over the dusty land, puffs of powdery red hung in the air behind each step. Nearing the soft sand she saw the beast just yards away and coming fast, almost running. Nora quickened her pace.

William's eyes grew to saucer size, as the boy mounted the snake, kicking it in the side like a horse. In a whirl of green and blue they sped off passed him toward the quicksand, toward Ms. Anderson, toward Ci'del.

Spot barked once then started after them.

The snake was amazingly fast, darting over the sand, scarcely touching it. Jonny crouched on top like a junior jockey. William began to run after them, grabbing his slingshot and ammo, loading a ball bearing into the pouch.

· ·3· ·

Nora reached the quicksand first, stopping just shy of the edge. On the other side Ci'del also stopped and was coldly glaring at her through yellow lizard eyes.

"I can get out this way, can't I." It wasn't a question.

Ci'del made no reply. It only stared at her, clacking its talons together.

Hon slithered to a stop, and Jonny slid from its back. "Ya don't wanna go in there," he said. "Not if ya wanna live." He was responsible for her safety, M said so.

The words were familiar to her, words of warning; words she didn't want to hear. Ignoring them Nora stepped closer. One more step and she'd be in, then there'd be no turning back. *Go ahead,* Joseph's voice said inside her head.

Spot and William ran up beside Jonny as that awful, terrible sound filled their ears a second time; alien laughter.

Spot barked.

Jonny and William put their hands to their ears trying to keep out that terrible noise.

Nora took another step forward, unaware.

Ci'del joined her there and together they disappeared into the quicksand, the noise disappearing with them.

Jonny glanced at William and saw in his eyes the terror they shared. Grabbing Hon by the scruff of the neck, he hoisted himself up then reached a hand to William. "C'mon," he nearly yelled.

William grabbed Jonny's hand and climbed aboard the giant snake behind him.

"Giddy-up," Jonny commanded.

The snake sped off back toward Ci'del's lair at an amazing speed, the dog running alongside as fast as his legs would go.

· ·4· ·

The soft, stuffed snake cruised across the desert floor with a swiftness William could hardly believe. *Hell, the whole damn thing's unbelievable.* All the same, the ride was rather enjoyable if it weren't for the fact that they were going back to the lair of the monster. When they finally entered the corridor which William had previously exited he said, "By the way, Jonny, thanks for saving my bacon back there. My name's William."

Jonny brought Hon to a stop and turned toward William. "You came in looking for her, didn't ya?"

William nodded.

"How come you weren't with the others?"

"Well, it's kinda embarrassing." William paused. "Ci'del tricked me."

"Yeah," Jonny replied. "That happens a lot around here."

"Yeah, I noticed."

· ·5· ·

Jonny glanced from side to side as Hon slowly slithered forward through the corridor; nothing was familiar, everything was familiar. It happened from time to time, much more lately, as the magic holding this place together was beginning to fade away. It wouldn't be long before all the magic was gone. Then what would be left?

Jonny shuddered as the question brought forth images of Ci'del sucking their bones; both those who were alive and those who weren't. He didn't really believe M's claim that they'd get out with a key, and he couldn't help but think of Lizzy; she'd been so brave, and stupid, to come in looking for him. The monster was right there, waiting for her. Jonny had seen it, as if he'd been there. But, he hadn't, not really. He'd seen it in a dream, a nightmare, a nightmare he had nearly every time he tried to sleep. He couldn't say every night, as there was no difference between day and night here; the days were days that ran together forever and ever. There was no setting sun or rising moon. There were no stars. There was no heaven. He remembered his mom telling him how all good little boys who said their prayers and minded their parents would go to heaven, but that was a lie. Jonny had prayed over and over and over, but all his prayers went unheard, unanswered. There was no god, no heaven, and no earth.

Spot barked once bringing Jonny out of his deep, dark thoughts. The corridor was changing. Right before his eyes several crossroads began to appear. Hon skidded to a halt, its head bobbing up and down. Spot barked a second time as a girl with super short hair ran out of one of the cross tunnels, almost plowing straight into the dog.

"Hey," Jonny called. "Up here."

"Ann," William croaked.

The girl looked up in surprise at the boys perched on the back of a giant green and blue snake. *Well*, she thought, *why not?* "William," she said. "Is that you?"

"Yep, it's me."

"What are you doing there?"

"It's a long story we ain't got time for. Climb up, we gotta save Ms. Anderson," he replied.

"You found her?"

"Nope, wasn't me. C'mon."

Ann grabbed hold of William's hand, swinging herself up onto the snake behind him.

"I'm Jonny," the other boy announced. "That's Spot, this is Hon."

"My name's Ann," she said, a smile crossing her thin lips.

The mark on her head reminded Jonny of his mother's rose garden. "Giddy-up," he said.

The snake lifted its head and took off.

Ann looked out passed the two boys and over the snake's head as they sped down the lighted corridor. It was nearly time for the gathering, the ending of all this. She looked toward the old dog running alongside them, panting all the way, and wondered how a dog would get into a mirror.

· ·6· ·

It was a comfortable ride upon the snake, and fast. Rose had little time to think about what was coming, their fate. Some of them would die, some would live. That was the way of it. She hoped the girl would survive. But Rose was not in control of this situation; there were higher powers at work here, much higher. It was no accident that caused Ann's memory loss. Destiny had created an opportunity, not an accident. Rose had needed a body; Ann was there for the choosing. A young, healthy teen who had just lost her parents and her memory; she was ready for emancipation. All she needed was a guide to lead her to the pendant, and the rest, as they say, is history.

Ann sighed.

"Whoa," Jonny commanded.

The snake slid to a stop.

"What is it?" Ann asked.

"The lair," Jonny whispered.

Ann shivered, a flood of memories washed over her, memories of bloodshed and death; memories belonging to Rose. "What're we doing here?" she whispered, feeling her heartbeat quicken as a heavy blanket of fear covered her.

"The red-haired woman," Jonny replied.

That was all the answer Ann needed.

· ·7· ·

Ann slid from the snake's back, William and Jonny followed. The entrance to the lair lay directly ahead. The smell of things long dead permeated the air surrounding them.

William stepped inside behind the others. His thoughts drifted back to his conversation with Ms. Anderson shortly after his Pa's timely death. She'd said he could stay with them, be a part of their family, hers and Scott's. It would've been great except for one thing. He was in love, as crazy as it sounded, with Ann. He loved her the minute he laid eyes on her angel face. It was that feeling deep in the pit of his stomach each and every time she looked at him with those big, brown, electrifying eyes. He was pretty sure he couldn't handle living in the same house, seeing her day and night in Scott's arms. *No, if we ever get outta here I'll just ride off into the sunset, never to be seen again. It'll be better that way; better for everybody.*

A hot breeze swept across William's grimy face. He could sure use some fresh air and water, lots of water. But that seemed ridiculous in this place. He hadn't seen any water since losing his backpack. *And just where was that?* He thought back to his last visit here, did he have it then? He couldn't remember, and he supposed it didn't matter. If they found Ms. Anderson alive, which was doubtful, he would probably die of thirst before they ever found the mirror.

And even if they did find it, could they get back to the real world? Scott's Uncle Ed claimed they'd need a key. William wondered just what kind of key he was talking about; surely not a real key. The answer was buried somewhere inside William's sub-conscious; all he had to do was remember. Only problem was, he couldn't. No mater how hard he tried to remember the meeting in the library, he couldn't. *Why?*

    Kismet, a voice whispered.

    William stopped. *Sure, that was it.*

· ·8· ·

Each breath brought a wave of nausea washing over her as the smell of death and decay filled her nose and the sight of it filled her eyes. Nora couldn't believe what she was seeing, didn't want to see what she was seeing. She closed her eyes. Now more than ever, she wanted a drink. Then a memory appeared in her brain; Rascal's nose poking out of Sucker Lake, and something else; the edge of the mirror. But how had it gotten there? When?

    Then it came to her. The Lane woman.

    Long before Joseph, Scott or Rascal, the woman and her husband had rented cabin number five. Cabin number five hadn't been rented in years, Nora couldn't remember why. The couple had begged and pleaded with her to open it and let them stay there, it was their honeymoon, they said. Later that evening Nora saw the Lane woman dragging the mirror from the cabin to the lake. Nora chalked it up to another bizarre dream, but the following morning, the Lanes were gone; and they hadn't taken their car.

    She opened her eyes. Scattered across the dimly lit lair were piles and piles of old dried bones. And then she saw them, William, Ann and Jonny, standing at the entrance; another hallucination. Beads of sweat peppered her brow, drenched her armpits. She felt it running in streams down her sides as she hung from her wrists on a wall next to . . .

    Nora quickly looked back toward the approaching hallucination of the children.

· ·9· ·

Ci'del was nowhere in sight, and that made William very nervous. Why would it steal Ms. Anderson and leave her there to be found? Was it that stupid? William knew better than that. It was waiting somewhere for them.

They started toward her.

DAY FIVE
THURSDAY

C·H·A·P·T·E·R 22

INVESTIGATIONS

··1··

Sheriff Mason Radcliff stood tall, six feet three inches to be exact, inside the open door of his pea green patrol car, his hat in one hand, radio mike in the other. The early morning haziness rolled across the only beach access to Seal Bay.

Sally Ferguson had discovered the body of a man, a big man, clothed only in a dirty tee-shirt, on the shore of their sleepy little town, during her morning run. An autopsy would reveal the actual cause of the man's death, but the Sheriff had his own conclusion, after seeing the man's battered face, the smashed bridge of his nose, and the marks on the sides of his big head, the bruises all over his body. In the Sheriff's opinion the man hadn't been in yesterday's turbulent sea for long. He didn't yet know the identity of the victim, but Sheriff Radcliff was pretty sure this man belonged to the abandoned Jeep he'd tagged out on 121 early yesterday morning. The Jeep was registered to a man by the name of William Joseph Wade with a rural address in Elk Valley, a little berg in northeast California along the Shahamas River. A *likely place for the man who washed up on my shore to hail from,* he thought sarcastically.

Gazing down the beach passed the dozing Sea Lions the Sheriff eyed the bluff with its jagged, steep cliffs of hard volcanic basalt. The towering Light Keeper's Inn and lighthouse stood tall on its ledge above the misty haze. He didn't know why, but he had a funny feeling there was something going on up there again, something deadly. The disappearance of the Reed family several years ago and now one of the town's caretakers, Sam Jacobs, who was also missing, just gnawed at him something fierce. There was something about that place, something eerie. Now there were new owners at the old Inn, and a dead man on his beach.

Mason looked back out to the ocean, calmed by the action of the waves washing in and out, the birds running along the surf, snatching live food from the water's edge. He'd come to Seal Bay just six years before. Tired of Portland, where crime ran rampant and the police there, in his opinion, were mostly crooks and murderers. There was no crime in this town, his town, and that's the way he liked it. With no crime it was unlikely he'd have to shoot somebody, either on purpose or by accident.

Hanging up the mike and placing the big green hat back on his graying head of hair, Sheriff Radcliff slid into his cruiser; he had an investigation to start.

· ·2· ·

The green cruiser pulled onto the cobblestone drive, under the stone arch entrance of the Light Keeper's Inn, for the second time that brisk Thursday morning. It was half-past-eight. It had taken about thirty minutes to obtain a search warrant from Judge Thompson; about three hours less time than it would have taken in Portland. Good old Portland, the city of roses, roses and crime, and police brutality. The number of police related killings of citizens had risen significantly since Mason's departure.

He stopped his car at the little turn-around and got out noticing the old pickup still parked there, thinking the owner's hadn't left by way of vehicle, at least not that vehicle. The Inn loomed over him; its twin towers piercing the blue sky overhead. He removed his hat, tossed it inside the cruiser's window, where it landed on the seat, smoothed back his thick, graying hair and proceeded toward the massive stone staircase leading to the Inn's entrance. Removing the search warrant from his shirt pocket, the Sheriff mounted the stairs and rang the bell. He hadn't gotten an answer on his first visit. He wasn't expecting anyone to answer this time; thus the need for a search warrant. But he rang the bell just the same, just a man doing his job. He waited a couple of minutes, then hollered, "Police, open up." He really hated the thought of having to break down the beautiful doors. Then another thought occurred to him.

During the investigation they had entered the Inn through an unlocked door around the south side. Sheriff Radcliff quickly dismounted the stairs and headed toward the south tower. He entered a breezeway that housed the spiral staircase. To his right a short corridor led to the door of the Inn's sitting room.

Peering through the glass door into the magnificent interior of the small Inn, he saw no one. He turned the crystal knob and the door silently swung open.

"Sheriff Radcliff, search warrant," he hollered. Emptiness washed over him; squeezing his heart. Something was wrong, deadly wrong. He hesitated briefly then entered. It looked very much the same as he remembered, with its crushed velvet furniture and tasseled lamp shades. He crossed the sitting room and entered the foyer. A large mirror hung on the wall opposite the grand, mahogany counter. It hadn't been there before, he was sure of that. *Probably brought by the new owners,* he thought. He stepped into the library, noticing the books above the huge rock fireplace, and proceeded toward them. It was a collection of science fiction and horror. Some of the titles he recognized. Many were red hardbacks.

Turning from the book collection toward the closed balcony doors he noticed one of the red books lying on a table next to a chair. Placing the search warrant on the table he picked up the book and opened it. On the inside cover he found a handwritten note.

Scott;
May you always enjoy great fiction,
have a wonderful life, and find true love.

Your teacher,
Miss Leeann

He stared at the words for a long time then closed the book, returning it to the table. Grabbing the search warrant, as he would need to produce it to anyone he might encounter inside the Inn, Sheriff Radcliff left the library and headed up the carpeted stairs to the penthouse.

· ·3· ·

The double doors stood wide open at the top of the stairs, there was no sound coming from up there. It was eerily similar to that day long ago when he'd been there investigating the disappearance of the Reed family, they'd not been found to this day. He'd met the family just once before they closed down to remodel. According to documents, the Reeds had just purchased the Inn shortly before that, shortly before the Sheriff started his new job as head honcho of the Seal Bay Sheriff's Department.

Sheriff Radcliff proceeded up the stairs, his hand on the butt of his revolver, just in case. He wouldn't draw yet, not until he was absolutely positive he needed to. He stepped into the large living room, noticing the just moved in look; piles of flattened boxes and wadded newspapers in the corner by the unlit fireplace. Framed photographs and mirrors; dozens of mirrors, another collection, hung on the wall to his right.

Crossing the room to the large window he looked out over the flowerless rose garden, the rose bushes being no more than thorny sticks this time of year. As he stood there gazing southeast his portable radio crackled to life.

"Sheriff, we've got an identity on the man and something else you'll be interested in. Copy?"

The Sheriff unclipped the radio from his belt and pressed the talk key. "Copy. What else? Over." He released the key on the outdated radio. They were a poor precinct, and made do with what they had.

"Abandoned motorcycle just south of the Inn in the bushes east of 121. Over."

"10-4, who's the stiff? Over,"

"William Joseph Wade. Over."

He nodded his head, he'd been right.

"And what about the motorcycle? Over."

"Running the plate right now. Over."

"10-4. Let me know as soon as it comes in. Over"

"10-4. Over."

An abandoned motorcycle in the bushes. He shook his head, things were getting weirder all the time. He clipped the radio back on his belt and left the living room to finish up with his search of the Inn so he could get back to the abandoned bike, wondering if the incidents were related.

• •4• •

He stood in the doorway of the master bedroom staring at the large rust colored stain on the beige carpet at the foot of the king size bed. Sheriff Radcliff was fairly certain the stain was not rust. Sheriff Radcliff was fairly certain in fact that the stain was blood, wiped up blood. When he had it analyzed he thought it likely to match the blood of the man that had washed ashore that morning. *But what happened here?* There was no sign of a disturbance. The place was immaculate. It didn't make any sense. *And where in hell is everybody?*

The Sheriff continued through the rest of the penthouse, the bathroom and the two other bedrooms. One of the bedrooms was vacant, the other was piled high with boxes, a weight bench, a pair of crutches beside the bed and a photograph on the nightstand. He picked up the framed photograph and looked closely at the family there. A young boy, about five years old with dark, curly hair and pale blue eyes smiled out of the picture along with a pretty redheaded woman, tiny lines feathering out from her green eyes, his mother most likely and an older couple, her parents, most likely. The Sheriff returned the photo to the nightstand.

His search of the Inn ended in the kitchen, finding no one and nothing indicating a problem other than that stain on the bedroom carpet. It reminded him of the investigation years ago. Both families disappearing without a trace, leaving all their belongings behind.

A banner on the kitchen wall caught his eye, a banner that had been there five years ago, it read;

The hurrier I go, the behinder I get

Like the written dedication in the book, the Sheriff stared at the words for a long time before turning and exiting.

Out in the driveway, next to his police cruiser was the old Dodge truck. Someone had spent a lot of time fixing it up. Wrapped around the steering column Sheriff Radcliff found the registration, still in the owner's old address. They'd been here a couple days and now they were gone. He looked back to the old Inn, wondering again what might have happened there. Suddenly feeling the need to go back in; perhaps he'd missed something.

Sheriff Radcliff crossed the cobblestone drive to the Inn's marble stairs, stood at the bottom for a couple of minutes contemplating if he really wanted to go back in there alone. Something deep inside was warning that it was not a good idea, that he should call Deputy Frank to assist. Deputy Frank worked the seven a.m. to three p.m. shift, then Deputy Richards came on from three p.m. to eleven p.m. Deputy Cane ended the night with the eleven p.m. to seven a.m. shift. The Sheriff got the twenty-four/seven shift, but he didn't mind. It just meant he might get a call in the middle of the night or very early in the morning, like this morning's call. No, he wouldn't call for assistance; that seemed absolutely absurd. He'd already been through the whole place once by himself, why would he need backup to return? There had been nothing there, nothing but that dried blood stain.

· ·5· ·

Dismissing his feelings of doubt, the Sheriff climbed the marble stairs to the front doors. He'd left them unlocked so that later the forensic team could get in without having to go around to the side entrance. He would radio in after one last look. He eyed the watch on his hairy wrist, noted the time then opened one side of the large entry doors and stepped in. The first thing he noticed was the heat. It seemed to be coming from the mirror in waves. It was a god damn big mirror. The rosebud frame was quite different from anything he'd ever seen before. He wondered if it was hand carved. Reaching out with one long finger he touched the closest rose. It was cool; cool and smooth, like satin. Each rosebud, he noticed upon closer examination, was different. Not only that, there seemed to be one missing, right at the very top. "Isn't that odd," he said aloud.

Suddenly the glass went black and an image appeared.

The Sheriff took a quick step back. The image in the mirror was that of the oldest Reed child, Elizabeth, he recognized from the photographs he'd seen during the investigation, and having met her once. Her image wavered. The long flowing hair surrounding her soft face was laced with red and blue ribbons. Her large eyes were the color of sapphires.

Sheriff Radcliff blinked, but the image remained. "What are you doing there?" he asked, feeling a little absurd at doing so. Did he really think she would answer? Did he really believe what he was seeing?

Then she spoke, *Beware the monster.*

The sound of her voice was sweet and innocent, that of a child, and yet somehow adult like. Her lips did not move. Had she really spoken or had he simply gone mad? Then a scene unfolded inside the mirror and he saw the swirling red sand of a desert. Running across the dusty valley was a gigantic black beast, a woman with red hair slung over its shoulder. Then the scene changed and he saw four people walking across the desert, an old man and three kids, teenagers. He continued to watch as the scene shifted again to a cave with glittering walls, a small pond surrounded by tall palm trees and grass huts. *Is any of this real?* he wondered. Then the girl reappeared, tears rolled down her translucent cheeks.

Please, she said. *You must save Jonny.*

Jonny, the Sheriff thought, *was the name of the youngest Reed child.* Then something so bizarre happened that Sheriff Radcliff almost turned and ran from the Inn, almost. But he didn't, he stood his ground there in front of the huge mirror, stood looking wide eyed at the ghostly hand coming through it.

Please, the tiny voice pleaded. *Please help.*

The Sheriff reached out, grabbed the girl's cold, immaterial hand, and stepped into the mirror.

RACE AGAINST TIME

·•1•·

T he black Bentley Continental GT crawled through the thick early morning fog as fast as the driver would dare, which wasn't nearly as fast as the car could go. Sarah Anderson hadn't much practice driving in quite some years; not since the accident.

The auto wasn't a loaner as Eddie had told Scott. Eddie had gone on a spending spree after selling their hotel in Hawaii. The car had cost him over a hundred and fifty thousand dollars. Sarah had been so furious at Eddie for buying a car that cost so much when they should be putting that money to good use by helping others that she had sulked in their room the entire day until Eddie promised her he would donate the car to a good cause, they didn't need such a fancy auto.

Sarah was grateful they still had the new car now however; the thought of driving the old car was frightening. Although she would have tried, and succeeded no matter what mode of transportation she used. The Bentley was fully equipped with power everything and there were two things the car did have that Sarah was extremely grateful for, one was the heated seats, the other the CD player. She selected her favorite Willie Nelson CD and plugged it in. Sarah loved Willie. She loved to sing along with him, even though Eddie said she couldn't carry a tune in a paper bag.

Fog shrouded exit signs came into view under the hazy lights. This was her exit. She veered the car toward it as a semi truck whipped passed her, the driver angrily blaring its horn. She didn't know what the problem was with drivers these days. She was going as fast as she could. She looked at the speedometer and saw the needle sitting at 40 mph. *Well,* she thought, *maybe that is a little slow, but I'm doing the best I can. Especially considering the fog is thicker than mushroom soup.*

Following the signs for Bristol Bay, Sarah merged the Bentley onto the highway and then into the nearest service station where she pulled up to the pump and got out. A young man in a blue work shirt rushed from a tiny island office out to where she stood. "Help ya?"

"Could you fill it with premium please?"

"Sure." He grabbed the hose from the pump.

"Is there a public restroom?"

"Over beside the bay," he said, pointing the nozzle in the direction of another building where a car was up on a rack.

"Thanks," she said, hurrying away.

Inside the dingy bathroom, Sarah splashed cold water on her face in an effort to wake up. She had nearly fallen asleep a couple of times on that last straight stretch from Howard Pass. They say that most accidents occur only a few miles from the intended destination. She didn't want to be having any accidents. She needed to get there in one piece; it was a matter of life and death. Life and death, how she hated that terminology.

Finishing up Sarah went back to the car. The man was just replacing the nozzle into the pump. "That'll be thirty nine sixty," he said.

Sarah handed him her credit card and got back into the car as he rushed off to the little office to collect the payment. He returned a couple minutes later with the credit card receipt for her signature.

"Do you know how far it is to Seal Cape?" Sarah asked, handing him back his copy of the credit card receipt, the little signing pad and his pen.

"'Bout a hundred miles, I guess."

"Thanks," Sarah replied.

"You're welcome," he said with a nod.

Sarah started the car and slowly drove out of the station's lot headed west down Highway 492 toward where there was certain trouble waiting. She was sure of it. She selected another CD from the stack. Hopefully the music would help keep her awake. She couldn't believe it was already morning. Time, it seemed, was racing away, faster and faster with each mile she drove.

· ·2· ·

Highway 492 was a nice little two-lane blacktop winding through the coastal range. The fog was beginning to thicken again, as the car crawled up the winding road higher into the mountains. The miles clicked passed as the hands on the clock moved forward at an alarming rate. The winding road lay ahead of her, its lines nearly non-existent. She swept through several small towns, their businesses and homes just starting to come to life in the fog. The last town had been quite good sized, and quite a long time ago, it seemed. Sarah felt she was making better time on this stretch of the drive, but she could feel the lack of sleep catching up with her. Perhaps she would stop for a cup of tea.

Sure, Eddie agreed, appearing in the seat next to her. *Stop and have tea.* Startled by his sudden appearance, Sarah nearly lost control, jerking the steering wheel, crossing the center lane as a telephone pole loomed directly ahead. She jerked the wheel the other way, sending her back into her own lane and close to the edge. Her heart galloping.

"Eddie, you startled me," she scolded, regaining control and looking his way, realizing then that it wasn't him, not really. It was just her imagination. The vision was nearly transparent, ghost-like, and Sarah felt heart squeezing fear that things were much worse than she wanted to imagine.

He was looking straight ahead through eyes that didn't really see, couldn't really see. Then the image changed and her grown daughter was sitting there, but not really. Again it could only be her imagination. She blinked away the tears. "Get hold there, girl," she said aloud, looking back toward the road.

Yes, an unfamiliar, yet familiar voice said. And in the seat where Eddie and her daughter had been the black monster appeared. It smiled a deadly, carving knife smile. Then reached out with a sharp, black talon and caressed her chin. The pain from it was nearly unbearable. In a voice that sounded much like her Eddie, it said; *Too late, my love . . .*

Sarah screamed as the Bentley slid out of control around a hair-pin corner, shot straight between two trees and plunged down a hillside. The air bag exploded from the steering wheel as the car crashed through a ton of brush and into a large tree. Steam rolled out from under the crumpled hood.

Sarah's passenger was gone, the air bag in her face. She didn't need a mechanic to tell her the car was totaled. She sat for a few moments wondering what she would do next.

No, she thought, *you don't have time for tea, and you don't have time for this. You've got to get there as soon as possible to do whatever it is you've got to do.* Sarah didn't know what that something was but whatever it was seemed more important than anything else. In fact it seemed that right now, it was the most important thing in the world, and had plenty to do with Eddie and that damned mirror. How she hated having it in their possession, a constant reminder of the loss of their only child. Even now, after all the years that had gone by since then, the thought brought tears to her gray eyes, a hitch in her breath, and a pain in her heart that would never go away. She would give anything to have Rose back.

· ·3 · ·

Sarah forced the door open with her shoulder and crawled out of the wrecked Bentley. *Not much of a donation now*, she thought. She stood on wobbly legs looking up the dark hillside toward where the fog covered roadway should be. She reached out for the nearest bush, grabbed hold of its wet, slimy branches and began to pull herself up the hill, one bush at a time.

She shivered as the damp, cold fog penetrated her clothing, chilling her to the bone. Why hadn't she grabbed her winter coat or her gloves instead of this light-weight jacket? Did she think it was summer time? No, she'd grabbed the nearest thing and had run out the door without even thinking. She looked up the hill, still unable to see the roadway through the dense fog.

All around her the smaller trees that she'd missed with the car while plunging down the hillside stood like statues in the still calmness. She could hear the rapid water of a nearby river below. She reached for the next slimy branch, wrapping her numb fingers around it. She pulled herself up another step and reached for the next branch. All the while she could hear Eddie's (not) voice telling her she was too late, she need not bother coming.

"Shut up," she said under her breath, knowing it wasn't really Eddie, knowing that creature was trying to stop her. She reached out for another branch, positioned her foot for the next shove when suddenly the foot slid out from under her and she went down on one knee in the muck. The cold spread from her knee all the way up her thigh as ground moisture soaked through her favorite pants. She looked down and saw the skid mark in the mud, raised her foot a second time, placed it beside the mark and pushed with her foot there as she clung to the next branch. She felt the bush give slightly and had visions of sliding all the way down the hillside back to the disabled Bentley. *At least it's warm inside the car*, she thought.

Yes, the voice spoke inside her head. *Go back to the car. It's safer there.*

Ignoring that voice Sarah continued her climb to the top of the hillside, slipping here and there but never giving up. Finally she reached level ground, and pulled herself up onto the gravel at the side of the road. Fog hung in the lightened sky.

After a short rest, Sarah slowly got to her feet. Pain flared in the small of her back. It was going to be a long walk. She wasn't much for hitchhiking, but if someone were to offer her a ride she just might accept, this time.

· ·4 · ·

Sarah kept her eyes and her mind focused on the road ahead, marching to the beat of Willie Nelson singing one of her favorite tunes. She figured she was making pretty good time even though she had no idea what time it was. The weather had not changed, and the fog was just as thick as it had been, if not thicker. She kept a steady pace going to get her old blood circulating. She hadn't walked like this in a long time and her feet and legs were letting her know about it. Not a single car had gone by. She was thinking that she might have to walk the entire way when she heard the beeping behind her.

Sarah turned to see a beat up, yellow Volkswagen beetle pulling up beside her. Inside was a young woman with long, straight hair, some of it purple, some green, some red. She had a nose ring attached to a chain which was attached to her right ear.

"Hey," she said. "Ya like, wanna ride?"

Sarah nodded her head. The woman with the multi-colored hair swung the passenger door open for her and said, "Hop in."

Sarah slid into the little car, noticing right away the distinct smell of pot. It didn't bother her any, she didn't understand the problem of legalization.

"Where ya headed?" the young woman asked.

"Seal Cape," Sarah replied.

"Awesome, I'm goin right passed there."

"That's wonderful, thank you."

"No problem. Hey what're ya doin way out here walkin? Looks like ya fell down or somethin, ya got blood or somethin on yer chin."

Sarah nodded and said, "Saw a ghost in my car right before I drove it off the road."

"No kidding?"

"No kidding. Had to climb out of a rather large, muddy ditch."

"Whose ghost?" the girl asked with wide eyes.

"A monster," Sarah replied.

The young woman with the brown eyes didn't quite know what to think about the old, old woman in the mud caked clothing talking about ghosts and monsters. Perhaps she was crazy. Mary suddenly felt a little uneasy about picking the old woman up; it was something she *never* did. But the minute she'd seen her bent over and walking hell bent for leather it just seemed the right thing to do. Now Mary wasn't so sure. Visions of the woman truck driver in an old Pee Wee Herman movie, with her bulging eyeballs, sprang to mind.

· ·5· ·

Sarah got out of the car feeling the pull of the mirror tugging at her, guiding her to some end. A gust of wind flew passed, catching her long silvery hair and lifting it from her aged face. She looked toward the ocean passed the green cop car and Nora's old black truck, could see the darker clouds hanging on the horizon. Somewhere along the way the fog had lifted. Slowly she turned and walked over the cobblestone toward the Inn, her muddied, soft soled tennis shoes made no sound. At the massive door she hesitated. *This is it*, she thought. Slowly she reached out and took hold of one crystal door knob. Pushing the door open she stepped inside, closing the door behind her.

The little yellow Volkswagen pulled out of the cobblestone driveway. Mary headed back to Highway 121 toward Bristol Bay, never to see the crazy old woman again.

JONNY DELIVERS

• •1• •

The place smelled of things long dead. Ann recognized the turtle lying at Ms. Anderson's feet right away. But how did it get there? The last time she'd seen it was at the pond. She snatched it up then looked back as the sound of something approaching touched her ears.

Nora and the others looked that way too.

Spot barked, once. His ears standing at attention, the stubby tail as still as a statue.

Ci'del entered the lair. Tall and black and bristly, it stood there glaring at them. It wanted them all, and eventually it would have them all, but right now Ci'del had agreed to let the youngest male go, along with the females.

Lumbering toward the older female, the tainted female, Ci'del pushed the others aside. Now was the time for magic. Reaching a long talon toward the woman, Ci'del stroked her chin, bringing the tainted blood to the surface. The woman screamed in agonizing pain. Ci'del smiled. The others looked on unable to move, as if a spell had been cast over them.

• •2• •

Then the spell was broken, and Nora fell from bondage, unconscious. Ann was still holding the turtle clutched to her chest, Jonny and Spot were standing beside her. But where was William? Where was Ci'del?

Ann hurried over to the fallen woman, cradling her head in her arms. She smelled bad, like death. A *death spell*, Ann thought. Then she had another thought.

"Jonny," she said. "We need to get her back to Paraiso, do you know the way?"

"I can find it," he replied.

"Can you make the turtle bigger, like the snake?"

"Sure," he said. "That's easy."

C·H·A·P·T·E·R 25

ELIZABETH'S GHOST

· · 1 · ·

I t was the pungent smell of decay. A stench he hadn't had the displeasure of smelling since his last investigation in Portland. *The straw that broke the proverbial camel's back,* he thought. *What in hell am I doing here?*

He no longer held the girl's hand, if he ever really had. She was hovering nearby pointing her phantom-like finger toward something behind him. Sheriff Radcliff didn't want to look, no he really didn't want to. But he had to, it was his job, and *if* he upchucked his breakfast, well then, so be it.

Slowly turning in the direction of the pointing phantom finger he saw with disgust, and an almost wrenching illness, the body of the missing caretaker, shriveled up and laying in a heap. He did indeed lose his breakfast.

After Mason regained his composure, he wiped his mouth with the back of his hand. Then he wiped the wetness from his eyes, still trying to understand what it was he was doing there. He could see early morning's bright light streaming passed the portal, hitting the foyer's pale purple tiles, just as if he were standing in a doorway, but when he tried to step back through, he couldn't. His booted foot felt the springy resistance of some unseen barrier. *What in hell?* Sheriff Radcliff stepped back from the mirror that wasn't really a mirror, drew his pistol and fired a shot at the glass that wasn't really glass. The bullet sunk into the spongy substance imprisoning him inside a mirror. *Like Alice,* he thought crazily.

Elizabeth's ghost hovered above another, smaller body dryer than last years jerky, a rifle lay beside it. Mason looked from the girl's ghostly, tormented face to the mummified carcass and suddenly understood. It was her body, her ravaged corpse in a pile next to a rifle. He snatched the rifle, looked into the chamber and saw one shell, ready to go, and so was he, he supposed.

"Lead the way," he said, hanging the rifle by its strap over his shoulder.

Elizabeth floated passed him, a bright light leading into the darkness. He only hoped there would be a bright spot at the end.

"Wake up Mason," he said to himself as he turned from the bodies. "You're fuckin nappin on the job!"

· ·2· ·

He stood just beyond the entrance to a world that couldn't possibly exist. A world connected to his own by a mirror that wasn't really a mirror. The ghost of a young girl missing for six, count 'em six long years, hovered by his side. She'd told him to stop there, or at least he *thought* she had told him. He never saw her lips moving. He smiled a little at the thought of it. Then he heard her again, in his mind, telling him to wait, telling him to remember the written words. But what did she mean and just what was he supposed to be waiting for?

Glancing again at the watch on his hairy wrist, he noted the time at quarter-to-ten. *Wait a minute,* he thought, *it can't still be quarter-to-ten!* He brought the watch up to his ear and heard nothing. He looked up, something strange was happening outside. The land was shrinking. The mountains were closer, then closer still, close enough that all he had to do was step from one entrance to the next.

Now, Elizabeth said. Together they stepped into the glittering mouth of another tunnel, or corridor or whatever, the Sheriff wasn't quite sure.

His thoughts traveled back to Portland as he followed Elizabeth's light down the long corridor. The call came in about midnight. The report of an odd smell coming from a single family dwelling located at 5010 Trenton Street, nobody seen in weeks coming from or going to the place. Four Officers, Portland's finest, were dispatched to investigate.

Officer Kelly knocks. "Police, open up!"

The door does not open.

Officer Kelly lifts his black polished boot from the ground and slams it into the door. The door splinters then flies off its hinges and lands on the dirty linoleum inside a filthy kitchen. A rat runs across the floor and disappears under the counter. A smell floats out, the officers exchange glances and wrinkle their noses. They draw their semi-automatic police issue 9mm pistols and enter the foul smelling home.

A young boy, demented to be sure, had somehow survived with his father's dead body, in a house filled with meth cooking chemicals. The boy charged at them, a needle that may have been filled with pure meth in his upraised hand. They shot him, each and every one of them, four officers plugging the crazy kid with the needle, sixty bullets lodged in or passing through the crazy kid's body. The thought of it was sickening. Sheriff Mason Radcliff no longer carried a police issue 9mm semi-automatic pistol, now he carried only his six shooter.

• •3• •

She led him down the dimly lit corridor, a fierce heat and the smell of dead things billowing around them. It was a reek the Sheriff would rather not smell, but he was on a rescue mission. He just hoped it wasn't all for nothing.

Sheriff Radcliff stopped when Elizabeth's ghost suddenly disappeared, leaving him standing in the shadowy darkness. A lump rose in his long neck. He thought about the flashlight he'd left in his cruiser, he could sure use it now. Then, as if she were still there he heard her say, *Beware the monster.*

• •4• •

In the backseat of the rusty old WILLYS William contemplates the sling shot inside his pack. All he has to do is load it up and shoot his Pa right in the back of his head. It should be easy. He reaches for the pack, retrieves the weapon and ammo (take two they're small), and then returns the pack to the floor. He watches closely as his disgusting, murderin Pa places a filthy hand on Ann's thigh. The fire of hate burns bright in William's brain.

In the rearview mirror William sees his own reflection, the older face of, *wait a minute; that's Scott's face in the mirror.* It doesn't matter. He looks away, loads the ball bearings into the sling shot's pouch and aims for the base of Pa's skull. He pulls the pouch back as far as he can and lets the shot fly, hearing the cartilage in Pa's neck snapping and popping as his head flops forward onto his chest. Green goo spurts from the gaping wound, and the jeeps veers off the road, down a steep embankment.

In an endless rolling motion, the jeep cascades down the hillside, plunging wheels down into the sparkling blue lake; a lake with waves. William rubs his eyes with his fists. Not a lake, he realizes; the ocean. The crashing waves roll in and out, in and out, over the vehicle.

William jumps from the WILLYS, swims frantically to the other side and with muscles he's never had, pulls the sleeping (unconscious) Ann from the vehicle. She's not bleeding, not hurt. William sighs with relief.

He carries her on wobbly legs toward the sandy beach, each step a chore of its own. He looks down and sees, with minor amusement, Scott's steel-reinforced leg braces and the huge shoes. He looks up toward the sandy beach, and then to the jagged cliffs supporting the old lighthouse and Inn. They were finally home.

· ·5· ·

There was a clicking sound. Then an opening appeared before him. Sheriff Radcliff slowly entered; an undeniable dead smell in the air. Across the semi-darkness he could see the backside of the beast he'd seen in the mirror image, hunched over something, someone. A quick glance around the dim, desiccated cave showed him other awful and disgusting things. Piles of bodies lay everywhere. Against one wall he saw a line of people, nearly naked, shriveled up and hanging by their arms, tiny puncture wounds below their navels. He tore his horrified gaze from them.

Raising the rifle toward the beast Mason pulled the trigger.

· ·6· ·

William slept, exhausted from the last couple of days, deep in the clutches of a dream where he's the hero, the savior; unaware of Ci'del's needle thin tail sucking the marrow from his bones.

Wake up. It was Ann's soft voice, but it was older, more mature.

William opened his eyes. Blurred vision gave way to the dimness surrounding him. He couldn't move, paralyzed. The smell of decay hung heavy in the air. His heart raced at the realization that he was still in the lair. He wanted to scream but couldn't. He was frozen in time and space.

Ci'del laughed through wicked teeth, the stinking breath wafting passed William's nose. He was done for, a goner for sure. Ci'del was sucking his life from him, it wouldn't be long now.

No, Ann's sweat voice spoke inside his melting brain. *You are not defeated, you must resist.*

Then another thought slammed into William's brain. He was not William, he was Scott and Scott had a disease, a terrible, rotten disease and now he was giving it to Ci'del, all of it, every single drop of the tainted marrow pulsating within his bones was being transferred to Ci'del. William smiled up at the creature towering over him. "You're dead," he said coldly.

Ci'del roared, quickly withdrawing the tail from the child's tainted marrow; tainted marrow that could kill Ci'del. Ci'del stumbled backwards, away from William, crashing to the floor.

A soft light appeared to William's right; a pulsating light in the darkness, a guiding light. William tried to stand on flimsy legs, legs that seemed uncooperative, legs that were not his own. He looked down at them, seeing the illusion of Scott's leg braces there. He looked up at the sound of her voice. *Hurry*, she said.

William looked down at his legs again, the braces were no longer there. The light moved away and William wanted to follow; he wanted to be as far away from Ci'del as possible; but he couldn't move.

· ·7· ·

The rifle's bullet ricocheted off the beast's black armor, striking the wall creating a small poof of dust. The beast then stumbled backward, falling to the ground. Mason dropped the empty rifle and raced over to the boy. "What's your name?" he asked grabbing him by the arm, hoisting him from the ground. The boy was as limp as a noodle, and not being very cooperative. *What had that beast been doing to him?*

"Follow that light," the boy croaked.

The Sheriff looked up to see the faint hovering light of Elizabeth's ghost, she'd come back. Hooking the boy under one arm Mason carried him down the corridor, looking back only once to see the beast still lying there, not moving.

The light led them down the dim corridor, side tunnels appearing every now and again, first to their left then their right, back and forth like the pendulum ticking away at time. Then the light stopped, throwing its glow across the entire width of the tunnel. The Sheriff stepped right into it, right into the spongy spring of magic.

Stop! A voice commanded.

The Sheriff took one step back, eyed the light curiously.

Patience.

The Sheriff thought he understood.

He set the boy down on his own two feet as something began to happen. The walls began to change, become transparent, thin; like the draperies at the Inn. Behind those thin draperies, colors swirled in a lavender mist. Then the light disappeared and the Sheriff and William were standing outside a little setting with grass huts, palm trees and a gurgling pond.

William hurried on wobbly legs over to the pond. All he needed was a great big drink of water, nice, cool water. He stopped abruptly at its edge, seeing the brown scum floating on the top of it, smelling the smell, the ungodly smell. He turned toward the sound of her voice.

"Will," she called.

Mason looked over to see a teenage girl with short, short hair, dressed in blue jeans and a plaid flannel shirt standing in the doorway of the largest hut, embracing a stuffed turtle in the crook of her left arm.

"Ann," the boy croaked, heading toward the hut.

Mason followed.

C·H·A·P·T·E·R 26

THE GATHERING

· · 1 · ·

A nn waited at the door for William and the cop, wondering just *when* the cop had entered the mirror. Was he one of the dead? She couldn't remember seeing him with the others at the pond, or in Ci'del's lair, but maybe that wasn't all there were. Who knew how many people, innocent people, had lost their lives, their souls, here? How many since Martin? Grabbing Will by the hand, Ann led him inside.

The cop followed.

The first thing William saw was Ms. Anderson lying on a pile of old clothes. A dark red line ran along the base of her chin. A familiar (although he couldn't remember from where) old man with long graying hair was bent over her doing some kind of weird voodoo thing.

"What happened to her?" William asked, unable to remember anything after they entered Ci'del's lair.

"It's no good," the old man said, sitting down hard on the floor beside Ms. Anderson, stroking her face.

Scott was seated at her feet, the dog lying beside him. The Sheriff stood beside Scott's uncle. Jonny stood next to them.

"We can't leave her here," Scott said.

William saw the tears glisten on Scott's stubble covered cheeks. "What happened?" he repeated.

"No," Uncle Ed agreed. "I'll carry her out." Scott's Uncle stepped toward Ms. Anderson just as the bearded man jumped up from his position on the floor. He stepped in front of Uncle Ed, his pale eyes glaring. "I don't think so," he snarled, "you've done quite enough already, don't you think brother dear?"

Edwin only looked calmly at his younger brother. It was a look Martin remembered from long ago, way before this business ever started. It was a look that said I forgive you for being such an idiot. But Martin wasn't looking for forgiveness this time, this time he was looking to make Edwin pay.

"I'll carry her," William offered.

All turned toward William, surprise in their eyes.

"She might be alive, if it weren't for me," he said.

"No," Ann said. "Not true, someone set you up." She looked hard at Martin, knowing what he'd done. Knowing she could strike him dead, if she chose to.

"Come," Edwin said. "It's time."

"Time for what?" the cop asked. "Just what is going on here?"

Edwin looked for the first time at the man in uniform, seeing the embroidered name on his shirt pocket. "Sheriff Radcliff," he said, extending his hand. "Name's Edwin Anderson."

The Sheriff gripped Edwin's hand.

"I'd like you to meet Martin, Ann, Scott, Jonny, William and Spot, or Rascal, he'll come to either."

The Sheriff let go Edwin's hand and did a little head nod at each introduction. What were they doing here? His eyes stopped momentarily at the small rose tattoo on the girl's forehead. He was strangely drawn to it, moved by it.

"What's going on here my friend," Martin stated coldly, looking not at the Sheriff but at the red-haired woman, "is madness. They think they can destroy Ci'del, and return safely to their home." He laughed, shaking his head. "They tried it before and failed, I wonder what makes them think today will be any different."

"Don't listen to him," Edwin said. "He doesn't know our plan."

"They have no plan," Martin spat back, this time looking directly into the eyes of his brother.

"We have a plan," Edwin replied calmly.

· ·2· ·

"How long have you been here, Sheriff?" Edwin asked, taking the equally tall man by the shoulder.

Sheriff Radcliff looked into the blue eyes of the man who had introduced himself as Edwin Anderson. "Not long. I was investigating the old Light Keeper's Inn when I was kind of coaxed in, by a," he paused. All eyes were on him. "A ghost." He finished.

"Ahhh," Edwin replied. "What I mean to say is, what day and time were you coaxed inside? Do you remember?"

"Absolutely, it was precisely quarter-to-ten a.m. on Thursday, October fourteenth. I know because my watch stopped." The Sheriff held out his watch-wearing arm for them to see.

"I think he saved my life," William said.

"It's very likely that he did William, very likely indeed," Uncle Ed replied. "But we don't have time for stories. That will come later, after we're finished here. We've got to get back to the portal. Straight away. We must be there to meet with Ci'del."

"Why?" the Sheriff asked.

"The exchange," Edwin replied. "We must hurry though." He sauntered toward the cloth doorway, holding it aside for the others and said, "Ci'del will be finished repairing the damages caused by sucking William's marrow soon."

Outside the grass hut, Edwin removed the small, lavender colored ball from the folds of his long, tan coat. Holding the ball closely to his old face, he whispered one word.

Mason thought the word was serpiente, and was thinking it odd until a giant green and blue snake appeared in the courtyard. He took a quick step back as the younger boy, Jonny, ran toward it, climbing aboard.

Jonny was in a hurry to get this over with. He'd seen the old man stash the magic ball under his coat. He had to get it somehow. Then he could end all this pretending. They didn't know what they were talking about, these older people. They had no idea.

The others joined Jonny on the long, long body behind the stuffed snake's head while William struggled to carry Ms. Anderson.

"Let me take her," Sheriff Radcliff offered.

William looked up at the tall man, the man who had saved his life without even knowing who he was or what he'd done. He felt ashamed. He would turn himself in to this man for his crimes, if they ever got out of here. He handed Ms. Anderson over to the Sheriff without argument. He was beat.

· •3• ·

Jonny sat directly behind the snake's head, followed by Ann, then Scott, then Edwin, then William, then Martin. Lastly was the Sheriff, holding the weightless woman in his arms, a woman who didn't appear to be alive. She didn't smell well, that was for sure. Mason held her head as if she were alive though, it seemed the proper thing to do. She was the woman he'd seen in the picture at the Inn, although the lines on her face were much more noticeable now. An angry, new scar ran along the line of her chin. He wondered what caused it.

"Giddy-up Hon," Jonny commanded.

The snake speedily slithered toward the exit leading back to the desert land of Ci'del's world. Spot tagged along beside.

Martin was seated backwards on the snake facing Nora and the Sheriff. He stroked her face with his withered hand. Such a lovely face it was, and now she was gone. They had just been reunited and now she was gone. He was going to get Edwin back for this, and he knew exactly how.

Sheriff Radcliff watched as the old man lovingly stroked the woman's hair and face. It occurred to him then that the man was probably her father, missing perhaps. It seemed a likely scenario. The other old guy was their uncle, they all called him that. The uncle knew some magic tricks, tricks Mason hadn't seen at any carnival he'd ever been to.

The Sheriff hadn't had much time to ask questions and get answers, but his job required good listening and observation. The beast was a marrow sucker; probably had sucked the marrow of those people hanging in the searing cave, its lair according to the others. It was sucking William's marrow when he'd come upon them. Now they were headed to meet with it, exchange something. It didn't make a lot of sense, but Mason knew doodley-squat about magic. He liked the crystal ball and the giant snake, though.

"Whoa," Jonny commanded.

The snake slithered to a halt at the entrance to the sand swirling desert. Its head bobbing up and down as usual. They all noticed right away that the swirling red dust was much worse than it had been; the effect of diminishing magic.

"Do you all have some sort of protective covering for your faces?" Edwin asked. "Can't go out there without protection."

They began to search their pockets for the swatches of cloth, when the Sheriff suddenly had an idea. "Wait," he said, remembering Elizabeth. "If we have patience," he quickly explained to the others, "the entrance to the other side will come to us, really." He saw the looks on their faces; wonder, doubt. The dog barked once.

The land outside shifted.

They waited.

The land shifted again.

Again they waited.

The Sheriff, along with the others, was beginning to wonder and doubt the veracity of his statement when the two entrances were suddenly within a step of each other.

"Giddy-up," Jonny commanded.

· ·4· ·

The snake slithered into the darkness of the other corridor, the corridor leading back to the mirror. The time was coming when they would meet face to face with Ci'del, as they had years before. There were differences this time. This time they were in a magic place, not Ci'del's real world. Here they had some advantages; some, not many.

Edwin felt the rose pendant inside his pocket; a gift for Ci'del. Their task would soon be finished. As soon as they reached the portal he would turn the pendant over to Ann. The experiment had worked; the one to test Ci'del's immunity to the disease. Edwin had considered the idea earlier, when Ci'del had posed as William and received a small taste of the real thing from Scott. A simple thought, later placed in William's mind had proven that Ci'del was vulnerable to it, even the thought. That was good news, good news indeed.

There was other good news, Martin. Martin was summoning Ci'del, informing Ci'del of the rose pendant, the key. Edwin relaxed, confident things were proceeding as planned.

· ·5· ·

The light from the portal came into view, growing brighter as the snake slithered closer. They stared at it with great expectations and wishes, before seeing the dried up bodies piled beside it. Reality was just beyond their reach.

One by one they slid from the snake's back. Edwin quickly, secretly removed the rose pendant from his pocket, handing it to Ann as he passed her making sure Martin was witness to the event. Then Edwin turned, whispering to the snake he extended his right hand, slowly bringing his thumb and index finger together. Before their very eyes it shrunk from a huge snake to a small stuffed animal. Jonny scooped the beloved snake into his arms; he'd given the turtle to the girl with the lightning eyes, after it had brought them back from Ci'del's lair with the woman.

Now all they had to do was wait for Ci'del, make the exchange and finish the job. But it wouldn't be that easy, it wouldn't be easy at all.

· ·6· ·

Sheriff Radcliff laid the woman named Nora down at the base of the portal. The others gathered in various places within the lighted area of the 'waiting room'. Soon Ci'del would arrive and the exchange would be made. At least that was the plan most of them knew, but there was another plan, a plan that no one knew, no one except Edwin and Rose. Once Ci'del had the key, then they could start with the real plan, the one that would actually destroy the creature of old; the last one of its kind.

Edwin glanced in the direction of Ann, the girl with the powers of Rose, the soul of Rose, the girl cradling the stuffed turtle in her delicate arms. How he and Sarah had cried over her demise. Only Edwin knew of her safety, he had not told Sarah. Sarah would never be able to stand the loss again, if it should happen that they didn't succeed this time. Fate had a funny way of prolonging its arrival sometimes, like their last encounter with Ci'del.

This time Edwin had told Sarah to sit tight, that all would be well and he would return as soon as possible, knowing she was destined to follow, knowing that in the end she was the key to their escape.

A shuffling noise from the darkness of the tunnel caused the entire group to look toward it in anticipation of the creature. They were not disappointed. It stood ten feet tall just inside the reach of the light, its sharp, black talons clacked together as its tail wagged high above the black, bulbous head. Carving knife teeth moved in and out with each labored breath. Green goo oozed from one eye. It looked at them through its other lizard eye, seeing them all. It did not know their names, nor did it care. It wanted the rose. It would destroy the jailer and his heir, and then worry about the others, the insignificant.

· ·7· ·

Jonny stood next to the old man everyone called Uncle Ed, waiting, waiting for his chance to get the ball. Then he would take care of everything. He glared at the monster, the killer of his family, his mom and dad, his sister. He glared at it, hated it. Wanted it dead more than anything else in the whole wide world.

It took a step toward them.

Jonny dropped his beloved stuffed snake and leapt for the old man, digging inside the folds of his long coat. Triumphantly he pulled the magic ball forward, holding it in his small hands. He gazed at its lavender color, raised it up in front of Ci'del. "Be gone," he said.

Ci'del eyed the boy then laughed, scraping alien laughter.

Jonny's eyes widened as the monster's tail shot out toward him. He jumped aside, the tail barely missing him. The deafening sound of Ci'del's roar blasted Johnny's ears. The tail shot out a second time as Johnny dodged and ducked away from it like a champion boxer. The triumphant smile on his young face fell as Ci'del's tail finally connected, knocking the boy to the ground, the ball rolling from his unconscious hands.

Spot barked and charged the beast, sharp teeth useless against the armored tail. Ci'del swatted the dog away, sending it crashing into a nearby wall.

Ann dropped the turtle and raced over to Jonny. Kneeling beside him she cradled the boy's bleeding head in her arms. "You bastard," she yelled up at Ci'del.

Alien laughter scraped through their minds again. Ci'del grabbed the girl around the waist with its hot, deadly talons. Jerking her away from the boy it flung her over its shoulder and ran from the lighted area into the dark corridor.

William and the Sheriff hurried through the darkness after them.

Sheriff Radcliff drew his revolver.

William drew his flashlight.

· ·8· ·

Scott, Edwin and Martin stood and stared out into the darkness. The magic ball came to a stop at Edwin's feet.

"What just happened?" Scott asked, not quite believing what he'd seen. Johnny's body lay on the cave floor where Ci'del had knocked him. Rascal lay in a heap close by, no longer breathing. It nearly made him sick, he quickly closed his eyes. Hot tears burned behind the closed lids, the feeling of illness growing, threatening to spew forth, had there been anything in his stomach to spew. His legs collapsed underneath him, he fell to the floor, wanting to die. He couldn't think straight. "Why?" he cried.

"Kismet," Edwin replied.

Scott opened his burning eyes, and glared at his Uncle. Ann had used that term. "What do you mean?" he spat.

Edwin retrieved the ball from the floor and stuffed it back into the folds of his coat. It was time for the truth.

Martin stood next to him with his arms crossed over his bare chest, a frown on his old face.

Edwin raised his hands over his head. Bringing them down he spoke the word invoking the magic cloak. "Ann holds the key," he said. "It's all in her hands now, hers, Rachel and Rose."

Scott didn't understand, couldn't understand. Rachel was gone, a prisoner in the rose pendant. "How?" he asked.

"The disease never belonged to you, Son, nor did the telepathy. Those curses belong to Rachel. Ci'del wants the key, the rose pendant. It was led to believe the pendant is the way out. It isn't. The pendant will be Ci'del's demise. Rachel's curse will be unleashed."

"So you lied?" Martin asked.

Edwin nodded.

"And Nora?"

"Safe. Remember I told you that destiny could not be changed. Nora's destiny is not to die in this place."

"And what about Jonny?" Scott asked. "Will he be alright?"

Edwin proceeded over to the fallen boy. Kneeling beside him Edwin lifted the youngster's hand feeling the steady pulse beat there in his small wrist. "Aye, he'll be fine."

C•H•A•P•T•E•R 27

KIDNAPPED

··1··

The thick jeans were a blessing in disguise, a shield against the hard, sharp bristles of Ci'del's outer amour and the heat generating from it. Ci'del gripped her legs tightly with the deadly, hot talons. She knew it was taking her back to the lair, a replay of their last encounter. Only this time she had the key, this time there was to be no interference from the others. Edwin would not send the turtle to save her, and Martin could no longer sacrifice Will.

Behind them she heard running footsteps, could see the tiny light shining out into the darkness. It was all she could see. The knowledge that someone was following brought the stinging tears, if only whoever it was would have stayed behind. There would be less bloodshed, less death if they all stayed behind.

Kismet, the familiar voice said.

God how she hated that word, and yet she knew it was true. She still had a job to do, no matter what the outcome. No matter who lived or died the job remained the same. She held the rose pendant tightly in her hand.

Ci'del ran out into the dusty, red desert.

Ann raised a hand to her eyes, blocking out the furious dust storm as Ci'del carried her passed the black limbless trees and up the hillside of the giant crater.

Lightning flashed across the red sky; no thunder followed.

Ci'del slid down the inside of the crater and disappeared into a large cavern at the bottom.

··2··

William and Mason raced along the dark tunnel, the flashlight barely any help at all.

"Do ya see 'em?" William was asking.

"No, can't see a damn, sorry, darn thing."

"No problem man."

They didn't really have the time or the breath for talking. Up ahead a lighter spot came into sight, and then was filled by the beast as it ran through the doorway and out into the swirling sandstorm. They ran toward it as William extinguished his flashlight, trading it for his sling shot.

Mason grabbed William's arm, stopping him from running out into certain, chocking death. "Wait," he said. He concentrated on the lair; it would most certainly be going to its lair. *Come on lair*, he thought, *show yourself. Come on, come on.* He was growing desperately impatient, knowing that the longer it took to find her the worse the situation would be. The vision of the mummified people hanging on the cave wall surfaced in his brain, he didn't want to find her that way.

William bucked and twisted against the tall man's grip, the cop's grip. "C'mon," he yelled. "They're gettin away!"

"Look," the cop remarked, pointing his gun in the direction of the tunnel's opening.

William stopped struggling as soon as he looked in the direction of the pointed gun, seeing the entrance to a cave and thousands, maybe even billions, of rocks of all sizes rolling toward them over the desolate, red land, like a run-a-way freight train. The doorways slammed together in a thunderous crash, the swirling dust falling to the floor. William instantly recognized the smell of decay.

They stepped into the entrance, the tunnel to the mirror vanished behind them. William saw his backpack lying on the floor next to a pile of bones. *Hey*, he thought, *I've still got two joints.* He grabbed the pack then noticed the people, who looked more like mummies than people, hanging on the wall. He turned from their ghastly faces, their hollow, vacant eyes. He would've lost his lunch, if he'd had any. "We gotta find a place to hide," he whispered.

Sheriff Radcliff nodded his agreement.

Dim light cast strange shadows inside the smelly and hot; stifling hot, lair. It sucked the moisture from their eyes. Grabbing his flashlight William shinned its beam into the shadows around the giant cave. There was no sign of Ci'del and Ann. "Where do ya think they are?" he whispered.

"We beat em, that's all."

William's light fell on two huge piles of mummified bodies and bones about ten feet away. "Come on," he said, heading for the pile on their left, shining his light on the pile to their right. "You go that way."

· ·3· ·

Ann removed her hands from her face as soon as they entered the tunnel leading to the bowels of the massive volcano, Ci'del's lair. In the dim light she saw the remains of many bodies scattered throughout as the beast ran by them. *How long?*

Since the dawn of man, Rose replied.

Ann shuddered. Then the lair's scathing heat sucked the moisture from her eyes and nose, like a raging inferno without the fire or perhaps a kiln like the one at school. A sudden memory entered her brain, that of an art class; and still the faces within the class were unrecognizable. *Why? Why can't I remember? Will I ever remember my past? Does it matter?* All these thoughts raced through her mind as Ci'del bound her to the wall beside the others with the invisible bonds of magic. Ann didn't want to see the others, knowing she'd seen them before standing at the pool of water, the healing water. Again she shuddered.

Ci'del stood before her, their faces within inches from one another. She crinkled her nose at its stinking breath.

"I have something you want," she said.

Ci'del took a step back nodding its head. *Yes,* the alien voice scraped inside her head. Yes, Ci'del wanted the rose; the memories, and the knowledge of a higher power. It was that power Ci'del lusted for; the power to conquer many, the power to control all.

Ann held the rose tightly in her closed fist.

Now, Rose whispered.

Ann opened her fist. "Here it is," she said.

· ·4· ·

William and Mason waited, watching from their separate hiding places. Each waiting for an opportunity to save the girl, although William knew Ann could most likely take care of her self. They watched as Ci'del entered the lair just moments after them, lifting Ann from its shoulder and placing her back against the wall facing them, attaching her there by some invisible means. She didn't struggle, didn't even put up a fight. In fact, she was smiling a bemused little smile with her dainty lips, the rose imprint on her forehead glowing in the dim light of Ci'del's lair.

Both William and Mason remained as still and quiet as possible, one false move, one tiny breath, could give them away.

Then Ann spoke, "I have something you want."

Ci'del stepped back, nodded its head.

"Here it is." Ann opened her hand and the small rose pendant slowly lifted from her palm and floated through the air.

C·H·A·P·T·E·R 28

KISMET

·· 1 ··

S cott glared at his Uncle then said in a near whisper, "How could you possibly know that; and what about Ann and William? Aren't we gonna go after them?"

Edwin did not answer the boy. Instead he handed the crystal ball to him. Scott looked up with questioning eyes.

"Ask it what you want to know," Edwin encouraged.

"But I don't know magic."

"You don't need to, Son."

Taking the lavender colored globe from his Uncle, Scott peered inside it, seeing the colors within the ball beginning to shift and swirl. Faint music flowed from it. Then the green goo splattered face of the monster appeared. Scott smelled its stinking breath. Then Ann's voice. "I have something you want."

Ci'del took a step back. In the background Scott saw a dimly lit cave littered with mummified bodies. Then there was another voice, as if inside his head, a female voice. It wasn't Ann or Rachel. No, it was another. *Now*, it whispered.

He heard Ann speak again, and watched through her eyes as her slender fingers opened and the rose pendant floated from her hand.

Suddenly the ball was snatched from his hands. He looked up to see his mother's father standing over him, a madman's grin on his face. Quickly Scott glanced around. His blue eyes widened as they fell upon the sight of the crumpled body of his Uncle lying nearby on the dusty floor. Tears sprang to his eyes. "You killed Uncle Ed!" he screamed.

"My brother knows nothing of destiny," Martin spat. "Ci'del is about to become ruler of all. And you, my boy, you and your friends, the ones that are left, will become his loyal subjects; whether you like it or not." Martin grabbed the boy by his arm, and jerked him from the ground. "La guardia," he said.

Blackness engulfed Scott as the burning fingers squeezed his arm, taking his breath away. The needle like stabbing pain was back in his legs. The feeling that all was lost washed over him, that same feeling he'd had in their new living room at the Inn, a feeling of impending doom, inevitable, unavoidable.

I've been waiting for you, the burning voice whispered in his ear.

··2··

The magic rose floated like a feather through the air. The opening petals sent a swirl of bright pink and red colors splashing against the walls and over the many piles of bones and bodies.

Sheriff Radcliff thought it beautiful, until the colors began to change from the bright pinks and reds to darker colors, sinister colors, deep purples and blacks. He heard a voice, unrecognizable. What was it saying? He couldn't quite catch the garbled words floating through his brain, words that seemed familiar. He listened closer, turning an ear toward the sound. It seemed to be coming from the pile of dried, mummified bodies, a million voices of a million beings screaming out in pain, agony.

You killed my grandson, a voice clearly whispered. The voice of the boy's grandfather came back to the Sheriff as it had been that gray day on the steps of the court house. *Murderer,* it accused.

Get out of my head! The Sheriff thought back, and was amazed and relieved when he could no longer hear them. The voices simply vanished. He glanced toward the boy, William, and saw that he was preparing to use his sling shot. The Sheriff aimed his pistol at the beast.

William had heard the voice of his dead, murdering Pa, a voice telling him that their time was up, they were about to lose. But William didn't believe it, he'd heard that voice before and he knew this time that it was a lie. He brought the loaded sling shot up, aimed it, and waited. This time, if he got the chance, he would shoot out its other eye, the first one shot out as the other's made their escape on the turtle earlier. He thought he recalled the incident now, although he couldn't be positive. And hadn't the old man been there as well?

Ci'del eyed the rose pendant as it floated from the girl's hand, perfectly aware of the others hiding behind the dried bodies, and smiled. They would soon be slaves, carbon copies, all of them. Now that the jailer was dead, their fate was sealed.

• •3• •

A thunderous boom filled the lair as a bright light split the hot air. The rose pendant quickly closed its petals, the dark colors disappearing into it. Ann knew right away something was amiss. Ci'del was supposed to be going for the pendant, sucking the innards from it, the glorious power of the rose (the diseased soul of Rachel).

A hand reached through the split, snatching the rose from the air seconds before the rest of the man, Scott's grandfather, materialized before her with Scott in tow. Scott's eyes were open yet unseeing, his body rigid.

"No!" Martin commanded.

Ci'del eyed the man (slave).

"A trick," Martin warned. Then he turned toward Ann and said, "What you want lies within the marrow of this young girl. She has the power of Rose. Edwin told me so, right before I killed him. That is the power you seek."

A small cry escaped Ann's lips. *My father is dead*, the tiny voice inside her head sobbed.

I'm sorry, Ann thought back.

Ci'del looked from the man to the girl and back again. The man was a liar. The man wanted out. The man would do anything to get out. *I grow tired of your constant babble*, Ci'del said, then slashing out with deadly sharp talons, sliced the man's useless head from his shoulders. The man's body stood for a second then collapsed to the floor.

Scott stood beside the collapsed corpse for a moment unaware. Then he regained his vision, the squeezing heat from the grip on his arm was gone. He looked around and saw Ann standing against the wall to his left, Ci'del to his right. On the floor at his feet was the headless body of his mother's father.

• •4• •

Ci'del approached the boy with the tainted, poisonous marrow. The boy was of no use to Ci'del, no use what-so-ever.

Scott backed away on legs that seemed to be working okay even though he wasn't wearing the legs braces and he didn't have his crutches. Suddenly an idea came into his head. Purposely collapsing his legs, he fell to the ground.

Ci'del stopped at the body of the headless man and sliced off the hand holding the rose. Stabbing the severed hand with the deadly talon, Ci'del brought the dead man's hand to its face, pried open the fist and snatched the magic rose from it. Ci'del held the rose in the tips of the black talons; again the rose began to open its petals. Again the bright pinks and reds shot out of the pendant washing the cave in its colors, then changed to the darker purples, the blacks. Ci'del's tail came up over its head, the needle tip plunging into the heart of the tiny rose.

William saw their chance and sprang from his hiding place, keeping the sling shot aimed at Ci'del as he sprinted toward Ann.

Sheriff Radcliff followed suit, toward Scott.

Ci'del was quite taken in the delightful absorption of the power of the rose, a dark, menacing power.

William reached Ann just about the same time the Sheriff reached down to help Scott. As before, William could see no bonds. But something (magic) was holding her to the wall. He didn't want to talk, didn't want to break the beast's concentration on the magic rose.

Sheriff Radcliff and Scott joined William at the wall.

"Martin's magic ball," Ann whispered in William's ear as he bent over her looking desperately for the release. He glanced toward the body of the dead man, the crystal ball within inches of his dead feet. Without saying a word William motioned for the cop to look in that direction.

Sheriff Radcliff understood. He said a quick prayer then snatched the ball from the floor and quickly returned to the others. The beast did not seem to notice.

Scott gently removed the globe from the Sheriff's hand. He held it in the palms of his own hands and whispered, "Release."

Ann's arms fell away from the wall, as did the others there, the ones that were more dead than alive.

Scott grabbed Ann's hand and placed it on the globe beside his, nodding his head once to indicate that the Sheriff and William should do so as well.

Quickly, they did.

"The portal," Scott whispered, and the four of them disappeared.

Ci'del smiled.

· ·5· ·

The old Inn's foyer was hot and stuffy. The ugly mirror hung on the wall just to Sarah's right. She leaned against the thick wood door; a twinge of fear squeezed her heart. Streamers of light flowed into the foyer through the door's stained glass inlays, casting colorful images on the tile floor. She jumped at the bonging of the old grandfather clock in the library. Then there was total silence and emptiness. The place was deserted. There was no one here, no one at all.

Sarah glanced around the entry, passed the mahogany counter, the arched doorway to the sitting room, the carpeted stairs, and the arched doorway to the library then back to the mirror. A bench seat sat in front of it. The last time she was here, the only other time she had ever stepped foot in this place, that mirror had not been there. The bench seat had been there, but the mirror had not. She didn't know much about the mirror, didn't want to know. But she knew enough. She knew it held a dangerous creature, the killer of her daughter, her Rose.

Cautiously Sarah approached the mirror. The glass sparkled with her reflection, the rose frame glistened. It was ugly with its hodge-podge of dead roses, the ugliest thing she'd ever seen, and it was scary. Scary like an atom bomb. She didn't like it, not at all.

Don't look at it, Eddie warned inside her head.

No, no she didn't want to look at it. Sarah hurried passed the ugly mirror and up the stairs to the penthouse. She had to find something. She wasn't quite sure what but she'd know it when she saw it, she hoped.

· ·6· ·

Scott, Ann, William and Sheriff Radcliff suddenly winked into existence at the portal, beside the caretaker's shriveled body, their four hands still firmly attached to the magic globe that had brought them there.

"How'd you do that?" William asked, as they removed their hands from the ball.

"Don't know," Scott replied.

Ann rushed over to and knelt beside the crumpled body of her (Rose's) father. The dead dog lay broken against the wall. Stinging tears filled her eyes. The sudden vision of Ci'del slicing off Martin's head slammed into her brain. Then another vision appeared there, Joe standing at Ms. Anderson's bedside, his dark eyes wide with surprise as the rifle butt swings toward him, the sickening sound of his cracking skull comes back to her in full force, followed by the vision of Jonny holding the magic ball out toward Ci'del as he said; Be gone. But where was Jonny? She looked around. He was gone and so was the snake. She'd call for him but doubted he would answer, and maybe he knew something they didn't.

Scott turned toward his mom, fear jumped up to meet him; fear that she was dead. Uncle Ed had said her destiny was not to die here. *How could he possibly know that? And if that's the case, how's she going to get out of here? Does it mean that Ann will survive? Will any of us?* He thought back to the library, Uncle Ed had told them something else, something important, but what was it?

"What do we do now?" William was asking.

"We use the ball to get out?" Sheriff Radcliff suggested.

The others all looked toward the Sheriff. Could it be that simple?

A stifling heat fell over them and a soft voice said, "Not likely."

· ·7· ·

Suddenly they were in a large room. The cave was gone, the desert was gone. Most everything was gone. All that remained were the piles upon piles of mummified bodies and bones, including those of the Caretaker, Spot, Martin and Edwin, and the smell, like an animal's cage at the zoo.

A stunning, red-haired woman, clothed in a long sleeved, black satin dress that hung to the floor, stood in the midst of it all. Behind her, eight smaller versions of Ci'del, bone eaters, stood at attention. Her brilliant green eyes glared at the foursome. Then her seductive lips curled into a smile and she said, "Name's Rachel." She started toward the little group of rookie warriors. They were no match for her army. It was the woman she was after; Mother.

Ann stood up from her position beside Uncle Ed's body, understanding right away that Ci'del had absorbed the essence of Rachel. She joined the others knowing that Rachel was still seeking her revenge. Taking Scott by the hand, the missing zap of electricity returning, they stepped in front of Ms. Anderson, who was still asleep at the portal, still under the influence of the death spell.

Rachel stopped, the smile fading from her lips as the other two, the man in the green uniform and the boy with the black hair joined her brother and Rose (oh, yes, she knew) in setting up a defense line around her intended target. But it didn't matter. She would kill them all if necessary. She had the key to escape. She had her army.

Again Rachel started forward, her little army of bone eaters fell in step behind her.

· ·8· ·

Behind the largest pile of bones, Jonny watched through teary eyes, Hon clutched to his bare chest. His head throbbed from colliding with the hard surface of the imaginary floor. The monster had killed his best friend. The monster had killed his family. He told himself he wouldn't cry, crying was for babies. He had to be brave. He had to save the red-haired woman, it was his job. M said so, right after killing the Uncle, right before disappearing with the crippled kid. But now M was dead and the magic land was gone. All that was left was the monster (who now looked like a woman), the newly dead bodies including Spot, and the piles of bones. He looked toward the body of the man he'd spent his last few years with, a man who had kept him safe from the monster, suddenly seeing the sheathed cattle prod still attached to his belt. A memory welled up in his mind. Jonny suddenly knew what to do.

· ·9· ·

The Sheriff drew his pistol from its holster and pointed it toward the woman, who was no older than Scott; he was pretty sure about that. Not only that but she resembled the boy, was almost identical. "Stop right there," he said.

"You wouldn't shoot an unarmed person, would you Sheriff?" Rachel asked, with a wicked smile.

The vision of the boy with the raised needle running toward him, the vision of the boy's bullet riddled body covered in blood, lying like so much hamburger on the filthy kitchen floor, slammed into his brain. The six-shooter melted in his hands, running through his fingers like water, he sat down hard on the ground. "Get out of my head!" he said through clenched teeth.

"No can do," she replied.

"Leave him alone!" Scott cried.

"Why should I listen to you?" she spat back.

"Because," Scott replied calmly. "I know something you don't."

Rachel glared at her twin brother. "Not possible. I know everything that's in your mind."

Scott stepped in front of Ann, closer to the image of his twin. "Do you? Do you know that you're not real? That you're just a figment of my imagination?"

Rachel laughed. "You wish," she said.

"I know. Uncle Ed told me."

Rachel stepped closer to the boy, wrapped her arms around his neck, standing nose to nose. Looking deeply into his blue eyes she said, "Uncle Ed lies."

· ·10· ·

Sarah stood in the doorway of the penthouse living room. The bright sunlight filtered in through the east window. She could hear the roll of the ocean waves from the open window in the hallway next to the elevator, could smell the ocean air. Whatever she was searching for was here, somewhere. *But where?* She glanced around the room passed the furniture, the flattened boxes, the massive fireplace, Nora's old hi-fi stereo, the pictures and mirrors hanging on the wall. *Was that it? Another mirror?* No, she shook her head.

You know, she heard Eddie say.

Sarah put her hands on her old hips and walked over to the window. Outside was the partially burned forest, the rose-less garden, the cobblestone drive, the old truck and the cop car, the rock archway. Then it hit her. She looked back to the rose-less garden. *Rose-less like me,* she thought.

· ·11· ·

Eleven year old Nora Anderson was finally asleep in her own cozy bed after spending most of the day in the closet with Papa's Precious Rum, a punishment that was more pleasure than punishment. She'd known better, but that hadn't stopped her from getting into the rum in the first place. It wasn't her fault. If those boys at school hadn't tried to hurt her, hadn't tried to put their filthy boy hands on her she might not have gotten into Papa's stash. It had helped to calm her nerves, helped to wipe away the filthy memories.

But even in her sleep she could hear people talking. Since she and Papa never had company other than string-bean Uncle Edwin and bird-brain Aunt Sarah, Nora figured it must be them. Couldn't they be a little quieter? Didn't they know she needed her beauty sleep?

Nora opened her eyes. Instant confusion filled her mind. She was lying on a dirt floor. Pairs of legs stood close by, and there was a foul smell in the air that made her nose crinkle. She looked up the legs to see backs. Where was she? She sat up, looking from side to side. What was she seeing? Piles of dried bodies?

Light laughter filled Nora's ears.

"You wish," a female voice said. There was something in the voice Nora didn't like, something evil, something familiar.

"I know." A familiar male voice spoke. "Uncle Ed told me."

Nora looked up, something was approaching. She watched as long black arms wrapped themselves around the boy's neck. She wanted to say something. What? What would she say?

"Uncle Ed lies," a grating voice said. "Doesn't he, Mother?"

Familiar green eyes inserted in the face of a creature that might have been her daughter, had she lived, peered around her son's shoulder at her. *Murderer*, that grating voice said inside her head.

"No," Nora said in a whisper. "You can't be real."

Rachel laughed again and shoved Scott aside, knocking him into Ann (Rose) and her into William. They fell to the ground like dominos. "Think again Mother dear," she said, stepping toward the woman on the floor.

Panic welled up inside Nora as the Rachel creature stepped closer. Nora tried to back up, but found herself already against a wall, a wall that wasn't going to move no matter how much she wanted it to.

Regaining a standing position William raised his loaded sling shot, aimed for what would have been the girl's ear, if she'd been a real girl, which she wasn't, and let the shot go. The Rachel thing reached out with her long fingers (talons) and batted it out of the air as if it were a pesky fly.

Rachel towered over Nora, a wicked grin on her unpleasant, alien face. "I've waited a long time for this moment," she said. "A fucking long time."

Nora cringed away from the foul words, like a slap in the face. This thing was not her daughter.

"Oh yes," Rachel said, reading Nora's mind. "I most certainly am what would have been your daughter had you not murdered me, murdered me in your womb."

"No," Nora said shaking her head, backing up the wall, coming in contact with the portal, the spongy magic barrier bouncing under her touch. She stepped to the left.

Rachel copied the move.

Nora took another step, Rachel followed.

Time stood still. Scott looked on as his imaginary sister played some kind of mind game with their mother, only that wasn't his sister and this was no game. There was no plan of action that Scott could recall. No actual plan to kill Ci'del, and there had been no mention of Rachel. Or had there? Why couldn't he remember?

Kismet, a voice said inside his head.

He looked toward Ann, her lightning eyes, the electric touch, and then it came to him.

· · 12 · ·

The heavy, accelerated beat of his heart thumped in his ears, his head, even his eyes. Jonny hugged the stuffed snake fiercely then set it down next to the pile of bones. He had to get the weapon then he could kill the monster, after all, it's what it deserved. It killed his family and now it was time for payback. His heart ached, knowing all that he ever cared about was gone, destroyed by the monster.

Jonny jumped from his hiding place, sprinted toward M, ripping the cattle prod from its sheath. M had shown him how to use it long ago, just in case. Jonny pushed the switch turning on the juice and ran toward the monster with it.

Rachel turned from Nora for a brief second, sensing the child.

"No, Jonny!" Ann yelled, seeing the boy running toward Ci'del, the cattle prod held up like a sword in the boy's hand. She tried to step forward and couldn't.

Jonny paid no attention. Instead he ran faster toward his target, passed the sitting Sheriff, and the others. When he reached Ci'del, the creature stood before him in the image of a woman. Jonny didn't care, he knew it wasn't real. Pointing the cattle prod at the beast he said, "You know I can kill you with this."

Ci'del smiled. *Go ahead, little man. Do your best.*

"Jonny," Ann coaxed. "Don't."

Nora and the others watched, unable to help.

Jonny reached out with the cattle prod, touching the beast with it. Surprise spread over his young face. The cattle prod was dead, not a single once of electricity was left in its old remains.

The woman (monster) reached out with long talon fingers, stroking the boy's lean chin. Jonny winced from the pain but didn't back away. He could feel the blood rising to the surface of his face, spilling out onto the woman creature's claw. He looked into her eyes and glimpsed his future, their future. He didn't like what he saw.

· · 13 · ·

Sarah hurried over to the large fireplace mantle. *Now which one is it?* She scanned the collection, a large yellow rose, a bouquet of purple violets, buttercups, a small red rose, a pink carnation, white daffodils. Her eyes went back to the small red rose with its petals closed up tightly. Three green leaves cupped its base. *That's it.*

She snatched the delicate water globe from the mantle, cradled it in her old arms and hurried out of the room and down the stairs.

· · 14 · ·

The Sheriff was sitting in the dirt looking into his hands, unable to comprehend what had happened to his pistol. Unaware of what was going on around him.

William, Ann and Scott stood staring at the dead body of the brave young Jonny. None of them had been able to move as the creature simply stopped the boy's heart. Nora couldn't believe what she was seeing, knew she was still dreaming, and wished with all her heart for a drink.

Rachel turned back toward Nora, releasing the others from her simple holding spell. Without thought or hesitation Scott reached into the pack on Ann's back. Pulling the plastic handled stun gun from inside he turned it over in his hand a couple of times. He had never used a stun gun before but Uncle Ed had said it would come in handy, and it seemed Jonny knew something. He looked toward Ann; saw the look of encouragement on her radiant face. She nodded. He took two large steps toward Rachel, grabbed her around the neck with one arm and reached out with the gun in his other hand, jamming it into her side, pulling the trigger as Ann and William snatched Nora from harm's way.

Scott held on as best he could, feeling the surging electricity while the Rachel creature thrashed and bucked and finally fell to the ground in a wave of frenzied, twitching convulsions. The illusion of Rachel vanished. Ci'del twitched under Scott.

Sheriff Radcliff looked up from his hands in a confused state of mind. "What in hell is going on?" he asked.

Scott released his neck hold on the black beast and said to the others, "I don't think its dead yet."

· ·15· ·

Sarah Anderson stood in front of the ancient mirror, the tiny water globe with its tiny, precious red rose safely in the palms of her old hands.

Break the globe, Eddie's voice coaxed.

Sarah slammed the globe onto the hard counter, shattering the glass ball into hundreds of pieces glittering in the light. The tiny red rosebud lay in a puddle of water. She picked it from the counter, held it in her fingertips. What was she to do with it now? She looked up at the mirror seeing her reflection there in the sparkling glass. She studied the rosebud frame, noticing for the first time a space at the top where a rosebud should be but wasn't. She glanced back to the rose in her fingertips. *Is this the one, Eddie?* She didn't really need to ask.

She approached the mirror and stepped up onto the bench. Not wanting to touch the glass, touching the glass could be unfavorable to her health; that much she knew. She also knew that as long as the glass was in its reflective state she would be okay, that is; the evil creature inside should not be able to get her as long as the mirror was a mirror, and not a portal. As long as the mirror reflected her image, as long as the mirror did not change to black, she'd be okay.

Quickly, Eddie's voice urged.

Standing on tip-toes, stretching her arms out as far as she could, Sarah could almost reach the spot in the frame where the missing rose would fit. But, she couldn't reach it. If she only had a couple more inches in the length of her arm. Try as she might Sarah was simply not tall enough, even standing on the bench, to reach the top of the mirror.

··16··

Sheriff Mason Radcliff got up off the dirt floor where he found himself sitting, his six-shooter in a melted puddle in front of him. Then it all came back to him. She had melted his gun. He looked toward the beast. The older boy, Scott, had pinned it on the ground. The other kids, Ann and William had gotten Nora off to the side of the portal, and were now helping Scott up. The young boy with the blonde braid lay on the ground, dead but not forgotten.

Near the center of the large room the eight little Ci'del look-alikes had come to a complete stop, as if they didn't know what to do. Perhaps they were no longer being controlled. About ten feet away lay the Uncle's body. Hanging on his shoulder was a rifle, the Sheriff wondered if it was loaded. There was only one way to find out. Quickly making his way over there and stripping the Uncle of it, he pointed it toward the little army and pulled the trigger. He wasn't waiting to find out if they were just playing opossum.

The sound was deafening, and the shot was true, hitting and shattering the skull of one of the little monsters. He fired seven more times, hitting and killing a creature with each shot.

As the creatures fell dead to the ground, their bodies began to revert back to the people they had once been, once upon a time. Mason felt bad for what they'd been through, but they were better off completely dead, he was positive of that. They were in God's hands now.

On the floor closer to the portal Ci'del, now in its real form, began to stir.

··17··

Sarah hopped down from the bench in front of the mirror and quickly made her way into the sitting room, grabbing one of the wicker chairs. She hurried back to the foyer, praying the glass in the mirror would still be glass. She knew time was running out, she was pretty sure that time, at least for Eddie, was gone. That thought brought a wrenching pain to her heart which she had to ignore, at least for now.

She set the wicker chair atop the bench in front of the still reflective mirror and climbed up onto it. She was plenty tall enough now, as long as the chair didn't fly out from under her. She reached out to the vacant place at the top of the frame, the chair wobbled. Sarah did a quick balancing act stretching her arms out to her sides as if she were a tight-rope walker. She was just getting ready to reach out again when a terrible vision swept into her mind. A blast from the past one could say.

She stood over the child, laying at the side of the road in the pouring rain, a child. She heard the wailing sirens. She felt the rising terror, the rising shame. She squeezed her eyes shut. Then she felt the grip of the father's hand around the back of her neck, the squeezing fingers forcing her to look at the dead boy. *You kilt my boy*, the father's voice burned in her ear.

Sarah's eyes rolled back as she and the chair tumbled to the hard, cold floor. The rosebud rolled from her hand, across the purple tiles.

· · 18 · ·

Nora Anderson looked at the thing lying in the dirt, the creature that had stolen her from her cozy, new home and taken her to a smelly desert place inside a mirror. She looked up at Scott, her son. He was still alive, as were Ann and William. A handsome man in a cop's uniform, a man she didn't know, stood nearby, the smoking rifle in his hands. The eight creatures, the ones that had been her Papa's friends lay dead, scattered across the room. Still she couldn't believe any of it was real, it had to be a dream. The boy, the dog, her father; all a dream and if she was lucky, she'd wake up soon.

Then the monster started to move, started to come to and Nora didn't like the idea one bit, not even if it was a dream. "It's moving," she said, trying to skitter away from the horrid thing, her eyes wide with fear.

The Sheriff raised the rifle toward Ci'del, knowing he already spent eight rounds out of a possible ten, wondering, hoping that the rifle was fully loaded when he picked it up; remembering the melted pistol. He wouldn't fire just yet, didn't want to waste the shot.

William raised his sling shot, this time he had loaded two of the ball bearings into the leather pouch.

Scott and Ann made their way back over to Nora, each grabbing an arm and helping her to stand. Then Scott yelled into the portal, "Aunt Sarah, are you there?"

The others looked at Scott as if he was crazy, all except Ann, and maybe he was, but for some reason he just knew that Aunt Sarah would or at least should be there.

Ci'del had now gained its full height, all ten feet of the black, bristle armored body stood before them. Its scratching laughter filled the room. It wasn't a cheerful sound, it was a deadly sound. Then it spoke; *Aunt Sarah is dead.*

"I don't believe you," Scott said.

Look. It pointing a long talon toward the portal.

They turned and saw the light shining into the foyer. Aunt Sarah lay on the sparkling floor.

"Aunt Sarah," Scott yelled. "Wake up."

Then the light faded, and with it darkness like dusk fell over them as the portal closed down, leaving a hole the size of a half dollar in the rock wall.

Ci'del advanced.

William let the two ball bearings fly.

Sheriff Radcliff fired the rifle.

Ci'del batted each thing away and continued to advance, continued to laugh, a sound that would surely drive any sane person crazy.

"I have a request," William said as Ci'del reached them.

Ci'del stopped, intrigued.

"A last request," William continued. "Everybody gets one before they die. It's the law."

Ci'del smiled wickedly with its carving knife teeth, clacked the black talons together. *Very well, what is your request, Billy?* This time it was not Pa's voice William heard. The voice he heard wasn't really a voice at all. It was almost unbearable, but William had an idea, an idea that just seemed to pop in and out of his brain in a single moment, like a whisper.

"A smoke," William replied. "I'd like a last smoke."

Ci'del contemplated the request, tried to read the boy's thoughts and found images of clear water and blue skies. *What is a smoke?*

William removed his backpack, pulled the small baggie from the side pocket and held it up for Ci'del to see. "Just a quick smoke," he said. "I only have two left."

Very well.

The others watched as William snagged one of the home rolled cigarettes from the baggie, pulled a lighter from his pocket, inserted one end of the cigarette in his mouth and lit it. The flame from the lighter brightened the dim room for a moment. He drew in the first hit not knowing if his idea would work, but there was only one way to find out. He offered the joint to the others who all declined to partake. They all knew it wasn't tobacco. It had a sweeter smell, a marijuana smell. Sheriff Radcliff knew right away, but he didn't care. It was William's last request, and he didn't think that was all it was.

"Ya wanna hit?" William asked Ci'del.

Ci'del looked at the boy through its one good lizard eye.

"I find it helps to calm my nerves," William confided, and took another toke, blowing the smoke in Ci'del's direction.

"Does it really work?" Scott asked, having an idea of his own, remembering something Miss Leeann had told him years ago; *There's no recorded case of death ever resulting from smoking marijuana.*

Ci'del heard the thought, confident that this was not a trick.

"Yeah," William said, taking another hit and blowing the smoke in Ci'del's direction.

"Let's see," Scott said, reaching out for the marijuana cigarette.

Nora, Ann and Mason looked on as William handed the joint to Scott. Scott had never smoked before, but that was not the issue here. He took a puff and without inhaling held it in his mouth for a couple seconds, and then blew the smoke toward Ci'del, handing the cigarette back to William. When it got short enough that they couldn't hold onto it any longer, William ate it then reached into the baggie fetching the last one. He rolled it over in his hands, his last forever joint, before inserting it into his mouth and lighting it.

The smoke from the joints swirled around them as the dust has swirled around them in the desert. It wasn't nearly as thick, but William could see that it was having some effect on Ci'del. He handed the second joint to Scott. Nora watched but was unable to comprehend what was going on, not only that, she didn't really care. Ann was in a position to see into the Inn's foyer through the small opening left in the cell's wall. She watched as Scott's Aunt Sarah continued to lie on the floor just on the other side. Then Sarah moved and Ann quickly looked away, masking her real thoughts with other thoughts. Thoughts about a relationship she might have if they survived this ordeal.

Ci'del hadn't moved since the lighting of the first joint. It stood there staring down at them, its stinking breath combined with the smell of the burning pot. William took the last hit from his last joint and then ate that roach as well. "All done," he said. Ci'del continued to stand there staring at them, unable to move.

"Come on," William coaxed the others. "We gotta get outta here, before it wears off."

••19••

Sarah Anderson awakened from her terrible nightmare with a start. Eddie's voice came out of the fog; *It wasn't your fault.* She looked up at the ancient mirror hanging on the wall and remembered. She scanned the Inn's foyer for the rosebud; the key to opening the jail cell. Then she heard something, voices; voices from the other side of the mirror. Faint voices yelling her name. She turned and looked toward the ugly mirror, the glass reflecting the image of the foyer, and still she heard the faint voices.

Get the key, Eddie's voice spoke inside her head.

Sarah turned toward the huge counter, seeing the red rosebud nestled against its foot. She quickly, as quickly as she could for an old woman, retrieved the rose. A toppled chair lay nearby which she also retrieved, and then Sarah Anderson approached the mirror. The keyhole to the mirror was at the very top, just beyond her reach without the chair. Placing the chair on the bench as before, she climbed aboard. Her gray eyes focused on the correct location. She reached out and stuffed the rosebud into the frame just as the chair wobbled, and toppled from the bench.

Sarah simply glided to the floor, quite amazed that she landed on her feet in an upright position and not on her ass on the hard tile. She turned toward the mirror, not knowing what to expect. Would it simply open up?

The mirror didn't *do* anything. It still looked like a mirror. It still worked like a mirror, her reflection nice and clear and sharp. *Pull em out Sarah*, Eddie's voice instructed. *You have to reach in.*

Sarah shivered at the thought, but Eddie knew what he was talking about, at least she hoped so.

· ·20· ·

Sheriff Radcliff clapped William on the back, "Way to go," he said.

William shrugged, "You're not gonna arrest me, are ya?"

The Sheriff shook his head. "Naw."

Ann looked back to the small opening that was the only thing left of the portal, back to seeing Sarah rising from the floor and coming toward the mirror. "Aunt Sarah," she yelled then pounded on the portal wall, the part that was now a solid object.

The others quickly joined Ann at the portal, pounding on the wall, yelling at the top of their lungs.

Suddenly a hand shot through it and into the little cove, and with it they could hear Sarah's voice. "Eddie, are you in there? Scott? Nora? It's Sarah. Grab my hand. For God's sake if you can hear me, grab my hand. Hurry."

Sheriff Radcliff grabbed hold of the hand and said, "I've seen this before, take my hand." Extending his other hand out to Nora. Nora looked into the man's eyes then grabbed the offered hand, then she grabbed Scott's hand and Scott grabbed Ann and Ann grabbed William, leaving William to feel the discharge of electricity from Ann, but he didn't mind. He would never mind.

C·H·A·P·T·E·R 29

ESCAPE

· · 1 · ·

A man nearly as tall as Eddie stepped from the mirror, his large hand firmly wrapped around Sarah's petite one. He had much darker skin, but he wasn't nearly as old, not nearly as handsome as her Eddie. He wore a cop's uniform and a badge. There was no gun in his holster, no radio on his belt. Nora stepped through next, looking like Jane of the Jungle followed by Scott, followed by an eye-catching girl with a rose tattoo on her forehead, whom Sarah didn't know, but there was something familiar about her, something about that rose tattoo. A younger boy, also unknown, was the last to step through. *Where was Eddie?* A burning deep down inside Sarah's guts told her Eddie was gone; Eddie wouldn't be coming back, ever. Just like her Rose, she had lost him to the monster. "Did you kill it, Scott? Please tell me you did, please tell me your uncle didn't die for nothing."

Scott shook his head. He hadn't had time to grieve for Uncle Ed and now he could feel the tears starting to burn inside his own eyes, could see the tears swelling in hers.

"Is there anybody left alive in there?" Sarah asked, turning toward the cop, tugging his sleeve.

"Sorry," he replied. "I wish there was."

"Which one's the key?" Scott asked.

Sarah looked at him through shocked gray eyes, tear filled eyes; her soul mate was dead.

"Aunt Sarah, the key!" Scott repeated himself. She wasn't taking the news well and he couldn't blame her. He looked toward the mirror. Where was it? His eyes scanned the mirror's frame. "Aunt Sarah," he tried again. Still there was no response. Turning toward the Sheriff, Scott asked, "Would you take my mom and aunt to the penthouse?"

"Sure," the Sheriff replied. "Come on ladies; let me be your escort."

When they were gone Scott turned toward Ann and William and said,

"Come on, we've got to find which one of these roses comes out, that's the key to containing it."

"No," Ann replied. "We have to destroy the mirror. That's the key." She turned and hurried out of the foyer.

• •2• •

Scott turned back to the mirror and started tugging at the roses along its bottom half, as William, who was taller, climbed aboard the cushioned bench and started tugging at the upper half. They didn't seem to be having much luck and Scott was beginning to get a bad feeling, even though the telepathy was gone. It was that same feeling he'd had on his arrival here, the light, hot fingertips touching his brain. Quickly he stepped back from the mirror just as black talons reached out followed by the rest of the bone eater. It swatted William out of its way, and then it locked its glare on Scott. A loud scraping sound filled his brain.

I hate you, it said. *And I'm going to kill you, but first . . .*Ci'del swung its deadly talons toward the mirror, the sharp, black talons collided with the ancient glass, shattering it into a million pieces raining down on them.

Then it advanced toward Scott, changing into the thing that resembled his twin. They hadn't killed it, they hadn't contained it and now it was out. It was out and the mirror, the cell-spell, was broken. It was out and it looked like his sister. No, he thought, *no it doesn't. It's a trick.* "You don't exist," he said.

The creature stopped and then it smiled and when it did Scott felt the strength, all that he had left, drain from his muscles, because that smile was the wickedest thing he'd ever seen. Scott stepped back from his advancing sister (monster). One step, two step, three step, four. On the fourth step he collided with Ann. What she saw she didn't like, not one bit. The mirror was shattered (seven years bad luck, don'tcha know) and Ci'del was standing there looking like Scott's twin, a person who had never lived, at least not outside of the womb.

Ann dropped the fireplace poker, grabbed Scott by the arm and yanked him from the foyer out into the sitting room. She then hurried him through the room, into the breezeway and out onto the lawn by the rose garden. Dark clouds began to appear in the blue sky overhead. Cupping her hand to his ear, she said, "I have an idea."

"What?" Scott leaned closer, breathing in her scent.

"You'll see," she replied.

· ·3· ·

William, having been pushed aside by Ci'del, landed up against the large entry doors, on the floor, a tiny piece of mirror glass stuck in the palm of his right hand. He winced from the piercing pain as he removed the shard. He then gazed at the broken glass littering the tiled floor, and wondered what the hell he was doing sitting there when the monster was chasing after Ann. He quickly got up and headed toward the sitting room. There was no one there. The door to the breezeway stood open.

From the breezeway, William looked out into the yard passed the rose-less garden and saw the monster, who had once again taken the form of a girl call-ing herself Rachel, a girl who looked a lot like Scott, in hot pursuit running down the cobblestone walkway that led to the lighthouse as Ann and Scott disappeared into it.

William took off after them, no plan in mind, but he couldn't do nothing; doing nothing would be like giving up.

· ·4· ·

Once inside the little house that had been the light keeper's home years ago, Ann slammed the exterior door shut, locking the deadbolt. Then she led Scott to the tower and up the iron stairs. Round and round they went, small ribbons of light shining in through its windows. About halfway up she heard the loud tearing sound of the door as Ci'del/Rachel ripped it from its hinges. From the window looking east Ann saw William running across the Inn's grounds after them, but she didn't stop. She couldn't stop. Rachel was very angry with them right now; they had thwarted her chance for revenge, revenge against Scott's mother. No, Rose said. *It wants your body, now. It cares of nothing else.*

Ann kept right on going, dragging Scott along with her. She had an idea.

· ·5· ·

In the penthouse, away from the mirror, the Sheriff escorted the women to one of the stuffed wicker sofas. Then he went over to the rock fireplace and flipped a wall switch. The gas fueled flames shot out over the fake log display. Mid-morning sunlight beat through the east window. The aroma of the fresh ocean air drifted in through the open window in the elevator hallway.

Nora, who was still clad in the ridiculous clothing her father had provided, rubbed her cold arms with her hands. *No,* she thought, *that wasn't my father. Papas been dead a long time.* She looked down at the broken arm, or rather the arm that should be broken. Her wristwatch was still missing, yet the arm didn't appear to be broken, confirming the fact that this was all still just a terrible dream. Her watch would be on the night stand when she awoke, you just wait and see. She stood up from the sofa she was sharing with her old Aunt, and proceeded out of the room. She had to change into some real clothes.

In her bedroom she noticed the dried blood on the carpet near the foot of the bed, the image of Ann swinging Joseph's blazing rifle at his head, slammed into her brain. She grabbed the silk PJs and put them on, and then hurried back out into the living room after grabbing her stashed bottle of rum from the night stand drawer. Her watch, she noticed, was not on the night stand.

Sheriff Radcliff stood at the fireplace, staring at the square clock on the mantle amongst the varied flower filled water globes. Then he looked at the watch on his wrist and back to the mantle clock, twice. The time difference between them was only half-an-hour. He didn't know how that could be. Then the woman with the red-hair, the woman he'd carried in his arms on an unbelievable journey in an unreal world, came back into the living room. She was dressed in a fancy, colorful pair of lounging wear; pajamas. They were quite cute, she was quite cute. She placed a bottle of Rum, Bacardi 151, on the table next to one of the wicker chairs then proceeded over to the old phonograph where she selected a record from a box on the floor next to it. Then she turned in his direction as he heard the familiar music begin to play.

"Hey," he said, "I know this."

"Yeah?"

"Beatles, Drive my car, Rubber Soul . . .UK 65."

"Wow, I'm impressed."

"Well, it's one of my favorites."

"Mine too, Sheriff."

"Call me Mason," he said.

"Mason, I'm Nora, and this is Sarah. I guess we weren't properly introduced, you know." Her green eyes flashed with embarrassment. Sarah remained seated on the sofa in front of the lighted fireplace.

Mason could see tears running down the crevasses of her old, mud splattered face, realizing for the first time that she was covered with mud, her long silver hair caked with it. A bright red line, a twin to the mark on Nora's chin, ran across her bony chin. *She lost someone, the old man, Uncle Ed,* he thought. *Maybe the man who washed up on the beach isn't important right now.*

"Are you here on official police business, Sher . . .I mean, Mason?" Nora asked.

"Fraid so," he replied.

Nora plopped down in the chair, grabbed the bottle from the table next to it and unscrewed the cap. "Would you like a shot, Mason?"

"Don't you think it's a little early for that?"

"Not in the dream I'm having. It's a doozey."

"You think this is a dream?" Mason asked.

"You bet your ass."

"What makes you think so?"

"Really, how could it be anything else?"

"You've got a point there. I think I'll see how the kids are doing."

"You go on ahead and do that Sheriff," Nora replied bringing the bottle to her lips, pouring the rum down her throat.

Sheriff Radcliff left the living room wondering why such a beautiful, intelligent woman, with so much to live for, was trying to commit suicide.

· ·6· ·

Mason stood at the bottom of the stairs staring into the foyer, the *empty* foyer. Large amounts of glass, mirrored glass, covered the tiled floor. He proceeded inside only to see that the mirror had been shattered into thousands of sharp, jagged pieces and the kids nowhere in sight. A fireplace poker lay amongst the debris. The mirror frame hung on the wall and as far as he could tell, all its roses were intact. He suddenly had a bad feeling, something wasn't right. Dream or not, things were adding up to trouble, big trouble.

Stepping over to the huge entry doors, he pulled them open and hurried down the marble stairs, only to see William, disappearing into the lighthouse across the field, and the roll of the dark storm clouds overhead. Mason raced to his patrol car and grabbed his police issue shotgun from the front seat. Then he took off after the boy, hoping to get there in time before something bad happened, something deadly. He didn't know why he was feeling that way, but he was beginning to believe that the monster from the mirror might be on the loose, on the loose in his town, sucking the marrow of his townsfolk, and he couldn't let that happen.

• •7• •

In the penthouse Sarah sat quietly in front of the rock fireplace staring into the flames when Eddie's voice spoke inside her head. *The children are in trouble*, he said.

"I know," she replied.

"What?" Nora asked.

"The children are in trouble."

"What do you mean? How do you know?"

"Eddie told me," Sarah replied, finally looking in Nora's direction, seeing the bottle of rum, that nasty rum, in Nora's hand. Sarah slowly rose from the sofa and approached her niece. "Give me that!" she demanded, snatching the bottle from Nora's hand.

"But I need it," Nora whined.

"No you don't. You never did and it's time for you to stop, right now. There are more important matters to take care of, and you know it." Sarah carried the bottle into the bathroom where she poured the remaining rum down the drain. When she returned to the living room, Nora was standing at the mantle fishing the other stashed bottle out from behind the clock. Sarah placed her old hands on her hips and said, "I'll take that one too." Then she reached out with one mud caked hand, motioning Nora to give her the stashed bottle.

Nora held the bottle close to her chest as if it were the most precious thing in the whole world.

"Are you trying to kill yourself?" Sarah asked.

"Of course not!"

"Then give me that bottle."

Nora looked down at the bottle cradled in her arms, her Precious Rum. "No," she said. "I don't want to."

"I don't care what you want. If you're not trying to kill yourself then what are you doing? Eddie won't be coming back, that puts me in charge. Hand it over."

"Or what?" Nora asked.

"Do you think Scott enjoys your drinking? Do you think he'll stick around now that he's in love? That he'll want to raise his children around you?"

"What do you mean?"

"You know perfectly well what I mean," Sarah replied.

With shaking hands Nora held the bottle out to Sarah who quickly snatched it away.

"Good," Sarah said. "Now you can start your long road to recovery. And I'll be there to help you Nora, I promise."

Nora glared at her old Aunt, she should have been happy for the support. But she wasn't, not yet.

· ·8· ·

Ann and Scott reached the top of the lighthouse stairs just as William entered through the door at the bottom; the echoing footfalls of Ci'del/Rachel on the stairs somewhere in between and getting closer. They hurried up the ladder to the lantern room. Once inside Ann slammed the iron gate in the wooden floor closed with a loud bang, and then secured the gate with its deadbolt lock. She didn't know how long it would keep Ci'del/Rachel out, nor did she care. Her only concern right now was the light, which had been changed from gas to electricity sometime in the past. Inside her head the voice of Rose guided her forward.

Scott looked out of the glass windows surrounding them, out to the rolling black clouds as lightning pierced the sky nearby and thunder rumbled overhead. The view was spectacular, but that wasn't the reason for their visit, not this time.

Ann approached the huge lenses, reached out with her hands and grabbed hold of the wire connecting the two incandescent light bulbs to the generator. Ripping it from its connection, the surge of electricity snapped in the air, making her short, golden hair stand on end. The rose tattoo grew brighter as she built the strength of her own electrically charged body. The music inside her head grew louder until it was the only thing she could hear, drowning out the ocean, the clap of thunder and Scott.

· ·9· ·

Mason was just about to the lighthouse door when he noticed it missing, ripped from its iron hinges and tossed on the ground. A flash of light, much brighter than the lighthouse light itself, shot out from the very top of the tower, electricity filled the air. Lightning stuck overhead. He hurried inside bumping into William who was standing just at the stairway door himself listening to the beast as it pounded up the stairs toward the top, toward Ann.

"What're we gonna do now?" William asked of the tall uniformed man now standing with him at the bottom of the long spiral stairs. "It's on the stairs, between us and the top."

Mason nodded and reached for his hand held radio. It was time to call for backup, however his radio was missing. Somewhere he'd lost it. "Damn it," he said.

"What?" William asked, his eyes wide with fear.

"Lost my radio, I guess it's up to us," he replied, and then pushed passed William and started up the stairs.

"Wait," William urged. "How're we gonna kill it? You can't kill it with bullets and I can't kill it with my sling shot."

"But, we have to try."

William agreed, but it seemed an impossible feat. The monster had powers they didn't have, had gotten away at every turn. How would they possibly destroy it? He didn't know the answer and apparently neither did the sheriff, but they followed the monster up the stairs just the same; the Sheriff with his shotgun and William with his high-powered sling shot.

· ·10· ·

Nora followed her aunt down the stairs to the foyer where broken glass from the mirror littered the floor. She followed Sarah out the entry door and down the marble stairs and onto the cobblestone walkway, the wind whipping their unbound hair around their faces. They had no weapons, but Sarah was determined to help in whatever way she could.

The Sheriff's police radio, Eddie instructed.

Sarah opened the door to the green cop car, reached inside and grabbed the radio mike. She depressed the button on the side. "Is anyone there?"

"10-4. Who is this?" A woman's voice came back to her.

"We have a situation out at the Light Keeper's Inn," Sarah replied. "Send help right away. All the help you can."

"What's your situation?" The woman's voice asked.

"Officer down, and fire," she lied. Then she tossed the radio mike back into the car, grabbed Nora by the hand and took off in the direction of the towering lighthouse as another blast of light from the tiny room at the top of the tower pierced the sky. Something was going on up there.

··11··

Scott yelled, unheard, as Ann collected an electrical charge that no human could possibly withstand. Her wheat-colored hair stood on end, crackling with sparks. He would later swear he saw her skeleton through nearly transparent skin, almost like a cartoon. But this was no laughing matter, no laughing mater at all. He turned at the sound of Ci'del's talons tapping against the iron gate covering the opening to the lantern room. It was trying to get in. It was no longer in the form of his twin.

"Ann," Scott yelled. She made no indication of hearing him. Then she turned from the light, placing a finger to her lips, shushing him. He reached for her, but she stepped back, shaking her head no. He was sure he understood that she was electrified and dangerous, but that didn't stop him from wanting her. He could hear the footfalls of others on the stairs and wondered who had followed. William? The Sheriff? His Mom or Aunt? He didn't know for sure but he suddenly wished with all his heart that whoever it was hadn't, for they were in bigger danger out there than he or Ann in here, he was pretty sure about that. Then he heard a voice, a male voice, and was fairly certain of the followers. Ci'del's deadly talons disappeared from the iron gate as two loud shotgun blasts rang through the tower.

· ·12· ·

William raced up the long stairs behind the Sheriff, his sling shot ready just in case he happened to get lucky. But luck, William was pretty sure, would not be on their side this time. The monster from the mirror was not something they could kill with bullets or ball bearings from even a high powered sling shot, they would need a miracle. If only he'd had more pot. He could have really smoked the thing dead if he'd had say a half an ounce instead of two measly joints. He was pretty sure about that. He didn't know the statistics of pot, he didn't care. He only knew the reaction of the monster after two joints of smoke had been blown in its direction.

Suddenly William plowed into the back end of the Sheriff.

Sheriff Radcliff had stopped on the last stair to the watch room. Ci'del was only a few steps away, working the lock of the iron gate with one long talon. "Hey you bitch," Sheriff Radcliff yelled.

Ci'del turned, removing its talon from the lock.

Aiming his twelve gauge shot gun at Ci'del, Sheriff Radcliff pulled the trigger. He pumped the gun a second time and fired again, Ci'del deflecting each shot before they reached their destination.

William raised his sling shot and fired two ball bearings at it, both hitting the armor and bouncing off.

Ci'del laughed and proceeded toward them.

William took two steps down the stairs.

The Sheriff remained where he was. Then much to William's surprise, and the Sheriff's as well, a ball of pure electricity came flying through the gate, connecting with the monster. It yowled, but kept coming their direction as another electric ball came flying down the ladder. Overhead they saw Ann glowing like a light bulb, a very bright light bulb.

· ·13· ·

Scott watched in fascination as Ann conjured up the first ball of electricity, held it in her hands for a second and then threw it through the iron gate toward Ci'del. Seconds later she threw a second ball. Then she reached for the deadbolt, unlocked it and flung the gate open. The thud of the gate hitting the wooden floor echoed throughout the tower.

Ann saw the Sheriff first, standing on the landing. William was on the stairs. Both were looking her direction, eyes wide with wonder. She motioned for them to move down the stairs, as Ci'del turned back toward her, seeing her unprotected by the open gate. It was then that Rachel reappeared.

"Come and get me, you bitch," Ann said.

"No!" Scott shouted, a look of pure horror crossed his face. *What is she doing?*

Ann looked his direction saying, "Its okay. I know how to destroy it. You just stay there." She looked back to the ladder. Rachel was almost to the top. Ann stepped back, waiting.

··14··

Rachel entered the tiny lantern room at the top of the tower. Her destiny was within her grasp. Finally she would live as she had never lived before. She eyed her brother standing on the opposite side of the room. Soon she would be part of the family, as she should've been long ago. And the first thing on her agenda, after getting her new body, would be the destruction of Mother. Something she deserved.

Rachel stepped closer to the girl, closer to her destiny.

Ann opened her mouth, the trapped tune inside her head poured forth. Her angelic voice rang through the lighthouse tower, stopping Rachel dead in her tracks, paralyzed by the sound, unable to move a muscle, unable to change back into the form of Ci'del.

Now, Rose spoke inside Ann's head.

She flung her arms around the paralyzed creature, flooding its body with electricity, shorting every circuit within it. When Ann let go, ten minutes later, Rachel fell to the floor, and the song that had been in Ann's brain vanished. When it did all her past memories flooded in.

Collapsing to the floor, she said, "It's over." Then closed her eyes as the memory flood washed over her.

Yes, Rose replied. *You've done well. It's time for me to go.*

NEW LIVES

·· 1 ··

Wailing sirens filled the air. Scott stood over the dead, mutating body of the creature that resembled his twin, if she had truly lived, which she hadn't. Ci'del had created her by using her essence, pulling it from the rose pendant. But she wasn't real, had never been more than a voice in his mind.

Sheriff Radcliff entered the tiny room followed by William.

Sarah and Nora stood at the bottom of the ladder, in the watch room below. "What's going on up there?" Sarah wanted to know.

"It's dead!" Scott replied.

Sarah sighed with relief, but her heart was broken. That monstrous beast had taken everything from her. Rose had been gone an age it seemed, and now Eddie . . .she looked at Nora, and for the first time saw the child she'd lost. She saw also the girl within Nora who'd lost her father to his selfish vanity, and her soul to a bottle of rum.

Eddie and his precious 'destiny' insisted Nora stay in that horrid place. But Eddie was gone now and nothing would bring him back. Nora was still here. Nora needed her more now than she ever had. *Maybe*, she mused, *you need Nora*. Either way it didn't matter, she would take Nora back to Nevada, at least for awhile. Eddie and destiny no longer had a say in the matter.

Scott wasn't a child anymore. He'd taken care of himself for most of his life, had taken care of his mother too. The Inn belonged to him now, Sarah would see to it. She didn't know if he would stay or not, he was in love and he would go or stay with the girl, she supposed. It would depend on the girl, the girl with the golden voice and the rose tattoo. Sarah was certain it was the girl who had destroyed the monster, finally. The girl had a spirit like *her* Rose, Scott was in trouble. Sarah smiled at the thought.

· ·2· ·

Scott helped Ann to her feet. She looked to Sheriff Radcliff and said, "I killed somebody."

Sheriff Radcliff narrowed his hazel eyes, "This thing?"

"Yes, no," she replied, shaking her head. "William's father."

"No," Scott and William said at the same time.

"No?" The Sheriff responded, somewhat confused.

"It was self defense," William said. "Pa was a bad man. He was trying to kill Ms. Anderson, trying to kill them both."

"So where is this man?" Sheriff Radcliff asked.

"We dumped him in the ocean," William replied.

Sheriff Radcliff nodded and said, "I think he washed up on shore this morning."

"I'm ready to go to jail now," Ann said, holding her wrists out toward the Sheriff.

He smiled at her and said, "That won't be necessary, Ann. You saved this town, maybe even the world. I don't think there'll be any charges."

"My name isn't Ann. It's Angelina, Angelina Spear. I'm from Mitchell, California. My parents died in a lightning storm in the Land of Many Lakes. I have nobody, no relatives," she said, bursting into tears.

Scott reached out and gathered her in his arms. The rose tattoo had faded from her forehead, the lightning was gone from her eyes, but he loved her regardless. If he could do anything at all to keep her with him, he would. "You can stay we me," he said, wiping the tears from her face. "And you're still Ann to me."

"Me too," William replied.

"Do you have any friends in Mitchell that you'd like to contact?" Sheriff Radcliff asked.

Ann shook her head. "No," she said remembering Jess, Jen and Gayle. It'd be better just to disappear. Her old life would never be the same. She felt empty inside. The music and the little voice, the voice of the rose, were gone.

"Come on," Scott said, taking her by the hand. "Let's go home." He led her over to the ladder and helped her down to the watch room below.

Mason Radcliff turned toward William and said, "What about you? Do you have any living relatives, any place to go?"

"I dunno," William said. "I should go to jail."

"And why's that?" Mason asked, crossing his arms over his large chest. The hint of a smile crossed his face.

William hung his head, the black curls falling over his dark eyes. "I shoulda stopped him. I shoulda done somethin a long time ago, but I didn't. He killed those girls, all those girls, and it's my fault. I was chicken!"

Mason didn't know whether to laugh or cry. That bastard had really screwed this kid up. He wasn't going to ask William about the dead girls yet, he'd get to that later. "Last time I checked William, bein afraid of someone twice your size wasn't exactly a hangin offence. I've stood beside you against this thing," he said pointing a finger at the body of the monster. "It's the scariest son of a bitch I've ever heard of, and son, you're no chicken." Mason put his arm around the boy's shoulder. "How'd you like to stay with me?" he asked.

William looked up at the tall man, the Sheriff. "I dunno," he said. "Maybe I otta just grab my stuff and go."

"And where would you go?"

William shrugged.

"I don't think I can just let you walk out of here," Mason replied.

"I understand."

"Do you?"

"Uhuh, a kid like me's gotta be disciplined."

Mason smiled. "Jesus Christ, William. Let me tell you something. I was a kid like you, and you'll do fine without *that* kinda discipline. Come on, help me get this monster over to the opening so we can hoist it down the stairs."

William looked down at the beast lying on the floor at their feet. "Why don't we just throw it over the side?"

"Now why didn't I think of that?"

Together they dragged the heavy creature over to the glass door leading out to the parapet. Once it was outside, they worked it, one limb at a time over the iron railing until it finally dropped to the ground 45 feet below.

Volunteer firefighters and other residents of Seal Bay, including Nora, Sarah, Ann and Scott, looked on as the blackened body hurled toward the ground, landing with a thud at the base of the lighthouse.

The small crowd was stunned by the shear mass of it, they stared at it in wonder. It was intimidating to them even dead, with its big, sharp teeth and claw like finger tips. And the most dangerous looking thing of all, they would all agree later, was the tip on its long prehistoric tail. Most wanted to know what it was, where it came from, and what they were going to do with it.

· ·3· ·

William and Sheriff Radcliff silently descended the 65 stairs to the bottom of the lighthouse tower. When they reached the bottom, inside the old light keeper's house, Mason stopped. Turning toward the following boy he said, "You did a good job. I just thought you should know."

William smiled, speechless.

Mason turned and stepped from the little house.

The red emergency lights from the fire truck flashed out over the gathering crowd. Deputy Frank stepped up to his commanding officer and asked, pointing toward the creature, "What're we gonna do with that?"

"I think we'll have a big bon fire," Mason replied.

"What the hell is it Mason?" Deputy Frank asked.

"It's called a Bone Eater," Scott replied, as he approached the smaller group that had gathered for 'official business'.

"A Bone Eater," the squat officer repeated. "Where'd it come from?"

"Doesn't matter, what does is getting the lighthouse lantern working," Mason interjected.

Deputy Frank nodded, looking up the tower, and then back to the Sheriff. "Right away Sir."

"Hey, Jeff!" Mason hollered at a robust fellow wearing a fireman's jacket and hat, leaning on the town's one and only fire truck, "Get rid of this thing, would ya?"

"Sure-nuff, Mason," he replied, turning to the others standing around the truck. "You heard the Sheriff boys, let's get busy!"

The volunteers of the Seal Bay Fire Department took care of the creature by dousing it in gasoline and lighting it on fire, as the Sheriff, and the small group of surviving adventurers returned to the Inn.

· ·4· ·

"There won't be any investigation," Sheriff Radcliff announced as he seated himself on the penthouse sofa. "Hell, I wouldn't know where to start that wouldn't get me a free vacation in a rubber room. This . . .isn't gonna be in any paper either, I'll see to that. Seal Bay just doesn't need that kind of tourism, so you folks are free to go about your business. I guess the only thing that hasn't been said is, Welcome to Seal Bay." He leaned back into the sofa as he scanned the faces around him, his gaze settling on Nora Anderson. "Stay as long as you like."

Sarah Anderson didn't miss the look in the sheriff's eyes, or the direction of his gaze as he extended his invitation. "Scott, I'm going to take Nora back to Nevada with me for awhile," she said. "We'll get her started on recovery, while I work on settling Edwin's estate. I figure you can take care of this place while she's gone."

Scott looked from his Mother to his Aunt and back again, "Is this what you want, Mom?"

Nora didn't hesitate. "Yes," she said. "Now that you're well you can do just about anything Scott, you don't need me. Least not drunk or dead."

Scott nodded. His legs would need some strengthening, but he was feeling pretty good so far. He hadn't needed the leg braces (a good thing, particularly since they were left inside the mirror) or his crutches since before their escape from the mirror. In the end that was one thing Uncle Ed hadn't lied about. The disease wasn't, had never been, his. Scott felt tears welling up as he thought of his uncle. It would be awhile before he was completely over the loss. "Ann," he said as he fought to focus on more pleasant issues. "Will you stay here with me?"

"Yes," she replied, taking his right hand into both of hers. From the corner of her eye she saw William's head drop slightly. Turning toward him, she asked, "What about you Will? Will you stay?"

William lifted his head to face the others. Would he stay? He didn't think so. Slowly he began to shake his head no.

"Come to Nevada with us," Nora offered. "Remember what I said?"

William nodded, he remembered, though it seemed a lifetime ago. He looked at the older woman, her long silver hair streaked with mud, nodding her affirmation. William had never had choices, life for him had never been about his wants.

Sheriff Radcliff stood from the sofa saying, "You don't have to decide the rest of your life right now William, but I really was hoping you'd stay with me. At least for awhile. I got a nice little two bedroom place on the beach. What'd ya say?"

Somehow that felt right to William. Just the two of them, like his pa and him, only a hundred times better. Mason Radcliff was no murderin bastard. He nodded his consent as a smile crept onto his face, like the first smile of an innocent child, with people who cared.

The Sheriff turned to Scott, "Will you be opening the Inn as scheduled?"

"You bet!" Scott replied.

"Good, can't wait, Fat Patty's got the best burgers on the Coast, but the only way she knows how to cook an egg is over done. You ready William?"

William nodded as he stood and picked up his pack.

Mason turned to the others as he and William reached the doorway. "Can't say it hasn't been a pleasure meeting you all. I hope the next time it'll be under more pleasant circumstances . . .It's surely been an adventure."

THE TWINS

· ·1· ·

They were born two years later, blonde, blue eyed and full of mischief, just like most kids, almost. One was a girl, the other a boy. The girl was older by a mere five minutes, but at the tender age of three it was quite apparent which one was in charge.

"I wanna do it first," Jonny said.

"I'm first," Elizabeth replied. "The oldest always gets to go first."

Both of the children were well spoken for their age, they had learned much from their parents. Listening attentively, eyes, ears, and minds wide open. They knew things far beyond their years, things they saw in other people's minds, like William and The Sheriff who often came to visit. William and The Sheriff were coming back today. Today was a good day, a day of celebration.

"Neither one of you are going to do it first," Ann scolded, entering the twins' bedroom. "And if I catch you doing it, there'll be no ice cream for a week!"

Elizabeth's blue eyes widened. "No ice cream?" she wined.

"That's what I said. And that goes for you too," Ann said, looking at her son. He was the spitting image of his father. The hair color may have been different, but that little face was exactly the same. She looked back to her daughter. "And since you're the oldest, you'll make sure neither one of you gets into trouble, right?"

Elizabeth chewed her lip. "Yeah," she lied. She lied because she knew she wouldn't be able to not do it. It was something she had to do. She was pretty sure it was the same for Jonny.

· ·2· ·

Scott was standing at the sitting room window when he saw the old truck pull in. "Hey," he yelled running toward the penthouse stairs. "Grammas here."

Upstairs Ann was busy getting the three year old twins ready when she heard

Scott below. "Come on," she said, tousling their blonde curls. She grabbed each one by a hand and led them down the stairs as Scott opened the door and Nora stepped in with Aunt Sarah in tow.

Scott grabbed his mother and hugged her fiercely, five years was a long time. Both of them burst into tears. Then he hugged his Aunt, the woman who'd saved his mother's life.

Ann stood at the bottom of the stairs waiting with the children. When Scott was finished hugging his mother and aunt, she stepped forward with the twins. "Mom, Aunt Sarah," she said. "I'd like you to meet Elizabeth and Jonathan."

Nora stared at the blonde headed, blued eyed twins. New tears sprang to her eyes as she knelt to one knee. Together the twins raced forward, grabbing her around the neck with their little arms. She scooped them up, hugging them tightly, kissing their little faces. There was a tingling sensation in her brain, and then it was gone.

A voice spoke.

"Nora," he said. "Welcome home."

Nora turned to see Mason standing in the bright sunlight at the Inn's door. Beside him stood a young man who could only be William, all grown up, with a young, dark haired woman hanging on his arm. "Mason," she said, stepping forward into his outstretched arms, the twins still held tightly to her bosom. Over the years she had fallen in love with him and him with her.

Elizabeth smiled, as did her brother.

Ann tried her best to determine if the children were behaving, sometimes it was hard to tell.

· • • ·

Kristi Olson lives with her husband James in rural Washington where they manage an apartment complex They have many grandchildren. This is Kristi's first book.

· • • ·